My Year of Dating Crazy

J.P. Gebbie

Published by J.P. Gebbie, 2020.

MY YEAR OF DATING CRAZY

First edition. December 7, 2020.

Written by J.P. Gebbie.

For Elin and Gebs. For everything.

Chapter One
December, 1995

The worst part of the move wasn't when Wes dropped a box of my CDs with an alarming crunch. It wasn't even when the girls put a massive scratch in the coffee table as they tried to get it through the door. No, the worst part was when Edwin tried to set the box of coffee mugs on the seat of Lainie's pint-sized vintage wicker rocking chair that had been in the family for three generations. The corner of the box punctured the delicate weaving, creating a fist-sized hole that only a trained craftsman could repair.

"Okay, guys, hold up," I said. "I think it's time for a break." Six young people nodded in agreement, four girls from my lacrosse team and two of their boyfriends who had been conscripted to help me move during Christmas break with the promise of pizza and my undying gratitude. Edwin turned three shades of red and apologized five times before I could calm him down, assuring him that the damage was easily fixable (keeping to myself the fact that it might take months to find a tradesperson who could do it properly.)

"But there are still boxes in the truck, Ms. Smyth," Angela protested.

"You guys have been amazing, and I've kept you from your families far too long; I'm sure they want you home. You did a great job of getting all the big stuff. I'm pretty sure I can handle the rest myself." I pointed Angela to the phone on the wall in the kitchen and told her to order at least three pizzas and whatever else they wanted.

"At least let's get a few more things up here while we wait for the pizza to come," Wes suggested.

I nodded. "I'll come down, and we can decide what needs to come up stairs now." On the way to the truck, Wes scooped up a handful of snow, balled it in his bare hands and tossed it at Edwin. I watched the two boys horsing around, the sun glinting off the snow-covered ground, thinking, *this could be so much worse.*

It had been pouring the day I signed the lease. Raindrops left dark spots on my olive silk suit. My black pumps were sopping wet. I sat in the rental office hoping I didn't look as pathetic as I felt, but the water spots on my sleeves and soaking wet hair weren't helping. I filled out the form: name: Alexandria Smythe. Number of people living in the apartment: two, me and my shadow, my daughter, Lainie. Marital status: Divorced. Place of business, etc., etc. I consulted my Filofax for names and numbers, realized I had spelled my boss's last name incorrectly and looked around the desk for some Wite-out. It was sitting there, inches away from the highly manicured hands of the rental agent. She shuffled papers as she waited for me to finish. It looked like she would rather be doing something else. So would I. I smiled, shrugged and took the Wite-out. She already thought I was an idiot. I hadn't asked the most intelligent questions during the tour of my future home, stammering about the stacking laundry unit in the hall closet; were those things safe? What if there was a problem with the utilities? What if there was a bad storm? At least I hadn't asked if I could make a burnt offering on the balcony to exorcize the spirit of my ex-husband, although I had been tempted.

"Done," I smiled and handed her the bottle of Wite-out and the papers.

"Okay." There was a long pause while she scanned the application, making sure all the information was complete. The industrial gray of the office desk, carpet and credenza were only relieved by a fake bush listing in the corner. Through the window, bare trees creaked in the rain. In the stillness of the office I could hear the rain shift with the wind. As I waited for her, the finality of the move hit me as it hadn't before. This was it. Marriage over. My bravado deflated, leaving me hollow and alone.

"There you go. You're all set." She looked me in the eye and gave me a reassuring smile. I realized that she was smarter than I usually credit people with fake nails. She knew exactly why I was there, why I was moving. Her smile wasn't phony.

"You can move in on Friday. Welcome to your new home." She handed me the keys and I managed to whisper, "Thank you." I choked up. Very Blanche DuBois, kindness of strangers and all that.

The fact that my husband and I had split had not remained quiet for long. I'd told Michael, my boss, one dreary morning while we were waiting in line for the copier. Anne from the English department was trying to clear a paper jam, every door of the machine was open, parts pulled out, paper shreds scattered on the floor. It was 6:30 am, the Tuesday before Christmas break. Our students were antsy. We were tired and marched toward vacation like soldiers crossing a muddy field. He knew things hadn't been going well, so what I said wasn't a shock, exactly, but I might have chosen a better venue.

"How's it going, Alex?"

"Okay," I yawned back at him.

"What are you and Ken doing for the holidays?" There it was.

"Well, Lainie and I are moving out. That should take most of the vacation." This wasn't the conversation I'd planned, but it slipped out like I'd instantly developed Tourette's. A demon was sitting on my tongue and the little bastard kept getting me into trouble.

"You're moving out?"

"Yeah, I signed the lease the other day."

"Oh." Michael frowned, sad and disappointed. He shuffled the papers in his hands for a few seconds before asking, "Are you okay?"

"I'm getting there."

"I'm so sorry you guys got to this point." He said softly, almost to himself. I actually felt worse telling my boss than I had telling my own dad. Weeks ago, I had been sitting on the edge of the work table in Michael's office. He sat at his desk, fiddling with the cigarettes he wasn't allowed to smoke at school because of the rules, or at home because of his wife.

"You know they have gum for that." I told him.

"I tried the gum. I hate it."

"So, sniffing at the box is helping?"

"I sense some snark today, Ms. Smythe."

"True. Sorry. I need to get my own act together before I start criticizing the nicotine folly you have going on there."

He raised his eyebrows at me.

"It's me and Ken. It's just not working." Michael set the box of Newports aside.

"Do you want to talk about it?" he asked.

"Not really."

"Okay." He picked up the pack of cigarettes again. I heaved myself off the table and started to go to the workroom when he stopped me. "Alex, I'm not one to give much advice, because this is really your business, but you have Lainie to think about. Call me old fashioned, but I do think it's important for parents to stay together for the kids."

There was so much to say to that, like: *You mean even if the parents are totally miserable? Or if one person feels like their every hope for a normal life is being sucked out of them every time the other person heads off to play Dungeons and Dragons with the high school cadre who still think it's cool to stay out till 4:00 a.m. living in a fantasy land?* But I knew Michael's heart was in the right place, so I just said, "Yeah, I know. I'll keep that in mind. Thanks. See you in the morning."

***

After my volunteer moving crew had finished hauling all the heavy, bulky things upstairs, I sent them home and was left to lug the smaller boxes up the stairs alone. It was Boxing Day, or Day of Boxes for me. Lainie was with Ken. I plodded along: truck, to sidewalk, to stairs, to apartment, random songs tracking through my head as I marched up and down the stairs.

"*I am the Egg Man, I am a sherpa, coo coo ca choo.*"

"*We all live in a tiny little space, it's only saving grace, is... well, we all live in a tiny little space.*"

"*Deck the Halls with Boughs of Holly, Fa La La La La.*" Fuck this Shit. *This the season to not fucking be Jolly, Fa la la la la...*"

With no warning, my legs flew out from under me, my head slammed into concrete, the huge box of books landed on my chest. Everything went black. Pain radiated from the very back of my head through my jaw and down my spine. It sucked the breath out of me. I couldn't move for a minute, or five, I couldn't tell. Slowly, the world came back into focus, and I watched bright fluffy clouds drift across the cold, clear blue sky. I eased the box off my chest. After another interval, the chill air returned to my lungs.

This isn't bad, I thought, *I could use the rest. Maybe I'll nap here for a minute.* But it was a parking lot and I didn't move to the Apartment of Independence to get run over on moving day. I rolled onto my stomach and gently pushed my way into a crawling position, marveling at pink and yellow blotches as they floated in front of my eyes. This was not good. On all fours, in a parking lot. I had been too embarrassed to tell anyone other than the helper-kids that I was moving that weekend. I was going to end up frozen to the pavement, like an elderly Eskimo sent off on an ice floe. *Get your shit to-*

gether Alex. Somehow, I got the rest of the boxes up to my apartment and the U-Haul back to the U-Haul people, I probably shouldn't have been driving anywhere. It was not an auspicious beginning.

Later, head only slightly throbbing, I started to unpack. The challenge: how to fit the remnants of my life from a three-bedroom town house into a 709 square foot, one-bedroom apartment. On the plus side, one could vacuum the entire abode without having to move the plug; the long cord could reach the whole thing. My office, once a sunny third bedroom, was now the back wall of our living/dining/family room.

I pawed through the random stuff packed in the box justifiably named, "Random Stuff." I hadn't had a lot of time to do a good sort before the move, so I grabbed a paper grocery bag and tossed things in for recycling. Outdated memos from Lainie's day care, old aerobics schedules from the gym, the 1995 Far Side Calendar. There were only five days left in that disastrous year, but I didn't want to keep any record of it.

A pile of love letters rested on the bottom of the box. Some were bundled with a red ribbon. My ex-husband had been prolific in his early protestations of affection. I tore the ribbon off and threw it aside. The sight of his tiny, anal-retentive handwriting that I had once considered elegant in its precision irritated me now. I scooped up the whole pile of letters and dumped them in the recycling bag, and went to start unpacking boxes of books. Tearing open the first one, I sliced my finger open on the cardboard. Blood dripped on the carpet. That wouldn't do.

Searching through three more boxes marked "Bathroom," I found a Sesame Street Band-Aid. Big Bird smiled up from my wound, making me miss Lainie even more. I had almost forgotten it was Christmas. As book after book filled the Ikea shelves, I tried a little mental calculus, *How many books have I moved in my lifetime?* Thousands, counting all the times I'd helped my mother relocate her personal library. Once, while unloading her poetry section (she had actual sections for her books, while my collection was shelved by which dust jackets looked pretty together), I came across an unfamiliar volume in my mother's bookcase. It was so slim, I must have shoved it in with other texts without noticing it in earlier moves. Elaine was particular about writing in books. She inscribed each one given as a gift with a carefully chosen quote and heart-felt note. She requested the same from those who gave her books, so her collection became a record of her friendships and travels. I opened the little anthology. The writing on the flyleaf was unmistakably that of my father, but younger, clearer, more upright and uniform. Funny how one's handwriting ages too.

"*Mairzy doats and dozey doats*
And liddlee lamzy divvy
A kiddly divey too, wouldn't you?"
I love you,
Richard, 1972

They had divorced a few years later. I could hear him singing that little ditty in my head with a jaunty lilt in his voice. I hadn't heard him sing it in years. The poem was the only evidence I had that my parents had actually loved each other once, that it wasn't all painful custody battles and property division.

I walked back over to the recycling bag and fished out the letters from Ken. I bound them together with a rubber band and slid the bundle into a large manila envelope and added the program from *Much Ado About Nothing* in another box.

I blame Shakespeare. If Ken hadn't been cast as Don Pedro and I as Beatrice, we might never have met. Our dorms were on opposite ends of campus, and we didn't have any classes in common. But we had fallen in love in the dusty black box theater and on long late-night walks after rehearsal, gazing at stars, talking about the future as a bright certainty. I had floated along on a soap bubble of academia, from class to library to rehearsal, sustained by Diet Coke and a sublime baked good called the "Monster Cookie." I had thought the idyllic life of the mind would smoothly melt into domesticated bliss. But esoteric discussions that ranged from Chaos Theory to the history of the Middle East and the current peace process didn't translate well into "take out the trash and do the dishes." I found some extra packing tape and sealed the envelope twice for good measure, buried it in the back of the filing cabinet for Lainie to find when she got older.

According to *Cosmopolitan* and *House Beautiful*, I should have been living a more sophisticated existence at this point in my life, one with a creamy color palate and matching furniture. My bedroom was supposed to be a large, airy room with an enormous sleigh bed for me and my hugely successful husband. We would have a reading area with a chaise lounge and cozy armchair in front of a fireplace. The whole chamber would be richly upholstered in various shades of white and ecru, and the pop of color would come from fresh flowers delivered to the house every week. Instead, I was reunited with the bed of my childhood; its antique brass head- and footboards had been my jungle gym and ballet barre. The rosy pink duvet cover and lace dust-ruffle were pressed back into service. That evening, after I had unpacked and set up the bedroom Lainie and I would share, I stood in the doorway and watched as the sun streamed in through the wide window, casting a golden glow across the tarnished brass bedstead and the faded pink and blue floral carpet. Lainie's white crib, bookcase, and pint-sized rocking chair on one side, my things on the other. It wasn't a bedroom designed for the seduction of gentleman callers, but it would do.

When Lainie got back from her dad's house, she ran through the apartment, inspecting all the closets, cupboards and corners. She especially liked her toy shelf and the gingham-lined basket reserved for her favorite stuffed friends.

"So, this is our house now?"

"Yes."

"And Daddy lives in his house?"

"Yes." *Please let this be all right.*

"Okay. Can I go out on the bal-cany?"

"Sure." *Thank you.*

That night, I scooped her up out of her crib and brought her into bed with me. The sweet smell of her baby shampoo and soft breath against my neck calmed me enough to sleep.

On New Year's Eve, before I went to bed at 10:00 p.m., I made a to-do list for the coming year:

1. Buy a new shower-curtain liner
2. Make sure Elaine has my new address
3. Start searching for a preschool for Lainie for next fall
4. Find a new husband
5. Get the oil changed in the Acura

Chapter Two

January, 1996

We moved in and life moved on. Lainie went to day care, I went to work. In the afternoon, we made our way to the gym where Lainie loved the playroom and I tried to muster enough enthusiasm to workout. At home, we had what one might loosely term "dinner". On pleasant evenings, we walked down to the duck pond before bath time. Then there were stories to read and lunches to pack.

Work, daycare pick-up, gym, dinner, books, bed. Repeat. But there was also the "stare into space" portion of the evening; wondering, hoping, planning.

At the gym, the spinning room had floor to ceiling windows overlooking the parking lot. As I was getting my bike ready, I glanced out and saw *her* pull up in her bright, shiny red SUV. Dianne. I knew her name from signing in after her at the nursery. She unstrapped her older kids first, and the tow-haired tots scrambled out of the truck. Then she gathered the baby in her carrier and, arms dripping with pink and purple blankets and sweaters, shepherded her brood past the window, her huge diamond glittering in the sun. Dianne had everything I wanted. I had to figure out how to get it.

I didn't have long to wait to get started. After what seemed, in their opinion, to be a decent mourning period for my marriage (two weeks), my colleagues launched *Operation Get Alex a Date*. One lunch hour, Gerry showed up in my classroom. I was eating a tuna sandwich in one hand and typing a lesson plan with the other.

"Hey Alex."

"Hey Gerry, what brings you to C Hall?"

Gerry perched on a student desk across from me and glanced at the board. "You on World War Two yet?"

"I wish. We're still stuck in World War One. Bogged down in trench warfare." I laughed at my own joke.

He cocked his head, examining the picture on the board, and then stood and pointed at something that could be a cross between a dog and a small horse. I had drawn a bunch of them, poorly. "What the heck are these?" he asked.

"They are supposed to be rats, you know, the main cause of death and disease."

"Keep your day job my dear. Also, hustle up, I'm at 1938. You need to get moving, I don't want to deal with different exams in January."

"Don't worry, I assigned extra reading over break, like the evil priestess of history that I am." I had a suspicion he hadn't stopped by to align curriculum, especially since he hadn't moved from his seat. There was something more he wanted to say.

"Alex, I have this friend," he began. I braced myself. "He was the contractor on my brother-in-law's house. He's a nice guy, pretty good looking. I think he makes good money." Gerry looked at me the way I look at students hoping that they will come up with the right answer in class. The wiser course of action would be to politely decline. This could set a dangerous precedent, opening doors for all the yentas in the history department, but it was impossible to say no to my sweet colleague with the wobbly jowls and kind eyes of a basset hound.

"Um, okay, give him my number." Gerry smiled and stood to walk to the door. "But don't set his expectations too high."

"Too late!" Gerry sauntered jauntily on his way out.

***

Tassos ("call me Ted") picked me up in his monster truck (okay, perhaps it was just a huge white SUV). For my first date in years, I had paired a black pencil skirt (the bottom half of one of my work suits) with a royal blue sweater left over from high school. The tight skirt was a poor choice. It took executing a gymnastic maneuver to vault off the running board into the car. I was grateful for the seatbelt that almost kept me from slipping across the king-sized leather seat when he took tight turns.

"This is a nice car," I gasped, gripping the door handle as I slid around like a rodeo clown on a greased pig.

"I'm glad you like it. I have four of them for my business." He steered around a traffic circle like a NASCAR driver and slotted the behemoth between a Mercedes and a BMW coupe.

Ted had chosen an expensive, romantic restaurant; a candle-lit country mansion where the waitresses wore starched, ruffled aprons and floppy white colonial hats with their gingham dresses and nurses' shoes. It was lovely. Ted held my chair as I sat down. I realized, with a mixture of dread and delight, that this also was the evening of the Winter Formal at my high school, and the entire senior class seemed to have chosen this restaurant for their pre-formal festivities. A large cohort had taken over a private room next to the area where Ted and I were seated. His back was to them. Once word spread that I was there with a date, my students, mostly girls, sneaked over two-at-a-time to peek around the door jam, give me a little wave, giggle and retreat. This happened throughout the meal and at some point, Ted caught on. He thought it was cute. I was mortified. I excused myself to the bathroom where I was ambushed.

"Hey Ms. Smythe! Who is that?" Angela and Marissa, the lacrosse girls who had helped me move, were waiting inside.

"Well, he's my date. It's a blind date, actually." I just wanted to pee. I looked at the three of us in the mirror. The girls in their jewel-toned gowns and up-do hairstyles looked older and more sophisticated than I could ever hope to be, *I could use some eye shadow.* They were touching up their lipstick, and I was about to ask them if I could borrow some mascara when I thought the better of it, best to maintain some professional decorum.

"Isn't he a little old for you?" asked Marissa.

"Yeah, he looks like he could be your uncle," Angela chimed in, "or your dad."

"Gee, thanks for the support, guys. A friend set us up. Now, you know I adore you but go away so I can use the bathroom in peace.," I said.

"I just have to finish my make up."

"Stop, you're perfect. Leave."

"Okay. Good luck." They tried to muffle their laughter on the way out.

Back at the table, I attempted conversation yet again.

"So, tell me about your work," I smiled.

"I build houses," he answered.

"Do you like it?"

"Yes. It is very good."

"What do you like about it?"

"It is a good business. We make good money."

Silence.

He smiled at me.

More silence.

"Um . . . do you like the people you work with?"

"Yes, they are very nice." And thus, we sat while the restaurant bustled around us. He gazed at me with the still calm of a slow loris. My feet began to twitch with impatience. I kept glancing toward the kitchen, desperate for a view of our waitress. The axiom that the nicer the restaurant, the longer the wait, was in full play.

Saved by the arrival of our entrées, I picked at my Cornish hen and considered a story I'd read in *Cosmo* once about what men look for in a woman's apartment when they start dating. It was a typical fluffy article probably written by an intern after a few beers with her buddies. I think the title was akin to *Your Place or His? Apartment Do's and Don'ts to Get Your Guy.* According to the author, men don't like clutter, or things that are too frilly or fussy; they want a comfortable couch with a sturdy place to put their feet up. When men ask to use your bathroom, they don't want it covered in pink fuzzy accessories, nor do they want to see a counter piled with beauty accoutrements. When decorating my new bachelorette pad, I tried to keep these factors in mind, and had arranged things with a potential Prince Charming in mind, tasteful but comfortable. About thirty minutes into our date, I decided that Ted wasn't going to get to try out my couch or test my bathroom.

After dinner, Ted, in an effort to prolong an evening that he seemed to be enjoying, suggested that we go somewhere else for dessert. Torn between not wanting to be rude and my desire to go home to watch sit-com reruns, I agreed. We went to the local "river walk," which was neither a river nor much of a walk, but rather a man-made lake around which the developer had constructed a boardwalk with restaurants and a few shops. People threw French fries to the ducks. Once there, we discovered that this, too, was a popular spot for pre-Winter Formal activities.

We strolled past taffeta and be-tuxed couples, the girls shivering with the boys' jackets draped over their shoulders. They called out, "Hi Ms. Smythe." My date grinned a little too broadly. He strutted a little and I kept glancing sideways, trying to discern what qualities Gerry had seen that led him to the delusion that this date was a good idea. Ted wasn't bad looking if I squinted. Even features, dark eyes, salt and pepper hair. Nice. Boring but nice. Just as I was about to relent and agree to a second date if asked, Ted stopped and stood, looking out at the pond. He shoved his hands deep into his pockets, tucked his chin to his chest, and then looked at me.

"Alex, I have a big house. It has seven bedrooms, plenty of room for my mother and my sister, and hopefully a wife and children."

"Really?"

"Yes, five and a half baths, four-car garage. I built it myself. I just put brick pavers in the driveway. Very nice."

"So . . . your mother and sister live with you?"

"Oh yes."

"And they will want to stay even when you get married and have children?"

"Of course, they will help with the babies. In my country, this is how it is done."

"That is very . . . family-oriented," I said.

"I hope to find a nice American girl to marry. My mother would prefer someone from home, but she can't find a suitable girl."

"So, what is a suitable girl?" I asked. Now, had this been another man, I might have positioned myself provocatively against the railing of the duck pond, batted my eyelashes and thrust out my chest to elicit the response of "You, my dear, you are the perfect woman." He would lean in for the kiss, the film would fade. But, in this case, I was simply curious. What American woman would fit his requirements? And what healthy, red-blooded American gal would willingly sign up for a house full of permanent in-laws?

"You know, nice woman, good cook, likes children."

"Hmmm," I said, and continued around the pond.

***

Three days later and against my better judgement, I was back in the dating saddle, having somehow agreed to meet one of my students' swim coaches from her team at the YMCA. How I acquiesced to another set-up date was beyond me, but there we were, headed off to a Smashing Pumpkins concert with a guy named Sam. At least for this one, I thought, the wardrobe would be easy: jeans, black T-shirt, chunky shoes. My date picked me up in an aged, rattling Honda. We had agreed that I would wait for him outside because it would be a crunch to get to the show on time. He cranked down the window to wave me into the car, not bothering to get out. I got into this stranger's death-trap vehicle on the slim recommendation of a sixteen-year-old who thought we might get along. After a brief introductory conversation, we drove to the concert listening to the *Mellon Collie and the Infinite Sadness* CD, blissfully not having to talk. I examined him while his eyes were on the road. Slim build. Reddish hair. Pimply face. Unfortunate, rodent-shaped jaw. Sam had back-stage passes for before the show. He was very proud of himself. I was fairly blasé about it, which proved to be a mistake. I should have feigned ecstasy at the mere prospect of meeting the band, but this is all I knew about the Smashing Pumpkins before the concert:

1. They had some popular songs on the radio. I didn't know the names of the songs, nor of any of their albums, but they sounded good.
2. The lead singer's name was Billy Corgan. He was tall, bald, and incredibly talented.
3. My students thought the band was cool.

That was all. I should have done some investigating before the concert, but since this was the dark time just before Google became a verb and YouTube was born, research wasn't easy. I could have at least asked the guy who worked in the library at my school if he had any more info; he was hip and into music. Instead, I just winged it.

Somehow, Sam navigated us through the bowels of the stadium to the back-stage area where he showed an immense bouncer our passes. Soon we were standing awkwardly in the 'Green room.' I read my *Entertainment Weekly* (while standing in line at the grocery store), so I knew that:

a. Green rooms are seldom green

b. Performers are often divas who require exotic foods like bowls of raw squid or red m & m's be available in green rooms

c. Green rooms are places where mere mortals rarely gain entry.

Only one wall of this particular room was painted green, perhaps an ironic touch. In front of the green wall was a buffet that would have pleased even Elaine DuBonnet Smythe. The table, draped in a crisp white cloth, held white china platters heaped with fresh fruit. Brie, chevre and camembert cheeses were arranged on wooden boards with whole-wheat crackers. Cold cuts rested on a large tray next to a basketful of handmade bread and condiments, not in jars but in bowls with spoons. I don't know what I expected, but certainly not this country club fare. So much luxurious fruit, I could almost taste the plump strawberries and juicy pineapple chunks. I contemplated, while standing there stiffly, how great a social gaffe it might be to sample the green room buffet. Enormous, I figured.

The dozen-or-so people with backstage passes clumped like fettered sheep in the center of the big room. *I should have asked Sam more questions: How did you get the passes? Do you know someone important? Who are all these people? What is the protocol? How long must we stand in painful, obsequious silence in this so-called green room?* I was about to try to whisper some of these queries to my date when there was a flurry by the door and a knot of people entered. We, the sheep, craned our necks to see who they were. Judging from their build and all-black attire, it was decided that they were roadies, and we sank back into waiting.

Five minutes later, the scene repeated itself: flurry, door opening, people entering, only this time, the unmistakable bald head of Billy Corgan towered above his coterie. Our flock of sheep drew in their collective breath and dared to inch closer. The musician bobbed his head in greeting to the roadies and made his way over to us. He murmured his thanks to us for being there and shook some hands. Sam stood, eyes wide, lips slightly parted, rooted to the floor. I shoved him toward his idol and Billy shook Sam's hand. Then the rock star meandered over to the buffet, pointed at several dishes and sauntered out. His assistant rushed to fill his plate with the indicated choices and hurried after him, grabbing a pitcher of water and two glasses as she left.

Sam had an odd look on his face as we were led out of the green room, back through the underground labyrinth.

"So, that was cool," I tried.

"Yeah."

Then nothing.

"How long have you been a Smashing Pumpkins fan?" I tried again.

"Long time." He looked like he might be on the verge of tears, his Adam's apple bobbing up and down in his neck, so I let it rest while we found our seats. The warm-up act gave Sam the time he needed to collect himself.

Four songs into the concert, I began to understand some of the emotion on Sam's face. The music went from melodic and orchestral to rage-filled and percussive to whimsical and nostalgic. The writing was rich, varied, and executed with superb musicianship. But, an hour into the awesomeness, I had to go to the bathroom.

I wove my way out to the perimeter of the stadium, ears throbbing and a little disoriented from the light show. The fluorescent light inside the Ladies room was so harsh I squeezed my eyes almost shut and groped my way to the stall. My eyes started to adjust as I was zipping up my jeans. I looked down at my T-shirt and thought, *Where did the pocket go? I thought I was wearing the black Limited t-shirt with the pocket. Oh Shit, that's the outline of the pocket. I am wearing my shirt inside out. WHAT FRESH HELL IS THIS? I met Billy Freaking Corgan with my shirt inside out. I am on a date wearing a shirt inside out. Jesus Christ. I can't even wear jeans and a T-shirt right. What is wrong with me?*

I stood in the stall, indulging in self-flagellation as I turned the offending garment right-side-out. Lainie could dress herself better than I could.

As we walked back toward the car after the concert, I was trying to make conversation when Sam turned to me, pointed to the pocket on my T-shirt and said, "I was wondering when you'd figure that out."

We drove home in silence again, listening to the Smashing Pumpkins through ringing ears. Back at my apartment Sam said good night as I got out of the car, and then he sped out of the parking lot. I wouldn't hear from him again, which was okay with me.

***

The next day, my best friend, Cynthia, laughed so hard at the inside-out shirt portion of my story that she stopped making noise. I worried for a moment until I could hear her gasping for air again.

"Let me get this straight," she said, "you met Billy Corgan with your shirt on INSIDE OUT?" More laughter. I continued folding laundry, phone tucked between chin and shoulder waiting for the hilarity to wane.

"Only you, Alex." She said.

"Okay, what would you have worn?"

"I have no idea! I haven't been out of my sweats in three weeks." More laughter.

"You do realize that this is not helping my self-confidence at all, right?" I asked while trying to match very small socks. "Let's talk about your life for a change, jeez."

"Okay, you need a laugh too."

"Yes, ma'am, I do." I agreed.

"So, the other day, I had Buster out with me to run a few errands and then we stopped in the park on the way home so he could get his ya-ya's out, and he was very bouncy, all over the place. I could hardly hold on to his leash."

"Yeah?"

"Yeah, and I've got my bag from Blockbuster and a coffee in the other hand, and then he sees another dog and the two of them completely lose their minds, and all of a sudden Buster is running circles around me, has the leash around my legs, so, of course I trip, the coffee goes flying and I land on my face. It was not cool."

Now it *was* my turn to laugh, imagining the scene, Cyn with her corkscrew brown curls and brightly patterned warm-up suit being dragged through the park by Buster, who weighed almost as much as she did.

"Okay, yeah, funny, but you are never, ever going to guess who was the other dog owner," she said.

"Probably not."

"Vanessa."

"No." I put down the socks. Vanessa was Cyn's ex-fiancé's sister. "What happened?"

"It's not as dramatic as it sounds. Or as it could have been, that's for sure. She helped me get untangled. was very civil," Cyn said.

"For once."

"It wasn't her fault."

"We're not talking about the dogs," I said.

"No, none of it was her fault really. Well yeah, she could have controlled her dog better, but she had nothing to do with the whole Steve thing."

"Well, you're right, she didn't make Steve cheat on you. But she could have been a whole lot nicer through it all. She didn't have to be such a bitch about returning the gifts and all that. And she could have, at some point, acknowledged what that jerk put you through," I said.

"I know. It's still hard to think about. And this is not going to entice me out of the basement again any time soon if I might run into ex-future-in-laws. I can live on pizza and Chinese for a very, very long time, my friend," Cynthia said.

"I know. I don't blame you."

"And you are very brave to go out on blind dates."

"I think 'foolhardy' is the word you're looking for," I said.

"Well, slow down, sister, you just moved out, there is no need to rush this."

"I know. Okay. Gotta run, talk to you later."

"Love ya."

"Love you too." I rang off.

**

If I'm being honest, three things had arrived in the mail that had led me to agree to the whole blind-date experiment:

1. My final divorce papers arrived in a thick, official envelope.

KENNETH PORTER

V

ALEXANDRIA SMYTHE PORTER

2. A letter from my mom, who was in Africa and therefore unavailable to talk me out of it.

Darling Alexandria:

I know this is a tough time for you, and you might be wondering why I didn't fly back to help you. I thought about it but decided that I would probably just be in the way, and that this is something you need to take charge of for yourself. I'll come visit when you're settled.

When I left your dad, I had so much anger. I got through it with vodka-tonics and pistachios. I'm sure you'll make more heathy choices. Honestly, honey, that was my biggest regret about my divorce, staying angry for too long. My only advice to you is to turn that anger into more productive energy. You need to find your own way like I eventually did. Decide what you want your life to be, and make it happen.

Well, that's my two-cents worth. Maybe a nickel. Kiss the fabulous Lainie for me.

Love you,
Mom
P.S. Please send me your new address soon. Xo

3. The alumni magazine from my prep school. In the Class Notes section I read:

Stanford Todd Pierce: *I am happy to report that I have joined Paine Webber in NYC, the hours are brutal, but having a blast entertaining clients. Look me up if you're in the city!*

Mackenzie Bowen: *I am pleased to announce that I have recently accepted a clerkship with the Honorable Joseph C. Tauro of the District Court of Massachusetts in Boston.*

Corey Sanderson: Hello from Ulaanbaatar! I am doing research on the economic patterns of nomadic peoples. Will return to Harvard next fall to continue my doctoral program.

Jessica Ann McDormand's parents report that she is working with the Peace Corps in Ecuador.

Six other classmates wrote in to tell us about their medical residencies, and another three talked about starting their PhDs. In the past quarter, no one, not a soul, had gotten married or had a baby. After college, I had started one career, abandoned it, done a quick fifteen months in grad school, started teaching, gotten married, had Lainie, and got divorced. I imagined that my peers all had fabulously chic condos or were bunking in yurts and living off of goats' milk. I had a crappy apartment in the suburbs and a few monumentally bad blind dates. My classmates were soaring. I was crashing and burning.

So, wanting to salvage my life and recreate a family for my kid, and not wanting to be set up on another date ever again, I chose another strategy.

I stumbled onto the personal ads one cold Sunday afternoon when Lainie was at her dad's house. I was snuggled on the couch, avoiding grading a huge stack of papers. Having exhausted the rest of the newspaper, I fell onto the personal ads. I blame Jane Austen. If Elizabeth Bennet could marry Mr. Darcy, I could imagine meeting Mr. Right in all his glory. He would be older, rich, handsome, wearing a blazer, waiting to sweep me off my feet. He would be a sexy-smart combination of Cary Grant and Richard Gere. There had to be a winner among the likes of: Successful Entrepreneur, Healthy & Humorous, Great Smile, and Dream Man.

***

Like an addicted gambler at a slot machine, I couldn't get enough of these ads. I became slightly obsessed. Every morning for two weeks, I'd drag us through the routine: rush to work, pick up Lainie, rush to the gym. In the evenings Lainie would eat some version of macaroni and cheese and carrots while I heated up a Lean Cuisine. Duck pond, books, bedtime. Then I'd plant my butt back on the couch with a sit-com on the TV, papers to grade next to me and the paper with the personal ads nearby for study breaks. It was a pathetic life, but it seemed to be working.

"Listen to this one," I said to Cyn. It was a little challenging having a best friend all the way in Houston, so the phone would have to do. I read to her:

"**Broker, Bad Boy,** SWM, 32, stocks by day, fun by night. Seeks fun-loving SWF for hot nights. No attachments, no tattoos, no fatties"

"Sounds like a self-absorbed ass," she said. "Find something else."

"Okay, how about: '**Smart, Successful** DWPM, 40, gym-built body, heart of a poet. Seeking similar, any race, for date nights, romance, and Possible LTR?'"

"'Gym-built' is a bit much," she said, "also, a little too old for you."

"Yeah, he lost me with the poetry."

"Alex, you know you're a feminist's nightmare," Cyn said.

"What are you talking about?" I asked, feigning naiveté. I had a feeling about where she was going with this.

"You don't need a man. Just take some time, enjoy yourself. What has gotten into you?"

I leaned back on the sofa and surveyed the apartment my friend had never seen. It was fine. It was clean. The white walls were freshly painted, the furniture had been cobbled together from past dwellings and thrift shops. Realizing that a full-sized couch would take up too much room, I'd purchased two love seats from an ad in the paper and had covered the ugly chintz with solid navy-blue fabric. With the over-loaded bookshelves, black-and-white photos on the wall and a few potted plants, it was fine. But it wasn't home.

"I want a family, Cyn."

"You have a family. You have Lainie."

"You know what I mean. And I am going to be thirty soon."

"So what?" she said.

"So, the clock is ticking. Guys want younger women. I want more kids. I don't have time to mess around." *And I am beginning to panic.*

"You are insane. This is the '90s, and you're acting like it's 1950 and you need a man and an apron," she said.

"Probably more neurotic than fully insane."

"Just promise me you'll be careful," she said.

"Yes, ma'am, I'll be careful."

I would have continued as a personal-ad voyeur had it not been for my calamitous dates with Ted and Sam, but, determined to set my own course, I called the number in the paper to ask how much this would cost me.

"It's free to place an ad, Ma'am," the operator explained.

"Then how does the paper make any money?"

"The people wanting to meet the advertisers call the number and they are charged a fee to listen to voice messages. If they like your message, they can leave a voice mail and you can decide if you want to call them back. No one gets your name or your phone number unless you want them to. It's really very safe." He sounded like he was reading off a script and had answered this question far too many times.

"So, since I am putting my heart and soul out for the world to see, I don't pay?"

"That is correct, ma'am."

Stop calling me ma'am.

"Okay, I'll call you back when I figure out what my ad should say."

"Suit yourself," he said.

Since I was broke, placing an ad was the only option. The key to these ads seemed to be in the first two words, which were printed in bold. If they weren't eye-catching, Mr. Right would blow right by my ad and call the **Aspiring Astronaut** instead. It had to reel them in while containing a kernel of truth. There was a fine line between sounding grossly egomaniacal and writing something that would actually attract someone.

Actual truth in advertising would have required that I write:

Mildly Myopic, or Slightly Neurotic, or Fairly Desperate
Seeks answers to life's questions and
unresolved relationship issues stemming from
unsettled matters with father and
insecurities about own self-worth.

I scribbled different ideas for twenty minutes before settling on:

Erudite Athlete
NS, DWPF, 29, seeks similar, 35-45

For fun, adventure, possible LTR.

'Athlete' may have been a stretch, but I was, in fact, an educated, non-smoking, divorced white professional female who happened to exercise.

Then there was the matter of recording my voice message. After seven or eight attempts I had recorded, "Hi, my name is Alex. Thank you for responding to my ad. First, you need to know that I have a two-and-a-half-year-old daughter." I stopped for a long, dramatic pause, then continued the message with, "Okay, if you haven't hung up yet, or run screaming from the room at the idea of a toddler, and you like what you saw in my ad, please leave a message. Thanks, and have a great day!" Hopefully the ad would lure them in. If the idea of a two-year-old made them squeamish, I didn't want to talk to them anyway. If nothing else, I rationalized, it would be interesting to meet new people, give me a reason to get out of my lair and back into the world. Maybe I would find the guy to help me on my mission of building the white-picket-fence life. I had no idea what I was in for.

Chapter Three
February, 1996

In the late '80s, *When Harry Met Sally* hit the movie theatres. I am sure it was meant to give solace and hope to those looking for love. But the only line I could remember was when Carrie Fisher's character is in bed with her boyfriend. She says, "Promise me I'll never be out there again." And he promises, but there I was, out there again.

Bill was the first man to respond to my ad. I liked the way his voice sounded, confident but not cocky. Bill Owens (if that was his real name) was handsome for an older guy. We met at a stylish, modern restaurant on M Street, above a law firm. I got there first, he trundled up the stairs soon after, clutching a small plastic bag in one hand and an expensive looking briefcase in the other. Navy suit, distinguished grey beard, neatly trimmed. Full head of hair, also very neat. Lively blue eyes danced over ruddy cheeks, a business-man dandy who might age like Santa Claus Also, probably older than adver-tised, but I focused on The Mission.

"Hi, Alex?"
"Yes, Bill?"

He nodded and, shifting the plastic bag, reached to shake my hand. He wasn't much taller than me. "I called ahead. They should have our table soon," he said, rising to his tip-toes to peer over my head at the maître d'. We were ushered to our table and ordered drinks.

"I brought a present for your kid. I was in Florida last week and thought..." struggling for the right pronoun. I had to give him points for re-membering that I had a young child. It was a small, stuffed Mickey Mouse toy.

"I'm sure she'll love it. Thank you." I graciously received his offering. He smiled, looked relieved and asked me a few questions about Lainie, how old she was and where she went to daycare.

"My ex and I never had kids." *Woah, pardner!* We slammed into that top-ic rather suddenly for first-date protocol; our drinks hadn't even arrived yet.

23

"Do you regret it?"

"Hard to say. She was pretty wrapped up in work, and I guess I was too. I like little kids, I just don't know if I was ready."

"I don't know if anyone is really ready until it happens to them," I said, making light of it.

It was a nice date: tasty food, easy conversation. No sparks flying, no detectable chemistry, but nice. Bill talked about how he was too busy with his job to work out like he wanted to. We discovered that we both wanted to travel, and that we had both wanted to see Hong Kong before it reverted back to Chinese control, but life got in the way of that dream. His self-confident manner was attractive enough to warrant a second date. Evidently, I too met whatever standard he had in his head, or at least, I wasn't a disappointment. A kiss on the cheek and an early weeknight departure. Not bad.

The second date was much like the first, but at an older, classier restaurant with dim lighting and plush decor. The carpet was thick and springy beneath my feet as we walked to our table. Bill was a savvy businessman and talented raconteur, I almost didn't have to be there, he carried the conversation with little effort. After a week of teaching classes full of hyper teenagers, it was a relief to take the conversational back seat. I sank into the deep velvety booth and enjoyed being treated so well. If I cocked my head to one side and took a deep breath, he could possibly be husband material. Maybe. We ordered our drinks and entrées, then Bill's beeper buzzed.

"Excuse me, this won't take long." He went to find a phone in the lobby.

"Hi." Our waitress appeared next to the table, another table's drink order balanced on her arm. "Can I ask you a question?" She was a small woman with soft eyes and a matronly smile.

"Sure," I said.

"Is your dad single?" I stared at her dumbly, thinking about my dad in Connecticut and his string of girlfriends. She nodded her head in the direction of the lobby. *Oh my God, she thinks Bill is my dad!* She stood expectantly, looking toward the door. I could see Bill's silhouette. He gestured with his free hand and was rocking back and forth, heel to toe, toe to heel. This woman just mistook my date for my father. I had no sharp comeback for that. I stammered, "N-No, actually, that's my date." There was a uncomfortable silence. I'm not sure which one of us was more embarrassed.

"Oh." She tilted her head, squinting to get a better look at me. "I'm very sorry, that was so rude of me. Uh, sorry." She scurried away as Bill returned. I watched him as he ambled back to the table, his belly leading the way, his arms slightly trailing behind like the wake of a tugboat. Perhaps this wasn't an ideal match.

We were waiting for our entrées when our waitress returned bearing a tray with a *brie en croûte* garnished with pecans.

"We apologize for the delay in your dinner, a large party was seated just before you. Chef thought you might like to sample this appetizer while you wait." That was a very smooth lie. She looked at me, smiling in a strange fashion that said: *Please don't tell your date that I thought he was old enough to be your dad.* Technically, though, he was.

"Great! What a nice surprise, thanks, doll," Bill said, and dove into the brie.

Throughout dinner, Bill checked his watch more times than might be considered polite. As the busboy cleared our entrée dishes, Bill said, "Let's go back to my place for coffee. The game is on and I have ice cream in the freezer." He was trying hard to make this sound casual, but I had a feeling that he was getting anxious.

I had no idea what kind of game he was referring to and frankly, I wasn't quite sure which sporting season we were in. I was not a fan of televised sports but I had come to the conclusion that most heterosexual American males have a biological need for televised athletic contests. They fear that without exposure to TV sports their manhood might shrivel and die. I had met men for whom this was not an issue, who ignore sports on TV for months on end. However, most of these had shown flaws in other traditionally masculine arenas, such as lawn care and automotive maintenance, so I had reconciled myself to the fact that my future mate might indeed, be a football or basketball fan. Televised golf, however, was a deal breaker. Period.

Bill's house was decorated in an early Divorced Guys R Us motif. His ex must have departed with any matching furniture and seemed to have stripped the windows of all their dressing for good measure. What hodgepodge of furniture he did have looked like it was recently acquired at a going-out-of-business sale. He threw his wallet and keys into the large decorative dish on the counter.

"Do you mind if I get out of my work clothes?"

"No, go right ahead."

"Help yourself to anything in the fridge," he shouted over his shoulder. When I was fairly sure he was in the bedroom, I gingerly picked up his wallet, just a peek. His driver's license told me that yes, he had lied about his age. He also carried far more cash than I would be comfortable with. Resisting the urge to help myself to a twenty, I slipped the wallet back and looked around the kitchen, barren but clean.

"All right! Let's get this game going!" Bill bellowed on his way into the living room. I turned and stood in shock; the man who had emerged from the bedroom was not my date. Gone were the polished wingtips and cashmere topcoat. Gone was the suave businessman in a sharp suit. In his place was a stocky troll-man with spindly, hairy legs sticking out of baggy shorts. His leg fur extended down over preternaturally long toes clearly visible in cheap rubber flip-flops. A light blue T-shirt stretched over his beer paunch. Before he was fully in the room, he spied a foul on the play and began shouting at the TV referee from four yards back. He looked like a lost Hobbit and sounded like a shrieking fishwife. It was time to go.

***

I spent most of the next day congratulating myself on only spending two evenings with Bill. It was Thursday, so Lainie was with Ken. I stayed at work late to lesson plan and grade papers. By the time I got home after the gym, at about 8:30, the red light on my answering machine was flashing. Four flashes, pause, four flashes, pause.

4:35 pm: "Hi Alex, it's Bill, please call me back." His voice was chipper.

5:40 pm: "Hi Alex, Bill again . . . um, I had a lot of fun last night, let's go out again. Call me!"

5:55 pm: "Hi Alex, me again..." Beep

7:30 pm: "Hi Alex, it's me, Bill, maybe you lost my number. It's . . . "

Why don't they just go away quietly? I stood in my tiny kitchen with my coat still on and picked up the phone. Best to get it over with quickly, rip off the band aid.

"Hi Bill, it's Alex— No, I really don't think I should go out with you again." He was very quiet on his end, so I started babbling to fill the empty space. "I had fun with you too, but I think it's best to be honest, and I just don't see this going anywhere." I blathered on for a bit before realizing the futility of it. I stopped. Silence.

"Um, okay, thanks, bye," he said and hung up. That was easier than expected. I started settling in, putting away my gym stuff, looking at the mail, putting my frozen dinner in the microwave. The phone rang again and I answered it out of habit.

"Hello?"

"Is it me?"

"Excuse me?"

"Is it me? Is there something wrong with me?" Bill asked. I knew that the minute I hung up from this call all manner of sharp retorts would come to mind, but in the moment all I could muster was, "What do you mean, Bill?"

"What is it about me that makes you not want to see me again?"

Why? Why was this guy calling me? What would happen if he didn't like my answer? At least he didn't know where I lived. Mother always said if you don't have anything nice to say, don't say anything, so, *you're a testosterone crazed potbellied troll man who yells at the TV and lies about his age to get girls* was probably a bit harsh.

"I, um . . . " I stabbed the plastic covering on the frozen lasagna with a fork a few times before putting it back in the microwave . . . "I'm just not ready for another relationship right now. I thought I was, but I'm not really. I'm sorry." Why the hell was I apologizing? I didn't interrupt *his* Budget Gourmet dinner.

"No, I know it's me. Please tell me what it is so I can change." All right, I thought, screw it. I am starving. What the hell?

"Okay Bill, it was you. Bye." I had the phone half-way to the receiver and heard, "PLEASE ALEX WHAT WAS IT ABOUT ME?" The microwave lasagna was just not going to cut it. I reached for the ice cream hidden behind the frozen peas. Screw it.

***

"Can I measure your couch?" I answered the door on a Tuesday evening to find an earnest and harried young man standing in the doorway, tape measure in hand.

"Excuse me?"

"Oh, I'm sorry, I'm Fred. We just rented the apartment upstairs but I don't get the keys until the day after tomorrow, and my wife just called from Salt Lake City and wants to know if she should have her brothers put the couch in the U-Haul because if it doesn't fit, why bother? Our apartments are all the same, so I thought I'd ask." He was about my age or a year younger, his cheeks shining like brightly polished apples.

"Come on in. I only have two small love-seats, but I'm sure it's more the width than the length." I thought about that for a moment. Any other male friend would have snickered at the penis joke, but it sailed right over my new friend's freshly tonsured hair. He attacked the love seat with the tape measure, efficiently jotted the numbers on a notepad that had materialized from his pocket, snapped the pad shut, gave the tape measure an expert flick and it wound back into itself.

"Thank you. Have a good evening." He smiled and was gone.

I heard his wife three days before I met her. At 1:00 a.m. I was still up, half-heartedly grading papers and painting my nails when I heard a disconcerting thumping in the ceiling. Convinced that the building was collapsing, I was planning how I'd snatch sleeping Lainie from her crib, fold her in a blanket and swing Tarzan-like from the balcony to safety, when I realized what the noise actually was.

Thump. Thump. Thump. Groan. Moan. Thump. Thump. The Mormons were making noisy midnight love.

On Sunday afternoon, she appeared at my door, bearing a plate of homemade lemon squares. She was cheery and, of course, wearing overalls. Surely she could wield a pitchfork and bake a pie. At the same time.

"Hi! I'm Lori! Fred told me you had been a help to him when we were moving in. I just wanted to say thank you, and we're looking forward to being neighbors." I should have been the one welcoming her with baked goods. Would my inadequacies never end? Turns out, I would learn a lot from my Mormon neighbors.

***

When someone calls and places a personal ad, it runs for two weeks, after which, one can call the paper and renew. Or not. After a short hiatus, I decided to try again. I ran the same ad two months after the first. Maybe it was a full moon, or perhaps there was a spate of bravado in the metropolis, but this time I was bombarded with voice mail responses to my ad. Some men sounded interesting; some sounded familiar, as though perhaps I had rejected them from the first go-round. I decided I needed a tracking system. God forbid I do something stupid like respond to the same guy twice, or accidently call Bill back. After much thought and doodling during a staff meeting, I came up with the following:

Name:
Date of message:
Phone number:
Age (alleged):
Occupation:
Hobbies:
Meeting Time, Place:
Notes:

I toyed with the idea of a point system, awarding points for fiscal solvency, level of tolerance for toddlers, willingness to have more children, interesting hobbies, education, etc. But that would take it beyond the limits of a 3 x 5 card, which was what I'd allotted for the task. Philosophically, it would also be like a university rejecting one solely based on one's SAT scores without reading the essay, which was unfair. So, on an evening when I should have been grading papers or cleaning the bathroom, I sat with the phone glued to my ear, going through the messages, filling out a card for every guy, even those who were not going to get a return call, just in case. I placed the cards in a little box, thankful that Lainie was still too young to read.

***

I love my gym. To be clear, not the actual working out, but the fact that it was a place to go between work and the yawning loneliness of home. And, there was Leon.

Leon came by, pretending to dust the StairMaster next to mine, and, like a character in a spy movie, he spoke out of the side of his mouth without looking at me.

"His name is Grant Grabowski. Thirty-four. Works for the DEA. No wife or kids listed on the membership."

"That explains why they call him G. I thought it was some stupid rap reference."

"Well that would be really stupid 'cause y'all are *white* and he's got 'I am a country music guy' written all over himself."

"Any idea what happened with the finger?"

"How would I know? Looks like a wood shop accident."

"But, DEA . . . maybe a cartel guy cut it off."

"Your imagination is rich, my friend."

"So why isn't he hitting on me?"

"I don't know, it doesn't make sense. You're age appropriate," he said.

"Thanks for the ego boost. Do we have to do the middle school thing? Do you want to go over and tell him I think he's cute for me?"

Leon had given up pretending to clean. "Maybe he'll meet you by the water fountain after recess." He waved the dust rag at me and strolled away to take his place behind the desk.

Grant had the most beautifully rounded shoulders I'd ever seen, with lines that cut sharp V's inside perfect circles. Of course, he wore tank tops for the express purpose of showing them off. Crew cut. Penetrating eyes, lopsided grin, but when I overheard him talking, he displayed a woeful lack of grammar and a thin vocabulary, I considered that, if I could get his attention, the resulting liaison might be more on the physical side of things.

I only saw Grant at the gym where we spent quality time in spinning class together. Sometimes I'd get there early and stand among the stationary bikes, analyzing where I might sit to attract maximum attention from the object of my lust. Directly opposite so we could stare intently and make eye contact, or off to the side for a more subtle approach? But then he might catch me staring sideways at him. Do I sit right next to him and let the pheromones do the trick? Better still, should I sit next to someone more chubby and less attractive, making myself look thinner and more glamorous by comparison? I was forgetting, however, that I would have to spend far more money on my workout wardrobe and sweat-proof makeup to even approach glamour in the cycle room. Old bike shorts and paint-stained T-shirts left over from high school just wouldn't cut it. I had also come to the conclusion a while ago that I have the type of body that other women like to look at to make them feel better about themselves. Seducing Grant was going to take some creativity.

After all my careful plotting, when I attempted to start a casual conversation after spinning class with nine-fingered G, The Blonde slid between us. I had seen her in the locker room before class, brushing bronzer into her cleavage. She had logged so many hours on the tanning bed that the bronzer was totally unnecessary, clearly a force of habit. Once she had cornered G, there was no way I could join the conversation without looking desperately obvious, or obviously desperate. This was doubly frustrating as The Blonde was wearing a huge, flashy diamond on her left hand. Didn't she know it was against the rules for a married or engaged woman to monopolize a legitimately single man? Didn't I know I was being an idiot, getting my hopes up, cycle class after cycle class? The agony of what T-shirt to wear, how much makeup to wear to look naturally sporty, yet pretty? All these mental machinations—only to be thwarted by a pair of bronzed boobs bubbling over a bright yellow sports bra. She completed her look with coiffed platinum hair and screaming pink lipstick. People had to reserve their space in this class weeks in advance and It irked me to no end that this girl took up a coveted bike for an entire class, then idly pedaled while the rest of us sweated and grunted through an actual workout. If Bimbina did sweat, it was only to work up a misty dew, which she dabbed away with a little yellow towel that matched her top.

I marched over to the front desk. As soon as Leon was off the phone I leaned over the counter and stage whispered, "Damn, that's what I'm missing, the yellow push-up bra and matching my lip color with my nail polish. Also, a hair style that resembles a giant piece of bubble gum being blown into a perfect sphere through a hole in the top of my skull." I didn't need to identify the object of my fury. Leon knew.

He laughed at me. "My friend, you're looking a little too sorry to attract the likes of him. Get yourself an outfit!"

"Shut up and sell a membership." I said. He smiled and waved me away. I went to pick Lainie up from the nursery, and stood for a moment, watching over the open top of the Dutch door as she played with another little girl sharing the mini kitchen, pretending to cook. She came away reluctantly when I called. *This kid needs a sibling* I thought as we headed back to our quiet home.

***

I am dreaming. I am in a sun-drenched field of tall purple flowers trying to walk across it, but moving slowly because I am dream-walking through thigh high purple flowers, and I am not really in a rush. Far away, I hear a bell ringing and ringing. The purple fades, so does the sun and the blissful heat, because the bell is the Goddamned phone at two o'clock in the morning.

"Sorry honey, I know this is a bad time, but it was the only time I could get to the village phone. Can you hear me? Alex? Alex?"

"Yes, Mom, I hear you." Actually, it was a remarkably good connection, but I stood with the wireless handset close to the base, just in case. If we got disconnected, I might not hear from my mother again for a month.

"Are there purple flowers in your village Mom?"

"What? Alex, did I wake you?" She was shouting.

"Of course you did, as you always do, don't worry about it. How are you?" I asked.

"Great, doing just great. Things here are progressing nicely. We're having a great time."

"Who's 'we'?"

"Oh, I have a few missionaries visiting from Iowa. It's nice to have new people here. They are fun to have around, especially when they aren't rambling on about Jesus." For a missionary, my mother had an interesting relationship with God. Her voice had toned down, realizing we had a decent connection. "How's my Lainie?"

"Fine. Fabulous, actually. She loves her school and her teachers."

"Is she reading yet?"

"Mom, let's remember, Lainie is two and a half."

"Oh, I know, she's just so smart. Listen, honey, I don't know how much longer I'll have the line, I just wanted you to know that I am planning a visit, mid-September. Does that work for you?"

"I'll be back at work. Can you come in August?"

"No, I know, it's not the best timing. I'll just be at your place for a week, okay? I'll mail you my flight info when I have it."

"Did you get my letter? With the drawings?"

"Yes, tell Lainie she's quite the artist."

"I will. Are you alright? Is there anything I can send you?"

"I'm fine. You have enough to deal with. I don't need a thing. Have you been going to church?" (This from a woman who could only take so much Jesus. It's complicated.)

"Yes," I lied.

"Good. Maybe you'll meet a nice guy there. I have to go, they need the line."

"Okay, I miss you Mom."

"I miss you too sweetie, but you're doing great. Love you."

"Love you too." The line went dead. I missed that crazy woman so much sometimes. You spend your entire adolescence wishing your parents would leave you alone. Then they do, and you wish you hadn't been so hasty.

The last time Elaine had been state-side was for Lainie's christening in 1993. I'd been a mess, running myself into the ground trying to obliterate every dust particle in the house and attempting to re-create the "simple" dinners from that propaganda rag designed to make one feel totally inferior, *Good Housekeeping*. Ken was somewhat helpful taking care of the baby as I scurried around the townhouse. I gained four stress pounds in the weeks before her arrival. The immaculate home of my youth and the exacting standards of my mother haunted my every move. Following the suggestion of an older colleague with a similarly demanding parent, I carefully mapped out, on lined legal paper, every hour of the ten days prior to her arrival. Each evening was dedicated to housework and pre-party culinary and decoration prep.

By the time the weekend arrived, the house was pristine, nutritious food was in the fridge, Lainie's entire lovely, tiny wardrobe was freshly laundered and the flower beds were weeded. Driving to the airport, all I wanted to do was listen to music and try to calm down. Instead, my mind began to predict the course of the visit. In this mental video, my elegant mother would run her manicured fingers across the furniture in an automatic, if unconscious, search for dust. She would look around the small rooms of our townhouse and immediately begin the campaign of suggestions: *This plant would look so nice over here. Why did you choose this color? Let me help you reorganize your kitchen cabinets. You really could use some window treatments. When was the last time you saw the inside of a salon? Eugene would be very disappointed in your hair. You don't have enough stimulating toys for the baby, you have to make her mind work all the time, you know."* The knot in my stomach was fully formed and pulling tighter as we reached the baggage claim.

Exhausted passengers plodded in a daze toward the baggage carousel. Eighteen-hour flights are one reason (among many) that I wouldn't be visiting Mom in Africa any time soon; the people trickling into the baggage claim area were emerging from airborne Purgatory. With growing anxiety, I watched the line of people leaving from the gate. A dozen travelers passed. Then another, and another. If she didn't appear soon, the space behind my eyes would start to throb. There hadn't been any messages on the machine; I'd checked before I left. Where was she? Lainie started to fuss. Guilt replaced anxiety; I should not have brought such a new baby to the airport. Germs were surely on their way to attack my infant. I was sure thousands of micro-organisms were settling into her clothing, her blankets, her car carrier. I made a mental note to Clorox everything as soon as we got home. Where the hell was my mother?

"Hey sweetheart," came a voice by my shoulder. I didn't recognize this person. It was Elaine, but a strange new hippie version instead of the chic, sophisticated mother I knew. I had taken Lainie out of her stroller, clutching her to my chest in a vain attempt to have her breathe less-contaminated air. Reaching out to hug my mom, I tripped over the stroller and almost fell, which provided good cover for the shock that would have otherwise been readily apparent on my face.

"It's so good to see you!" We held each other for a long time, baby Lainie and my arm squished between our bodies, three generations united for the first time in baggage claim.

"Let me see this little angel." Her voice was hoarse. I settled Lainie into the arms of her namesake and pulled tissues out of my purse. "She's so beautiful. So beautiful. So perfect." Elaine gazed at her first grandchild. I refrained from asking if she had washed her hands.

"I think she has your chin," I said.

"Yes, and your eyes. Our DuBonnet genes will win every time."

"Well you have to give the Porter side some credit," I offered in defense of my husband. "I'm sure we'll see a little of him in her as she gets older."

"Maybe, maybe not." Elaine grinned.

"Which suitcase did you bring, the usual?" I asked. She nodded in response, not looking up from Lainie's face. I left the baby-bonding to find her black bag. Fortunately, this was a flight from Malawi. I hate trying to find her bag when she flies from New York where everyone's bags are black. The luggage carousel is much more interesting after international flights; boxes with strange labels, bags in all shapes and colors come tumbling down to be plucked from the belt by men in kaftans and women in bright dresses. Elaine's squat black bag floated past between a box crisscrossed with duct tape marked *Apon Ogbongo Bobo* and a green striped carpet bag. Knowing that her gear always pushed the upper limits of the weight restriction, I bent at the knees and heaved. Overestimating, I flew backward, the suitcase sailing high over my head. Taking three huge steps backward, I wobbled, then regained my balance, somehow managing to keep hold of the handle.

"Mom, I think you've been robbed! There's hardly anything left in your bag!" I bent to open it, fumbling with the zippers and mentally preparing to confront the airport staff.

"No, honey, don't worry, I'm just traveling light." She said this without looking away from Lainie. They were making silly noises at each other. I stared at them. This was so . . . unexpected. Elaine's hair, normally stylishly arranged and perpetually auburn, had grown out halfway, so that she looked to be wearing a muddy gray cap. It was pulled into a low ponytail, as if an aged beaver with a short chestnut tail had perched on her head. Where had she gotten that dress? What happened to the St. John Knit travel outfit? The Elaine DuBonnet Smythe I knew wouldn't be caught dead in a shapeless denim dress or Birkenstocks. There was no polish on her toes or fingers. When she'd departed for Africa a year earlier, Elaine had boarded the airplane with her usual ensemble of matching Fendi handbag and tote full of magazines and moisturizers. Now, this person had a batik cloth backpack slung across her shoulders. It, too, was nearly empty.

We talked nonstop on the way home. It was like she never left, until I glanced sideways and saw her hair. Ugh.

"I'm really sorry about the christening gown. I didn't expect this to happen so soon," Elaine said.

"We've been married three years, Mom, what did you think? You knew we wanted to start having kids right away." I decided not to discuss how disappointed I was that Lainie would not be baptized in the gown I had worn.

"I should have had Janet separate some of that stuff out before—"

"Before what?"

"Didn't I tell you? I had Janet pack and move all of my things into a storage unit so the workers could come in." Elaine was speaking absently, twisting around so she could look at Lainie in the back seat.

"What workers? What are you talking about?" I was confused.

"I'm getting ready to sell the house. I'm just going to stay in Malawi for a while. It's too much bother having two homes."

What the hell? She was just supposed to be gone for a year. Get the Isak Dinesen Karen Blixen Mother Theresa nonsense out of her system and come home. *Oh My God, how am I supposed to raise my kid without having my mom around?* Or at least close enough that a phone call doesn't entail staying up until the middle of the night and dealing with international operators just to ask if green poop warrants a trip to the doctor? I thought grandmas lived for this moment. What was she thinking? She was missing it. Missing her namesake's babyhood, missing me becoming a mother. I felt a mounting inward panic.

"Um, Mom, I thought Dr. Ramback told you not to make big decisions on your own. Have you spoken to him? Have you spoken to anyone about this?" I changed lanes to the far-right side of the highway. I needed to drive very slowly.

"I've meditated. You should try it."

"But what about me?" I blurted. The filter mechanism on my mouth failed. "What about me and Lainie? You can't leave us now. We need you!"

"No you don't. You'll be fine. I am happy." I recognized the end-of-discussion tone. "Look at that baby. She's just wonderful."

"Don't change the subject," I pushed.

"It's settled, Alex. The house has been on the market for three months. I'll be in the States long enough to sell it, then I'll be on my way. While I'm here we can talk about shipping some things from my house to you. Then you can come visit me in Malawi when Lainie gets a little older."

So, that was it, my last parental refuge in the Western Hemisphere was gone. I knew what this meant. Holidays at the in-laws. Always. Or so I had thought.

Chapter Four
February, 1996, Continued

My date that night was to be with one Marty Klein, who sounded fairly nice on the phone. While he met criteria one, three, four and five for a first date: proper use of grammar, decent conversationalist, fairly well educated, gainfully employed, he lost points in the interesting category. I would discover that he only sounded boring because he was hiding his life's passion, one that he only revealed in person.

This wasn't a date I was excited about. More of a what-do-I-have–to-lose-on-a-Friday-when-Lainie-is-with-Ken kind of date. The evening air was crisp and the moon shone bright out of a navy sky. I parked on a side street off Wisconsin Avenue and took my time, peeping into the windows of stately townhouses as I crossed the cobblestones; the rich, warmly lit interiors welcoming yet elusive. I lingered outside the restaurant for a few minutes, reluctant to enter. It was as narrow as the neighborhood townhouses with roughly a dozen tables covered in traditional red and white table cloths. As the host walked me back to the table, I scanned the restaurant for single males, hoping to get a look at my date before he saw me. When I got the first look, I felt far more confident, but this game was getting so old that I almost turned around and left to enjoy the evening on my own. I should have followed my instincts.

Marty had a head of full, beautiful dark hair, and a face one could live with. We got through the preliminaries, what do you do . . . where did you grow up . . . do you have family . . . without incident. His answers: research scientist, Minnesota, parents still alive, one younger brother. Things were going well enough to order dinner, so we did. Which was a mistake. Disaster struck moments after the waitress walked away. I remember the intensity of his blue eyes as Marty leaned in close over the table. He looked into my face, earnestly as a foreigner trying to communicate in a strange language and said to me, "Alex, do you ever wonder what is out there?" He gestured up and outward with his chin.

"You mean up beyond the Rockville Pike?"

"No, further."

"Um, what do you mean?"

"Alex, I believe that we are going to colonize the moon in my lifetime, and I want to be part of it." I waited. For a moment, I thought he was joking, testing my sense of humor. I waited for the laughter, the "just kidding." But it didn't happen. Marty continued without the slightest ironic inflection, his face the essence of absolute sincerity.

This man fully, whole-heartedly believed that he was destined to live on the moon, perhaps commuting back to Earth every six months or so on the space shuttle for a Costco run. He talked about sustainability and renewable fuel and food sources. Marty believed that it would be a multi-national effort funded with a combination of government money and charitable contributions. He went on to say what may well have been many other interesting things about colonizing the moon, but I couldn't hear them over the voice screaming in my head to *GET OUT NOW.*

I reviewed my options: pretend the babysitter had paged me, feign illness, set myself ablaze with the candle on the table. I sat staring at my date, paralyzed in disbelief. The light behind his head illuminated the edges of his thick hair, bringing to mind the phrase *lunatic fringe*. Lunatic: people rendered insane by the moon.

He rambled on about extraterrestrial colonization and how the space shuttle could deliver future pilgrims to a place they would call New Plymouth. I'd seen Plymouth Rock during a camp outing one summer. It was a disappointingly unobtrusive brownish stone, not even the size of a decent boulder. I hoped that Marty and his fellow lunar colonists had something more majestic planned to commemorate their achievement. Marty, pulling himself out of his moon-lit reverie, finally noticed I wasn't responding the way he had hoped. There was an uncomfortable pause while he stared at me, his vivid eyes fading.

I had been about to offer my observations about Plymouth Rock but didn't want him to think I was mocking him. He said, "I have been dreaming about space travel all my life. Buzz Aldren and John Glenn are American heroes and we need to continue their work. I am very serious about this."

"I can tell. It's good. Everyone needs a, ah,, an avocation." *Even if it's a little off.* I struggled with what to say next. "When did you first become interested," and here I almost choked on my bread stick, "in colonizing the moon?" There was no going back; we had already ordered, and the linguini at the next table smelled really good. Looking relieved, Marty carried on. There was a sizable fish tank near the bar where one large silver fish turned slowly toward me. He stayed in the same spot, opening and closing his mouth, like he was trying to breathe without the benefit of his gills. *I feel you man. I do.*

***

After the incident with the self-appointed head of Future Lunar Colonists of North America, I decided I needed to set more concrete criteria for my dates. Careful consideration yielded the List of Qualifications for Second Husband. As a long-time resident of the Metro DC area, I, of course, gave it an acronym: LoQuaSH, catchy and somewhat French sounding. It follows, in no particular order:

1. No Golf
2. Plays sports, doesn't watch sports (sports telecasts once a week, max, ok)
3. No obnoxious jewelry, cologne or grooming habits
4. Likes kids, especially my kid, and wants more kids
5. No living with parents (but good relationship with parents a plus)
6. Limited emotional baggage
7. Well spoken, well read, well educated
8. Financially solvent
9. Interesting and socially acceptable hobbies and interests
    a. No fantasy fiction or role-playing games. No spacemen. No exceptions
10. Bonus points awarded for charity work, church attendance, home maintenance skills

I placed this list near my box of index cards by the phone. Sometimes I was tempted to respond to a guy who sounded really sexy on the phone, even though he mentioned living with his mother or inviting *the guys* over to "game". I hoped LoQuaSH would help me to just say NO.

***

During our monthly CVS run, I picked up the prints from a roll of film I'd dropped off on our previous trip and made the calamitous mistake of looking at them right as we got into the car. I almost never saw Lainie as she must have looked to other people. Maybe that's typical of parents, but Lainie's personality was so much bigger than her little two-and-a-half-year-old body, how could I see what she really looked like when I got sucked in by her smile and the intensity of her chatter? How could one get past the bombardment of incessant questions? Leafing through the bundle of photos, the reality of our situation hit me: we both looked dreadful. Well, of course, she just looked like a cute ragamuffin, whereas I looked like an inhabitant of Hades. I had been completely delusional thinking that I could attract an attractive, successful man looking like this. I'd be lucky to attract a blind octogenarian.

"What's wrong, Mama?"

"Nothing Pumpkin."

"See pictures?"

"Mm hmm"

"Let me see. Let me see. See my pretty dress?"

I handed her a duplicate of her feeding ducks. She embarked on a running commentary about the flora and fauna of our local pond. I stared at the other pictures. What the heck was I thinking wearing those pants? My butt looked enormous. How in God's name am I going to get a date when I find my own eyebrows offensive? And my hair, my hair is stuck in eighth grade: mousy, limp, lifeless.

"Come Mama, go home." She was strapped in her car seat. We hadn't left the parking lot. I was still staring in dismay at the pictures. *No honey, we can't go home now. Mommy looks scary and wants to burn the photos in the toaster oven.* When had my face gotten pudgy looking? What made me think I was qualified to cut my daughter's hair? She looked like a gang of preschoolers had attacked her head with safety scissors. Could I afford a trip to the salon for both of us?

We couldn't head home; we needed beauty supplies. STAT. In her pre-Africa days, my mom dragged me to the Estée Lauder counter and had the

perfumed saleswomen give me a make-over. I had wanted to go to the Clin-
ique counter, but Mom had her favorites. In an effort to camouflage my acne,
she handed me over to a woman wearing so much mascara I wondered if her
vision was compromised. Tonight, however, I'd have to settle for the cosmet-
ic offerings of the drug store. Frankly, part of me was glad I only could afford Maybelline. I wasn't up for the fussing and gentle chiding about my lack
of a daily cleansing regimen I would get from the department store ladies. I
dragged us back into the CVS.

"Oh, Mama, pink lipstick. Like pink. Pink nail polish? What that?"

"Blush."

"Get that, get pink one!" She jumped up and down in place. *How did I
get such a girly girl?* As I stood in the aisle, trying to imagine what else I might
need for this emergency transformation, Lainie pulled at my sleeve.

"Mama, Mama, Mamamammamamammamamamama."

It was so hard to concentrate on cosmetology this way.

"What is it Lainie?"

"Potty!"

"Okay, hold on." Scrolling through the checklist: face, skin, nails, conditioner—

"Mommy, NOW!" The urgency in her voice propelled me into action. I
had less than sixty seconds to find a bathroom. A bearded pharmacist, recognizing that this was a true emergency, showed us through the storeroom to
the euphemistically labeled, Powder Room. Cringing, I wiped down the seat
and then covered it with toilet paper as Lainie was too small to stand and
crouch over the commode. She sat happily singing her potty song while she
tinkled. It took about three verses for her to finish.

The Powder Room was jammed with paraphernalia that should have
been stored elsewhere: filthy mop, pile of broken boxes, bins of unwanted
clearance items. The mop probably hadn't actually been used on this floor in
a decade. *This little shopping excursion is lovely, Alexandria.* At 6:49 p.m. we
should have been home starting the dinner, bath, book, bed routine. Instead,
some idiot decided to pick up the film, and here we were gathering supplies
for a beauty-school-drop-out makeover.

Before we left, I grabbed Super Moisturizing Restorative Conditioner, face cream, eyeshadow, tweezers and a Snickers bar. None of which were in the budget.

***

"Hmm. So, whom are we trying to impress tonight?" Michael, my boss, asked as he sat down across from me at lunch.

"No one. What are you taking about?" I continued to grade the stack of quizzes with my right hand while eating a peanut butter and jelly sandwich with my left. Evidently, the marathon sessions in the bathroom with tweezers, moisturizer and nail polish were paying off.

"You look, well, a little snappier than usual today." My boss remarked.

"Snappy, that's right out of the '50s. Move up a decade or two and call me *hip* or *cool* at least."

"How's groovy?" he asked.

"Too Marsha Brady, but slightly better than snappy."

"Hm. What about that nice guy Gerry set you up with?"

"He wanted to set up housekeeping in his big house with me and his mom and sisters."

"Ouch."

"Yeah."

"What about the other guy? Fred, Frank, the businessman?"

"You mean Bill."

"Right, I can't keep up. What about him?"

"The waitress thought he was my dad."

"Oh boy." He bit into an enormous meatball sub from the cafeteria. Marinera sauce leaked out the end. Cheese oozed over the top.

"You're going to kill yourself, eating those things," I remarked.

"Lois doesn't let me eat them at home. Did you have your Snickers and Diet Coke breakfast today, Ms. Nutrition?"

"No, for your information, I have upgraded to granola bars."

"Yeah, but still addicted to Diet Coke."

"It's better than that vile swill you call coffee." I remarked. Michael just shrugged.

Chapter Five
March, 1996

Blind date number four took place in a little, out-of-the-way chophouse far from any likelihood of running into my students. It took my eyes a minute to adjust to the dark interior. I walked slowly toward the back, trying to not look anxious or desperate. This was always the worst moment; the knot in my stomach came not from being nervous about meeting my date, but by the fear of making a fool out of myself by approaching the wrong guy. I had this picture of myself, abandoned in a smoky bar, going from one man to the next, pitiful, like the little match girl, asking, "Are you my date?" and having the men turn away in disgust.

I spotted a single man sitting in a booth, and quickly checked the rest of the room to see if there might be more than one. He was it. It looked as though he had bits of tissue stuck to his face, but because there were so many white spots, I convinced myself that my eyes must be playing tricks in the dim light. From a distance, his face looked like a fallen mossy log sprouting tiny white flowers.

"Hi, Terry?" I asked.

"Oh, yes, hi!" He stood and held out his hand. "You're Alex?" He and I were wearing identical facial expressions, a mixture of hope and embarrassment. There were, indeed, bits of toilet paper plastered across his face.

"Please excuse my appearance," he said, "I made the mistake of using a new brand of razor this afternoon and it made a real mess of my face."

Once, when I was in middle school art class, we each were given a balloon and covered one half of it in paper-mâché to make a mask. We painted them with bright colors and decorated the masks with sequins and feathers for Mardi Gras. It was like someone had started to paper-mâché Terry's face but got bored and walked away from the project. I had to give him serious points for his lack of pretension.

"If you don't mind, I'll go see if I can straighten myself out. Please order yourself a drink or something." He excused himself and I reflected for a moment on first impressions. Terry reappeared, looking hen-pecked but no longer blooming toilet tissue. I ordered a salad. He ordered a club sandwich. The restaurant was dim, wood-paneled, more hunting cabin than gentleman's club. We chatted a bit before launching into the heavy stuff.

Terry had twin nineteen-year-old sons attending rival universities. They were both varsity swimmers and had met several times in competition. Terry smiled broadly talking about traveling to see their swim meets. "Yeah, you think you're done with all of that when they graduate from high school." I calculated that I was closer in age to his boys than to Terry.

"Well, we're still working on potty training at our place."

By the time dinner arrived, we had decided to get the icky 'Why did you get divorced?' question out of the way. I explained that Ken and I were like salad dressing, oil and vinegar, good when you shake us up, but in a constant state of separating. (I'd stolen that analogy from a friend, but played it off as my own bit of clever wisdom.) "So, what's your story?"

Terry picked up his fork and fiddled with the coleslaw. "My wife left me, after eighteen years."

"Wow, that's a long time to invest in a relationship to just walk away," I said.

"Well, evidently, it had been a long time coming." I didn't say anything. He looked at me with an expression I couldn't read. "She left me for another woman."

What can I say to something like that?

"That must have been something of a shock."

"To say the least. I felt really stupid. She was with this woman constantly. They were best friends. You know, shopping, girls' nights. The boys even called her Aunt Jill. I can't believe I was that oblivious."

"How did you find out?"

"Three years ago, right after we had all spent Thanksgiving together, Donna told me she was moving out and going to live with Jill."

"I can only imagine how that made you feel. How did the boys take it?"

"Actually, not too badly. They were half-way out the door to college, and so busy with swimming and their girlfriends, it didn't faze them too much. And we still have holidays together."

"Jeez, that's huge. That must take, I don't know, patience, self-confidence. Extreme love of your kids?" I asked.

"And a really, really good therapist." We laughed. So far, this guy seemed to be the most mentally healthy specimen I'd seen in a while.

"My shrink says my boys would have had a harder time if it had been me who had the sexual identity shift. So we have that in the plus column."

We ordered dessert. He took his coffee with milk. I asked for tea. We talked about kids and a little about life. Then came the tricky part, do we try again or walk away? I think the world needs a dating referee. This neutral party would observe the date from a distance, seated at a distant table in the restaurant. He would have a dossier for each party at his disposal. To avoid the troublesome moment at the end of a date, the referee would step forward and dictate: "Shake Hands" or "Kiss on the cheek." It would be so very helpful if such a person could then say, "I'll let you know in a few days if you two have been chosen to date again."

Dating Ref would also keep one from making the common, yet often ill-advised move of having sex on the first date. In advanced societies, Dating Ref would be blessed with a special knowledge of how relationships might progress, and be able to stop something fruitless and ugly before poor people like me spent too much of their time agonizing over date-night outfits to please the wrong man. I must grudgingly admit that I was beginning to understand the practice of arranged marriage. Anything had to be better than this.

We walked toward the door. I think we were both trying to figure out the next step. Terry walked me to my car.

"This is the worst part, isn't it?" He looked at me with a sheepish smile.

"Yes." It was nice that we were both on the same page.

"Tell you what," he said, "I'm away at a conference most of next week. If you want to see me again, give me a call after I get back in town. I enjoyed tonight."

Well, that was civilized.

I told him I had a good time. He kissed me on the cheek and drove off. I drove sedately home, no rush back to the empty apartment. I considered Terry of the Toilet Paper. It struck me that he was really skinny. Something about his cheeks and eyes looked like he was being consumed from inside out. It took a lot of energy to play it off like everyone has a lesbian wife who brings her partner to Thanksgiving dinner. But Terry had such an air of hope that I knew someone would breathe life back into him and fill him like a balloon back to his proper proportions. I wished I was mature enough to be that person, but I wasn't. I needed someone less like a raisin, and more like a melon, which was a shame.

***

One's friends can only take so much secondhand depression. It's worse than secondhand smoke. One's family can alternate their reactions from, "I told you so," to, "Hang in there, kiddo," to, "Okay, time to move on." None of which were very helpful. That left me talking to Dr. Sheldon.

I don't recommend picking a therapist out of the phone book, and the insurance company's provider directory isn't much better. Dr. Sheldon was a guy somewhere in his mid-forties sporting a running watch and a red mustache. He folded his tall, lanky frame into his office chair like a wooden marionette.

During the first two sessions I cried a lot and worried that he'd start charging me extra for the Kleenex. I'm not sure he understood much of what I said through the blubbering, but he withstood it. The next few sessions were fun free-for-all-bitch sessions on the scummy nature of men (which Dr. Sheldon let go without comment), the fact that I was being abandoned by my mother in my hour of need, and how none of my friends understood me. Finally, the ranting proved too much even for mild Dr. Sheldon. In the middle of my sixth session (insurance would cover ten) he interrupted me mid-rave.

"Alex, listen to yourself."

"Excuse me?"

"Are you really listening to what you're saying?"

I stopped for a moment. No, I wasn't listening, I was talking. *That's why I'm here, right?*

"I am going to read some things back to you that you've been saying over our past few sessions. Are you ready?" He was stern. Caught completely off-guard, I sat back in the chair and nodded.

"Okay."

Dr. Sheldon folded back several sheets of yellow legal paper. He paused for a moment, finding his place and making sure he had my full attention. He then proceeded to read a whiny diatribe against everyone who had wronged me. In the lengthy quotes I recognized my own voice complaining about the injustices of the world in general and my life in particular. Evidently, I thought I was the only person to suffer the tragedy of divorce and single-motherhood. Dr. Sheldon continued. My mother had neglected me to self-ishly pursue her lifelong dreams. My friends were all happier than I was and it was unfair. Life was unfair. It was unfair that the phone bill was so expensive and Ken was late paying the day care bill. It was unfair that I was stuck way out in the suburbs while all the cool stuff must be happening downtown. It was unfair that babysitters cost so much. My psychologist's slightly nasal voice droned on. It was embarrassing. It was appalling. If I had to listen to that, I'd have kicked myself out of therapy. I was getting ready to disown my-self when he stopped reading.

"Does this sound accurate?" he asked.

"Yes." Chagrin filled my whole being.

"Alex," he explained with calm patience, "I am a *reality* therapist. The *re-ality* is that you are not the only human being involved here. You are alien-ating your friends and family by being so wrapped up in your problems. You need to start adding other thoughts and activities to your repertoire before you become bitter."

This was not what I was paying this man for. Who cared if he was right? My co-pay entitled me to gripe. We sat in silence. The truth and shame of it spread from the pit of my stomach up to my hairline.

"You need a perspective check. Your marriage failed, it doesn't make you a failure. You're bright, you have a good job. You have resources and support. Things could be much worse."

"So, you're telling me to get over it?"

"Look, I'm not the type of shrink who wants to delve into your child-hood and keep you in therapy for ten years. You're very strong. You need to be done with me. You also need to get used to being on your own before you keep dating and trying to make things work with another person. This relent-less quest for another husband is not a productive path."

I waited. I felt like I did when I was in fifth grade and broke a perfect discipline record by whispering to Connie Lowe in math class and getting detention. He was right.

He continued, "You need a cheerleading squad, but since you're not on the football team, you're going to have to do it yourself."

Oh my God, he is now going to try to sell me some self-help tapes from some find-yourself guru. That's the last thing I need. Instead, he sat back in his chair and waited for me to say something.

"Um, I guess you're right." He raised his red bushy eyebrows at me, urging me to continue. "I am fortunate. I do need to get on with my life."

"Yes, I wish you well. Next time we will work on strategies to move you toward independence, but I am only going to see you for two more sessions. Our time is up."

I left the office in a daze. I didn't turn the radio on in the car. I wallowed in shame for the ride home. I had behaved badly and I was selfish, but I wasn't ready to do this on my own. My shrink had kicked me out and my mom was in Africa. As I turned into the driveway of Lainie's day care, it hit me. Church. I need to get back to church. God can't kick me out.

My last venture back to the land of the righteous last fall had been so traumatic that I'd given up on church. There was a Presbyterian church near my house. I felt badly about not having Lainie inside a church since her baptism, and, though the chances were slim, there might be a cute guy at the coffee hour. One Sunday last October, we gave it a try. Lainie was doll-like in a charming dress and pink ribbons in her dark hair. She twirled around in the parking lot to make her dress pouf out. Tugging at my skirt, I took a deep breath and put on my church face as we walked into the modern glass and brick structure. I found the nursery, signed Lainie in, and then made my way to the sanctuary. Suddenly I was overwhelmed with self-consciousness. It was so odd to walk into church alone. I couldn't remember the last time I did that, maybe never. It felt like people were staring at me. Most likely, they were not.

We were welcomed by the pastor.

We sang a hymn.

We confessed our sins and were assured forgiveness.

So far, so good. The sermon began innocuously, the minister speaking about fall, the change of seasons, the glory of God in Nature and changing leaves, etc. The minimalist sanctuary was filled with well-scrubbed suburbanites, dressed, for the most part, in dark blue. Bright morning sun shone through clear windows. I was contemplating the lack of stained glass when things got ugly.

From the pulpit, the preacher was saying, "Parents, a time is coming that will test you. A time is coming that will test your strength as a Christian, a night that will test the resolve of your parenthood. Halloween is two weeks away. Halloween is a time of evil, a time when Satan can sneak into the corners."

Whoa. I sat straight up in the pew. The pastor's face was grim. He clutched the pulpit and began to sway.

"Satan is in every hideous mask, in the bloody make-up, hiding behind sheets that are cut to look like ghosts. Do not let your children wear the mask of that godless mass-murderer, Jason, or whatever they call him. Do not let your children wear pagan witches' robes or the pale faces of ghosts and zombies." His pitch increased. His eyes bugged out from his face as though he could see Beelzebub hovering over the sanctuary doors. So Nathaniel Hawthorne. *He cannot be for real* . . . I looked around. A few parishioners were giving each other sideways glances with raised eyebrows, but far more frightening was the number of good folk nodding in numb agreement. A couple clenched each other by the hand at the repeated mention of the Devil. "Do not play into Satan's hands. Do not let your children trick-or-treat. Celebrate the harvest if you must. Celebrate God's bounty, but DO NOT ALLOW SATAN TO SNEAK INTO THE CORNERS. Amen." The pastor mopped his sweaty forehead.

Everyone stood for the hymn. I stood and went for the door.

So, now, after Dr. Sheldon's verbal butt-kicking, I decided to try God again. The next church's unofficial moniker was "Church of the Aged." Mine was the youngest face there by decades, and there wasn't a nursery for Lainie. After about twenty minutes of her squirming on my lap, we abandoned that one too.

Working my way south, I came upon an enormous, beautiful church with not one but three separate nurseries for tots under the age of four. More importantly, however, it also seemed to have a selection of single, available men.

Lainie and I were greeted at the door by a tall older woman whose name tag read "Madge." Her floral dress hung off her bony shoulders as it would from a boutique hanger. Madge started to give me complex directions to the nursery, but seeing the bewildered look on my face, she abandoned her post, and with the determination of a skinny mother rhino, took Lainie by the hand and marched us there herself.

The congregants were pleasant, orderly Presbyterians, even the reluctant teenagers were well groomed. The sermon was rational and uplifting; the choir was sincere and well-rehearsed. Satan was not mentioned and the tune to the *Gloria Patri* was the one I had been raised on. At one point, I stopped my compare/contrast exercise to actively contemplate God. He and I had a tenuous relationship, but I did acknowledge that I probably needed Him more than He needed me at that moment. After the last hymn, I collected Lainie to hunt down juice and cookies.

At the coffee hour, I noted a man of medium height, about my age, standing alone and filed it for later. People smiled at us, not noticing the blazing red **D** for Divorce stamped on my forehead. We headed out into a perfect, sunny blue morning, Lainie munching on her last cookie as we walked toward the car.

"Yoo-hoo, yoo-hoo!" A woman's voice floated toward us. I turned and looked back toward the gleaming white church. Madge was waving her long arms, trotting down the sidewalk, her coat flapping, her feet in flat shoes making slapping noises on the pavement.

"I just wanted to see how the little one did in the nursery," Madge panted.

"My name is Lainie. I liked the nursery. They have good toys. I played with Tyler. Tyler has a boo-boo. The lady read us Bible stories. We play blocks—"

Lainie was on a roll and could continue without oxygen re-supply for ten minutes, so I interjected, "Everything was great; thank you so much."

"Well Honey, I'll be looking for you next Sunday, I hope you'll make us your church home." She smiled and looked like she wanted to hug us. "Take care."

As she turned back toward the church, my throat tightened. I watched her angular frame walk away and I was thankful. Thankful for Madge, for the Beauty of the Earth and the Glory of the Skies, and for the cookie that prevented Lainie from seeing me cry.

***

Against Dr. Sheldon's advice, and ignoring Cynthia's admonitions to take things more slowly, I agreed to meet Royce Parish after work for a quick dinner in Bethesda. Having done a presentation at the staff meeting that day, I was wearing a sharp suit with a short skirt. I got to the restaurant first, which gave me the first look.

Royce came in from the sun looking a little unsure of the situation. His suit and walk said, "I am a confident businessman," but there was a nervous hunch in his shoulders and he was squinting through his steel-rimmed glasses like he expected to be hit in the face by a swarm of bats. I strode toward him as his eyes adjusted to the interior and saw the anxiety melt into relief at my appearance. That was a nice ego boost.

"Hi, I'm Alex." I extended my hand.

"Royce. Nice to meet you. Sorry I'm a bit late."

"Not at all; I think I'm a little early." I was working on being cool but approachable. We had a quick, business-like supper at a restaurant that was all exposed beams and glass with efficient waiters.

Royce ran his own company. He was obviously used to being in charge. His suit was not off-the-rack. His Rolex matched the silver and gold cufflinks that had a subtle monogram. I wondered what an obviously wealthy, successful guy was doing answering a personal ad, so, I asked.

"The ladies in the office tried to set me up once." He shook his head. "It was terrible. But I don't know what was worse, the date or all the fuss it caused in the office." I waited for him to continue. "For days before the date, and then days afterward, all they could do was talk about it. When I didn't ask her out again, they wanted to know what went wrong. I'm just not comfortable with all that stuff at work."

"What did go wrong?"

"Trailer trash."

"Oh." I didn't know how to react to such brunt appraisal. "Probably not an explanation you could give the ladies at work."

"No."

We finished eating quickly. He had to get back to the office for a late client meeting. I spent a moment wondering if I was going to be relegated to the Trailer Trash pile when he said, "I'd like to see you again." He stood to leave and casually threw enough cash on the table to cover our bill, tip and then some.

"That would be lovely. Thank you for dinner. It was nice getting to know you." I answered in my best Katherine Hepburn classy yet independent manner. I may have batted my eyelashes.

For the next few days, I rolled the prospect of Royce Parish around in my mind like a marble. He was nice, decent looking, and the money was nice. Very nice. But there was no zing. One quick meal doesn't give one a full picture of a human being, but there should have been . . . something. Diagnosis: chemistry deficiency. Maybe he was just reserved. By Wednesday I came to the conclusion that he must have been badly hurt in the past and was exercising caution. That night, he called. I had just put Lainie to sleep. The apartment was quiet.

"Hi Alex, it's Royce."

"Hi Royce." I tried to drag out the syllables of his name a little to make it sound a little sexy.

We chatted for a while. He asked me to go out with him on Friday. I pretended to look at my calendar for a second before saying yes. I grew bold and said, "So, Royce, I recall from our lunch that you said you've never been married."

"Yes, that's true."

"Well, I was wondering if you ever came close, like getting engaged or living with someone?" This may have been abrupt, but I was on a mission. The clock was ticking. If this guy was just messing around, I needed to move on, Rolex or no Rolex. There was a long pause at the other end of the phone.

"It's not something I really like to talk about." I was right, he had been hurt badly. I needed to exercise caution.

"Oh, I'm sorry."

"No, no, it's okay. It's just been a little while since I've thought about it."

I waited for Royce to continue. "Her name was Jiao. She had been teaching about Christianity out of her home in China. One of my friends met her on a business trip. He put her in touch with some missionaries who helped her come to the states. They worked through the Chinese bureaucracy for weeks and finally secured travel visas for Jiao and two other Chinese nationals.

"That's really unusual," I said.

"Yeah, when they got to the States, my friend thought she and I should meet."

"Are you involved in your church, Royce?" Too much to hope for, it didn't seem to fit.

"No, my friend was the wife of a colleague. She took on the job of getting me set up very seriously and she thought Jaio and I would hit it off. She told me Jiao was really a knock-out."

"Was she?"

"Yes." He paused for a minute. "She was beautiful and sweet. Very bright. She didn't speak much English when she got here, but it seemed like she picked up more every day, like a little kid." I heard the sound of ice clinking in a glass. He swallowed. I remained silent. "Anyway, we fell in love. I wanted to marry her, not just to help her with the green card, you know."

"How long ago was this?"

"Six years now. She didn't want to get married without her parents' consent."

"Was she very young?" I asked.

"No, just very traditional. We tried to get through to her hometown, but the phones never worked. Then we wrote letters. Then she got pregnant."

"I thought you said she was traditional?"

"Only in some ways. When we finally heard from her parents, they gave us their blessing but couldn't afford to travel for a wedding, and there was a question about them being able to get visas. Anyway, we got engaged, but she refused to get married without her parents." I could hear him take another drink. "I went to all of the doctor's appointments with her. We started getting really excited."

I was sitting on the linoleum floor of my tiny kitchen, resting my back against the fridge. Royce was speaking very softly and I didn't want to miss a word. Hopefully, Lainie would stay in bed.

"We had one of those Pregnancy by the Week calendars. At twenty weeks she had a sonogram. It was a boy. Jiao kept saying how proud her father would be. Every time she crossed off another week on that calendar she'd cry. I thought it was just the pregnancy hormones, but I was wrong. She didn't want to have the baby without her mother. I kept trying to explain that everything was going to be okay."

"That must have been so tough."

"I tried to find her a Chinese doctor; I thought maybe the medical terms were too hard for her to understand in English. She was afraid for the baby and I really thought a doctor who spoke her language could explain things better than I could and maybe make her more comfortable with the situation." He sounded increasingly forlorn.

"So, what happened?" At this point in his story, all I could think was that she had lost the baby, and I was trying to suppress the lump in my throat. Just the thought of such things could send me into a tailspin. My love for Lainie made me so empathetic to other moms, it didn't matter if the story was second or third hand. I'd stopped watching the evening news after Lainie was born, too many hurt babies or murdered children. I was afraid of what Royce would say next.

"I came home from work the evening after she had been to the Chinese doctor. She was gone. She had taken two big suitcases, and she left."

"Did she leave a note?"

"No, her writing wasn't that good. She had called from the airport and left a message on the answering machine telling me she was getting on the plane to Beijing."

"What happened to the baby? Wasn't she too pregnant to fly?"

"He's fine. Or, he was fine." Royce took another swig of his drink. I still hadn't moved from my place on the floor. "His mother sent photos of him off and on until about two years ago. Then she stopped."

There were so many questions I wanted to ask, I didn't know where to start, but I also didn't know what to say. Why didn't he go after her? What did he do with all of the baby stuff they must have bought? Had they decorated a nursery for his son? How much that must have hurt, to get rid of all the baby things. This man was telling me the saddest story of his life after one newspaper-ad date.

"Did you try to find them?" I asked.

"I did. I knew where they were. I was advised against following them to China. I sent money for the first few years. Then I got a letter. Jiao asked me to stop; her husband wanted to adopt the boy. I signed the papers, what else could I do?" Royce said.

"Good thing that baby was a boy." I let that slip without really thinking about it. It sounded crude.

"Well, I don't know. Maybe she'd still be here if the baby had been a girl." We sat in companionable silence, each in our own lonely homes.

***

To say that our second date was disastrous would be a gross understatement. It was the Hindenburg of all dates, and it was my fault. I'd called ahead and asked Royce what I should wear. "Casual," he had said. Casual is the sartorial equivalent of a barbed wire-laced minefield surrounded by a moat and crocodiles. There are thousands of iterations of female casual attire, so many that they are impossible to list or codify. Fashion magazines are kept running on the insecurities of people like me who never know what to wear. Tell a guy *casual* and he has a maximum of three choices during any given season. Slacks with a polo or slacks with a button-down shirt. Throw on a blue blazer and he's good to go almost anywhere. I was in a total quandary, and in denial of the sad state of my wardrobe. So, I left the decision making to the last minute. To make matters worse, we were experiencing a mid-March heatwave, and I had nothing to wear. I put on, for lack of a better word, a muumuu. It was a black, sleeveless, ankle-length sun dress. A few years ago, the sales lady had assured me it was the height of casual dressing and had used the magic word *slimming*. I wore sandals, not cute strappy high-heeled sandals, but unisex things I'd heard referred to as *fisherman's sandals*. I did my hair and make-up, and was ready (I thought) when Royce arrived.

I opened the door and Royce recoiled in horror. *Oh God, I'd gravely miscalculated.* His *casual* meant spaghetti-strap-clingy-knee-length-cocktail-dress-with-sky-high-heeled-sandals-and-a-feminine-little-clutch. Not the Earth Mother from Berkeley. Oh no. I could see the confusion on his face. Where had the sexy gal in the business suit gone? I am sure he was asking himself if he really had to be seen in public with me.

"Hi," I said. This was followed by a silence during which I had time to think the following:

I should offer to change. I have nothing to change into. Cosmo says that if you have the right attitude and self-confidence, you can carry off any outfit. Fuck him for being so judgmental and criticizing me.

Royce had only said "Hi" at this point. *I am such a loser. What am I going to do?*

"Well," he said, "are you ready to go?" I hesitated and took a step away from the door as if to go back to the bedroom to change. Then I stopped and nodded and we got in the car.

It was a long, quiet ride to the restaurant. He'd chosen one of the new hot-spots in DC, but being locked into my own little teaching/toddler world, I was unaware of what was hip and cool until we were right on top of it. *I should have called the restaurant. No, I should have scouted out the restaurant and then gone shopping at someplace trendy. It would be worth adding to the credit card bill. I should have thought this through. I am an idiot.*

The new, flashy place was filled with twenty-year-old beauties with nothing better to do with their time than primp, spa, exercise, shop and repeat. They swiveled on their bar stools to examine us as we entered. Royce received high marks, I got dismissive glances. And, of course, there was a mirror on the wall behind Royce's head, so, throughout the whole torturous dinner, I was forced to face myself in full frontal frumpiness. The only thing to be proud of was the fact that I didn't burst into tears.

Before our entrée arrived, I excused myself to the bathroom where I spent seven minutes engaged in self-loathing. I didn't look in the mirror as I washed my hands.

Walking back to the table, I stopped and ducked behind a pillar by the bar. There was a strange woman at the table with Royce. She perched half a butt cheek on my chair, ready to leap out of it when I returned. Her bright aqua, thigh-high mini dress was snug, but verged on classy. The heels on her sandals had to be five inches tall. Smiling provocatively at my date, she settled her elbows on the table. She folded her hands beneath her chin and arched her back so that her breasts poked through the triangle created by the table and her forearms. That was a trick I'd have to remember. *Another woman was hitting on my date during my date.* She reached into a little matching aqua leather clutch and drew out a business card. She handed it to him and they shook hands. She held onto his hand a bit longer than necessary. As she turned to walk back to the table she was sharing with similarly clad girl-friends, she gave them a triumphant smile.

Royce watched her saunter away with the look of a hungry animal on his face. I wanted to hide. I checked for possible exit routes. I might be able to crawl behind the bar and sneak through the kitchen; there had to be a back way out. But I didn't have enough money for cab fare all the way back to the suburbs, so I walked back to the table feeling nauseous. I slipped back into my seat, the right half of which was still warm. We did not order dessert. Nor coffee.

Our phone conversation the other night had lulled me into thinking we had made a connection, that what I looked like wasn't so important. I was so wrong. Royce was looking for polish and sophistication and it stung to ac-knowledge that I wasn't up to par to be Mrs. Parish. Strangely, I was irritated with myself for the screw-up, not with him for wanting a Barbie wife. But it was also a relief, I can only meet Barbie standards for a date or two, anything more is exhausting.

If there was one lesson to be learned, it boiled down to one thing: high heels, baby, high heels.

***

Obviously, I needed some date-worthy clothes. I chose a Thursday evening when Lainie was with Ken to go to the mall straight from work, forage for deals and reward myself with a solo dining experience and a good book.

There are people who genuinely love to shop. They get together with friends and intentionally participate in shopping as a recreational activity, happily spending hours hunting and gathering clothes and objects both nec-essary and frivolous. I would rather do a thousand things, including cleaning bathrooms, than shop. But one must. For two and-a-half hours I wandered aimlessly among dresses, pants and shoes. I bought a cute little top at one store, and then returned it fifteen minutes later, confusing the sales girl.

"I realized that my mom bought me something similar for my birthday." I fibbed. "Sorry to waste your time."

"No problem." She popped her gum. I got sidetracked in the bookstore for thirty minutes, enjoying browsing the magazines without a small person trying to pull me over to the kids' section. *Okay, I really have to focus.* I was determined that the next store I went into, I would find someone to help me and I WOULD purchase one sexy outfit. And I did. My angel of fashion mercy was a sweet brunette whom I'd taught three years before. She came rushing to the front as I walked into the store.

"Ms. Smythe! How are you?"

Oh please, let me remember your name.

"Hi . . . Cece!" (*Phew.*) "It's good to see you. What are you doing here?" We gave each other a sideways hug.

"I'm taking some time off from school. I didn't do so well last semester. My parents wanted me to come home and make some money before I kept wasting theirs." She laughed.

"That sounds like a good idea."

"Yeah, after I changed my major three times, they thought I should quit playing around and figure out what I really want to do."

"Have you figured it out yet?" I asked.

"No."

"Me neither." Cece looked a little puzzled. "Anyway, I need your help if you have a minute."

I explained my predicament while omitting the wardrobe catastrophe that was my date with Royce. That still smarted. In no time, Cece had collected no fewer than eight complete outfits that one could categorize as sophisticated yet sexy, ushered me into the fitting room and commented on each selection with tact beyond her years. I chose two ensembles: one that, with some modification, could be used both at school and on a date, and one that was purely for seduction purposes, and rationalized them as business expenses, which they were.

Happy and with the confident swagger that comes with loaded shopping bags at your side, I walked through the mall sure that I could meet future wardrobe challenges without fear. I was beginning to hum when it happened. I rounded the corner, and there he was: Stuart with his wife. They were walking towards me, hand in hand, too far away for me to read their facial expressions, but the wife had a definite bounce in her step. Reeling as though punched in the gut by a heavyweight champion, I staggered into the nearest store and crouched behind a tall rack of frilly dresses. I didn't think they had seen me. Gripping the cold metal fixture, my knees weak, I watched them stroll by, passing time in the mall. They weren't talking, they hadn't seen me. Deflated, I collapsed into one of the cushy chairs put there for fatigued husbands and tucked my head in my hands, trying to breathe.

After a few minutes, I sat up in the wide leather chair, staring past the three-way mirror, not really seeing anything until I thought I might be able to get up and walk without throwing up. Ten minutes passed. Then fifteen. *Get a grip Alex. This is ridiculous. Let it go.* Five more minutes went by until one of the store managers asked if I was alright. I nodded, mouth dry, underarms damp. Things were supposed to be so different now. We should have been together, that had been the plan. But things changed. He went back to her and I went on alone.

Many years later, my yoga instructor would tell me that you can hold two conflicting emotions at once. He instructed us to imagine them as two birds' eggs of different colors in the same nest. He was trying to get us to acknowledge our feelings and observe them without reaction. What he didn't know, but I did, was they weren't birds' eggs. They were hot coals, burning in my hand. Love. And Shame.

This was so demeaning, the sight of my former lover leaving me limp and useless. Our bodies betray the state of our minds, and clearly, I was still a wreck. Now the biggest challenge was to escape from the mall without falling victim to 1500 calories of Cinnabon comfort food.

Chapter Six
April, 1996

Brian had arms that could have been used on the illustration on the side of the bicep curl machine at the gym, which was where we met. He was wearing a Merrill Lynch T-shirt. (One check for physically fit, another check in the financial stability column if he actually was a broker.) I sat across from him on the large stretching mat. This seemed to be a good way to meet people: stretch with studied nonchalance, see if they start a conversation.

Brian had one leg bent toward him, the other stretched out in front, and was doing an admirable job of holding his flexed toes with both hands. His head dropped toward his knee, giving me a view of his balding scalp and ample time to stare at those arms.

When he looked up, I was startled by his eyes, an azure clear as a Caribbean lagoon. The mat we were sitting on was a dull gray, and the rest of the gym had been decorated in stark black and white, making the color of his eyes dance in contrast. The shirt and thinning hair led me to believe that he was older and wealthier than he was. I would learn that he was prematurely balding and his healthy income went to three passions: his car, his dog, and his mountain biking habit. But we'd get to all of that later. We smiled at each other.

"Hey." He opened.

"Hey." I volleyed.

"How's it going?"

"Good, good. You?" Stunningly intellectual start.

"I've seen you in spinning class," he said.

"I like it, it's a good break from running."

"Yeah, me too."

"Do you work at Merrill?"

"Five years now."

"Do you like it?"

"Love it, it gives me time to bike. Market closes at 4:00." Okay, respectable job, outdoorsy type, I was getting a little excited. We chatted for a few minutes and I got up to leave.

"My name is Brian, Brian Jarvis."

"I'm Alex." He asked for my number and I did a little happy jig inside my head.

If you were to set the vocal rhythm of the country to a metronome, you might find that the New York has the fastest setting, perhaps followed by Chicago and maybe L.A. Washington DC, of which my hamlet was a suburb, lagged about half to three-quarters of a beat behind New York. Brian was a New Yorker, born and raised, and while higher education had softened the street vernacular, he still spoke with the speed and directness of home. Hearing him talk, I could be sitting at my grandmother's dining table, listening to my uncles argue about politics and road construction.

Our first date was at the local steak house on a Thursday. I had found that mid-week was best for a first date, as one had the excuse for an early evening due to working the next day. One could skip dessert and coffee if things weren't progressing toward a second date. We talked about growing up in New England, sports and the great outdoors. I learned that the guys call him "Jarvo" and that his best friend was his dog, Ralph. We ordered dessert and coffee.

In the middle of the second date at some forgettable chain restaurant, the conversation progressed past "Who are you and what do you do" to "What makes you tick?"

"I don't know, I mean, all I know is that I *don't* want to end up like my parents." Brian took a long swallow of beer and scooped up the last two French fries from his plate. "They're great people, don't get me wrong. I love 'em, I just don't think they have done anything new or different in the past twenty years. I go home and have the same conversations with them, every time. My dad bitches about their budget and the Giants. I don't know why he's still bitching about money, my brother and I have been out of the house and out of college for years. They haven't bought anything new since the Reagan administration, including their car. It makes me crazy, you know? I know they can afford better, but it's like they're waiting for another Depression, or world war, like they're disappointed they missed out on the chance to prove their skills and frugality."

"Are they unhappy?" I asked.

"I don't know. How do you tell? They seem happy. They're probably happy. My mom walks the mall with her girlfriends most mornings. The old man could use more exercise. I guess they're pretty typical," he replied.

"It's funny, you don't like that your parents have been static for twenty years. I don't like the fact that my mom can't seem to stay on this continent for more than two to three weeks at a time."

"Let's just resolve not to be like them when we grow old," he said. I perseverated over the when–we-get-old comment for days.

Brian arrived to pick me up for date number three on a mild early-spring day. He pulled up in front of my apartment building in his bright red Subaru wagon, bike on top. I buckled Lainie's car seat in the back and put the baby backpack in the cargo area with Brian's golden retriever, Ralph, who looked inordinately happy to see us. Jarvo looked at the big frame backpack contraption designed to safely transport a tot of up to forty-five pounds across the Himalayas and asked, "Are you sure you can handle that and Ralph at the same time?"

"Yeah, no problem, Lainie's pretty light and that thing is really well balanced."

"Okay." When we got to the trailhead parking lot, I busied myself getting Lainie ready while Brian unloaded the bike and strapped on his gear. He donned a red-and-yellow helmet that matched his bike, clear plastic wraparound glasses to deflect branches, a hydropack of water strapped around his waist and various other things to help navigate the mountain bike trails. I slipped Lainie into her backpack and used different brightly colored ribbons to attach her hat, a sippy cup and two small toys to the frame of the pack. I balanced the whole contraption on the fender of the Subaru and did my contortionist act to get her onto my back. Lainie giggled.

"I would have helped you with that," Brian said, looking up from his bike.

"That's okay, I'm used to it."

"Here's his leash. I'm going to make two loops. It will take an hour, maybe an hour-ten. Meet you back here?"

"Okay." I said.

"Be careful on the back side of the hill, the trail gets really narrow. Most bikers will give a shout, give them some room, the hill is really steep at that spot. Ralph usually stays pretty calm, but I'd talk to him while people are trying to pass you. Keep his attention on you, not the bikes."

"I think we'll be okay." He gave Lainie a dubious look. He seemed to like her, but clearly hadn't spent much time with little kids. I found his concern endearing.

"Ok. Bye." He set off, pumping the pedals with gusto. He may have been showing off. I was impressed, but nature was calling, in more ways than one.

With Lainie strapped in and Ralph ready to go, I was the one holding things up. There was a Porta John there at the trailhead. I tied Ralph's leash to a tree and left the door ajar so I could keep an eye on him. A little personal embarrassment would be nothing next to a lost or stolen Ralph, so I just muttered a little prayer that no other outdoor enthusiast would need the facilities.

Keeping one eye on the dog, I wiggled out of my jeans and crouched over the toilet seat. The cold metal frame of the backpack brushed my rear. Lainie giggled as I leaned forward. Luckily, I didn't have to worry about her toppling out as she was firmly buckled in with a five-point harness, the creators of which, I'm sure, envisioned hearty hikers climbing over fallen trees or negotiating tricky rock formations, not single moms crouching over porta-potties because no one else was around to hold their kids.

Finished, I pulled up my clothes as best I could and lurched out of the smelly outhouse. Pulling my pants all the way up required hefting the weight of the kiddie pack off my hips several times. Ralph looked at me quizzically and Lainie giggled even harder as I jumped up and down, tucking, buttoning and zipping. I was terrified that her shrill laughter would draw the attention of other hikers while my rear end was hanging out. This was not glamorous. How many L.L. Bean models jumped up and down outside of a porta-potty near a trailhead hoping that no one came along in time to catch a glimpse of underwear, or worse?

"What you doing, Mommy?" Lainie asked.

"Just trying to get my act together, Sweetie." The clothing calisthenics left me winded.

We started walking, Ralph nosing ahead, keeping the leash taut between us. The ground was soft from the spring rain and the woods smelled of things slowly awakening. Here and there, pale buds appeared on branches. Small patches of grass were beginning to lose the dormant look they had worn all winter.

"Where's Ralph, Mommy?" Lainie pressed her feet into the bottom of the backpack and tried to stand up to see over my head.

"Right in front of us, Honey."

"What's he doing?"

"Smelling things."

"Smelling what?"

"Stuff, people, animals that might live here."

"Flowers?"

"I don't think there are any flowers yet." I said.

"Up here." I looked up. There were tiny blossoms on the tree we were passing. I had almost missed them.

"Good job, Lainie." We carried on, the trail rising steeply in front of us. I had to put my hand down to launch over boulders. More giggling from the back. For a while, Lainie carried on a one-sided conversation about *The Little Mermaid* while I concentrated on my footing. About a half-mile later, I felt her head slump against my neck.

"Good news, Ralph, the kiddo is napping, we can hike in peace and quiet for a while." The trail narrowed along the back side of the hill. I reached out and grabbed the trunk of a sapling to pull myself up. An imprint of wet bicycle tires looked like the trail of a resolute snake where Brian (I assumed) had crossed over a flat rock. I left a muddy footprint next to it on the rock. Ralph was good company, venturing out the end of his leash and circling back to check on us. He was a little slow getting up the trail too.

"I think we're the junior varsity team, Buddy." Judging by my watch, we'd be lucky to make it back to the car within the hour. The trail met up with a gravel road, and we followed it a little way. Just as we were about to turn back down the trail where it left the road again, I heard a voice demand from behind, "Trail, trail!" I moved aside and pulled Ralph in.

"Come here boy, stay by me. Let's let this guy pass." Two bikers charged up the road, locked in a competition no one had overtly declared. Their faces set and determined, recalling footage of the Tour De France. Standing, pumping with straining quads, the riders bent low over the handle bars, eyes boring aggressively forward. Brian was in front, chased closely by a second rider.

They charged along the gravel road, one of the few places wide enough for one to pass the other, dirt and pebbles flying in their wake. Jarvo wasn't going to yield. The competitor was a younger, smaller guy in a garish red and blue biking shirt and neon green helmet. They looked straight ahead as they passed, beads of sweat rolling down Brian's face as he zoomed past. We watched him turn down the narrow dirt path back into the woods and relax into the saddle for a moment, knowing that the kid couldn't pass him for the next two hundred yards. Frustrated, the other rider followed down the trail, his front wheel inches away from Brian's rear wheel.

Ralph had been sitting quietly by my side. He gave a little yelp when he saw Brian, but otherwise was still. After the bikes blew by, we stood for a moment in the quiet. The leaves that had stirred as the bikes sped by settled their rustling. We continued on.

Brian beat us back to the car.
"How was your ride?" I asked.

"Great!" He was grinning, "Hey pup, did you have a good walk?" He bent and grabbed Ralph's neck with both hands, petting and rubbing and letting his face be licked. "How's my good boy?" Brian reached into the trunk and pulled out a dog bowl, which he set on the ground and filled with water from a gallon jug. He looked at Ralph. "Sit." Ralph sat. "Okay." I watched Ralph drink, sloppily and happily, tail wagging. Brian was more prepared for fatherhood than he gave himself credit for, but I kept that thought to myself.

After two restaurant dates and the mountain hiking/biking adventure, Jarvo invited me over to his apartment for dinner. I love going to people's homes, it's similar to meeting my students' parents at Back to School Night when all the oddity and behavior of their progeny is explained. Bookshelves and CD collections are abundant with clues, even better if there are lots of photos on display. It's like an archaeological dig, so I channel my inner Louis Leakey and carefully examine the artifacts for hints of erudition and genius, or minimally, decent taste. A dog-eared copy of the collected *Calvin and Hobbes* or *Bloom County* would be a good sign. I was anxious to see the inside of my new suitor's abode.

Brian rented a first-floor condo so Ralph could dash out the sliding glass doors and terrorize squirrels. Jarvo also used the glass door as the general egress for bikes and large sporting equipment. The apartment building was tucked into a hill, so the front of his apartment opened onto an expansive yard, but the back half was underground. The descent to Brian's door was murky, an institutional, yellowing off-white stairwell that smelled of old socks and mildew. Brian opened the door with a shy smile and invited me in. His apartment wasn't much of an improvement on the entryway, decorated in Early Frat House with a nod to Men's Locker Room. The entire home budget went to an enormous entertainment center with a mammoth TV that dominated the living room. A few things hung on the walls; their placement determined by preexisting nails left by the previous tenant.

"It's really more like a dorm room than an apartment," he said, "considering how little time I spend here."

"Well, you're a busy guy," I offered.

"Yeah, and I like to be outside a lot. I hate it when winter really sets in. It sucks when I can't ride."

"Maybe you should take up cross-country skiing," I said.

"Yeah, that's supposed to be great cardio. I just don't know how Ralph would do in the snow." For a moment, we stood stiffly in the living room. "Here, I'll show you around." He led the way to the bedroom, which was simply a laundry pile with a bed, hard to tell where one started and the other ended. "Here's the second bedroom, which I just use for storage." This room was packed with every variety of sporting gear imaginable: spare bikes and parts, downhill skis, lacrosse sticks, pads and jerseys. It seemed that each corner had its designated sport. The bike corner was immaculate. Brian had set up a workbench along one wall with two gooseneck lamps peering down each side. Tools were neatly arranged on a shelf above the table. This man needed a garage. But then, lurking behind the door, I saw something that could be a deal breaker.

"Brian," I asked cautiously, "Do you golf?"

"No, no. I tried it a few times but God, how slow is that? Hit the ball, walk. Hit the ball, walk. No thank you. Those were my Uncle Ray's clubs. He upgraded to titanium and gave me those. The nine iron comes in handy sometimes, though." I didn't ask for what.

He invited me to sit down while he finished the steaks. Ralph followed so close behind, hoping for some juicy morsel to fall, that Brian tripped over him twice. I watched through the sliding glass door as they did a six-legged tango around the grill. Brian brandished the spatula at Ralph. Ralph ignored him.

I stood up from the brown and yellow plaid couch and wandered out to the patio to be social. Jarvo had set up a table between two ancient lawn chairs, the kind with multi-colored plastic tubing running across the backs and seats, all lightly coated with residue from the last rainstorm. A stubby candle sat in the middle of the twenty-four-inch square table. Two paper towels had been folded lengthwise and were anchored by mismatched forks. I found the whole scene endearing.

"I'll put him inside while we eat."

"I don't know how much he'll like that."

"Tough potatoes for him." Brian said this with affection.

"Can I help you with anything?"

"No, no, just sit. Well, there are drinks in the fridge if you'd like something,"

"Okay." I stood up.

"Could you grab me a beer?"

"Sure." This was nice. Cozy. Almost familial. *Grab me a beer.* If he'd said *Grab me a beer, Honey* I might have fainted.

Pulling a Diet Coke and a St. Pauli Girl out of the fridge, I contemplated Ralph. He was a nice dog. It's not his fault I'm not a pet person. I keep promising myself to get over that, kids and men love dogs, right? I can adapt. I made a point of rubbing Ralph under the chin on my way back out. Jarvo had loaded my plate with a steak big enough to feed three people, a mound of potato salad and an ear of corn. Sinking my teeth into the meat, I closed my eyes and chewed. It was perfection.

"Wow, Brian, this steak is delicious." And it was, I wasn't just flirting.

"Yeah, I do good grill." He grinned. We ate in silence. Evidently, we were both very hungry. He stood to clear our paper plates. "I'd better let Ralph out of jail."

I leaned back in my lawn chair as he tidied up. The evening had softened to twilight, neighborhood kids were playing in the distance, their happy shouts floating over the hill. It was getting brisk. Now was about the time I could expect to be invited for a long make-out session in front of the enormous TV. A chill ran across my arms and I couldn't decide if it was caused by the breeze or anticipation. Brian's hands were like fireplace bellows, large and strong. Curiosity and lust led me to the living room where I tried to arrange myself provocatively on the couch.

Brian emerged from the kitchen carrying a carton of Ben and Jerry's ice cream and two spoons. God love him. Dessert before *dessert*. He handed me the spoon and sat down wordlessly as if this were a routine with us, or at least with him. Or, how many other girls had he seduced in this casual steak and ice cream ploy? *Shut up Alex*, I told my brain. We sank so far into the sofa that our knees almost hit our chins. There was a game on, but before I could worry about making a fool of myself and confusing offense with defense or not know which team was which, Brian put the ice cream on the coffee table and in one smooth movement managed to kiss me, scoop my legs up and lay me horizontal. From this angle, the couch wasn't so bad.

Simply put, the sex was breathtaking. While I was kissing him I didn't care if I was being slutty or not *holding out long enough*. I wondered why we had even waited for three dates. Everything he lacked in decorating and conversational skills was more than amply compensated for by sheer sexual mastery. Somehow, he had worked out the physics of his physique and I never felt squashed or endangered by his 220-pound frame. I don't know how he did it and I didn't really care to analyze it. He knew every little place to touch that would send shivers through me and clear my mind of any sensible thought. I wanted to hold on to that feeling of cool liquid glass pouring over and through me, but it was as elusive as it was exhilarating.

***

During our commute one day, Lainie piped up from the back and said, "Our car is red like Brian's."

"Yeah?"

"Daddy's car is beige. Stuart's car is black." I gasped, gripped the steering wheel, and held my breath to see where this was going next. Out of the mouths of babes.

"I miss Stuart." Lainie said this in a matter-of-fact tone, playing with the tail of her toy Dalmatian puppy. "Can we see Stuart?" *Never, unless the gods don't favor us and we run into him in the mall again.*

"I don't know, sweetie, Stuart is very busy."

"Okay, listen to happy tunes?"

"Which happy tunes do you want to listen to?"

"'Little Mermaid,' please." That, I could manage.

A few weeks later, Brian and I had the "It's not you, it's me" talk. In addition to being a sex maestro, Brian had a talent for brutal honesty. We finished doing the dishes from our dinner of tortellini and salad, and headed to the living room. We started kissing, and I was expecting the rapid amp-up to amazing sex when Brian pulled back, looked me in the eyes and said the words no one ever, ever wants to here.

"Alex, we need to talk." I'm not exactly sure what he said because the blood was rushing through my ears and my brain was in full retreat to the panic place, but I think his words went something like this: "Alex, you're a great girl, and I love hanging out with you, but I'm not ready for all the stuff you want. I'm having a good time and I'm not ready for all that responsibility. I don't want to be a dad before I get to be a husband, and I don't want to be a husband any time soon." In other words, he was saying, "You need to seek Happily Ever After elsewhere."

"Are we breaking up?" I held myself very, very still, afraid that if I moved I would shatter into a thousand little pieces. Or cry. Ugly, sobbing, snotty cry.

"No, no. That's not what I'm saying. I don't think." I didn't say anything. I just waited. His big hands still held mine. He turned one of my hands over and stroked my palm. "No, I could love you. I've half-fallen for you as it is. I could fall hard, but I can't. You are pushing me to be something I'm not ready for. Part of me wants to be the person you want me to be, but part of me still wants to have fun."

"I'm not fun?" I tried to say this without shrieking. I think I failed. "What about the hiking and biking and picnics . . ." I stopped before I added *And the sex?*.

"No! That's not what I meant." He turned his beautiful eyes to me, and I wanted to smack and kiss him at the same time. "I just need to make sure that you know where I stand on this. You are trying to drive at warp speed to, I don't know, to your white picket fence or something. I kinda need you to hit the brakes a little." He said this very gently. "I still want to hang out with you, and you know, do more of this." He leaned in and gave me one of his soft but solid kisses, and I let him. Then I pushed him off of me.

"So, to clarify, you're not ready to settle down, you just want to hang out, have sex, and go on the occasional date?" I asked.

"Well, when you say it that way, I sound like a jerk."

I sat back and looked at him. I couldn't fault the guy for his honesty. In fact, I realized right then, with the Tangerine Dream make-out mix playing fruitlessly on my boom box, that I should be the one thanking him.

Brian continued, "I just wanted you to know that I think you should keep looking for someone who can give you all that you want, now. But in the meantime, I'm here if you want someone to do things with."

"So," I asked, "is this the, 'it's not you, it's me' talk?"

"Kind of. I'm sorry."

I stood up and walked into the kitchen where I waited a minute for the tears to come. But they didn't. I was, oddly, okay with this. I was okay with this sweet guy being truthful. For the first time in months, I wasn't overcome with a deluge of sadness, guilt, self-loathing or shame in this moment of disappointment. So, I went back to the couch and gave in to my more basic instincts.

The weekend after Brian and I had our clarifying conversation, I took Lainie hiking again. I timed our walk to coincide with Lainie's nap so I could have a quiet moment. We drove to a nature preserve where the main trail followed the path of a wide, meandering stream. The rippling, gurgling water had a soothing effect on us both. I strapped Lainie into the backpack again. Stuart had taken one look at the flimsy contraption I used to carry her in and paraded us through the nearest camping outfitter. He gently placed Lainie in three different child packs, inspecting the straps, the safety features and the weight rating. Before making his final choice, Stuart lifted the pack loaded with Lainie onto my shoulders, making sure that I felt comfortable in the harness. Then he insisted that I help him put the pack on to ensure that the straps were easily adjustable between the two of us so we could take turns carrying her.

As I walked next to the stream I wondered why I loved Stuart, and why things had fallen apart with Ken. It wasn't an easy question to answer. Ken was happy to do anything I asked of him. He would willingly pitch in under my direction, usually with good cheer, but I was weary of asking and directing. We were two planets orbiting one another but each spinning on our own axis, our energy flying out into the universe in all different directions. Ken pursued his own wants and desires and didn't seem to think of us as a family unit. We didn't plan together, or dream together. We existed together comfortably, but to me, it always had a temporary quality, an impermanence that I couldn't define.

***

During the time we were together, Stuart and I talked constantly about the future. Our future. We talked about our goals and together we planned how we would balance work and grad school and more kids. We contemplated the home we would build and the places we wanted to take our children. We were both married to other people and were going about creating our lives together without addressing the fact that neither of us was free to do so, yet. Maybe if we had done things properly, put our relationship on hold while we each ended our marriages, things would have gone differently.

As we neared the parking lot, Lainie woke from her nap and began to squirm. I slid the backpack off my shoulder to the ground, and let her out to run around. She ran straight to the bank of the stream and squatted down. I followed and watched her examine the stones and moss at the water's edge.

As Lainie picked through the pebbles, the quiet of the woods and the babbling of the stream settled around us. We were on our own.

I hadn't gotten around to unpacking all of the boxes from my move. Some of them sat huddled under a bright blue tarp on my balcony labeled "Frames and Photos," "Extra Kitchen Stuff" and "Baby Clothes". Obviously, I didn't need the stuff if I'd lived so long without it. I thought I would go through them and only keep the stuff that was really important, so I opened "Frames and Photos" first.

There were some of my favorite pictures that I had missed having around, one of me and mom having tea at the Plaza. One of me and Cyn on a park bench in Florence. Had I really been there? It seemed so long ago and distant. Another little silver framed photo of me and Margaret on the Klein Matterhorn. I placed that one at eye level on the bookcase. A large, flat parcel lay on the bottom of the box. I hesitated. I should have just pitched it in the garbage pile, but my frugal half thought maybe I could salvage the frame. I sat holding it on my lap. Inside was our one and only family Christmas portrait, taken two years, almost to the day, before I moved out.

December, 1993

It had been a frantic day. I'd made the portrait appointment a month prior, careful to schedule it so we would have time to package the photos as gifts for our family, but not too early so Lainie would have time to grow into her green velvet First-Christmas dress. I dashed home from work that day to change into my matching velvet dress, a detail that seemed at the time to be of utmost importance. Running through the mall in high heels, pushing the stroller with one hand and carrying Lainie's freshly pressed dress on a Lilliputian hanger in the other, I was sweating and nauseous with the idea that if we were late, they would give our appointment away and all my meticulous orchestration would have been for naught.

Lainie and I arrived on time, and I carefully changed her into her dress, tying a bib around her neck to protect against the unpredictable but still frequent drool and spit-up. The bib would be removed an instant before the photo shoot.

Then we waited. And waited. Ken moseyed in twenty minutes late for the sitting, wearing two days of beard growth and a blazer that looked as if it had spent the better part of the week rolled up in the trunk of his Yugo. I knew if I looked at him I'd snap and cause a scene, so I busied myself buckling Lainie's petite black Mary Jane's onto her feet while we waited.

Didn't he realize what it took to pull this off? The timing of the last feeding so as to minimize the potential spit-up during the photo? The hunt for the perfect outfits and accessories? The search for pantyhose with no runs? That this picture would be the evidence we would present to our parents that we had our act together? Ken apologized and offered to help. I ignored him.

The photo is a good one, I have to admit. Baby Lainie's toothless grin is gleeful. Ken is his handsome self, the wrinkles in his blazer don't really show. And I, though I am not sure how, am wearing a serene maternal smile. We look like the perfect young family, which was exactly what I wanted to project to the world.

There was a nice diner in the mall, which would have been perfect for a post-portrait supper. I had hoped we could talk over a good burger and fries. There was so much to sort out for Christmas, our plans, the gifts, the travel. But Ken had somewhere he had to be. He gave Lainie a squeeze and tickled her as he buckled her in the stroller. He kissed me on the cheek and left.

I put the picture and the frame, unopened, back in the box.

***

The next voice on my answering machine had a French accent. Josef said that he was in imports and had a little boy. Would I like to meet him for café? Ooh la la! Café bébé! I let my hopes balloon out of control. A good job (one presumes), parent of a toddler and thus broken-in to tantrums and fits. Did I mention he was French?

Our first phone call was a bit stilted, so distracted was I by his melodious accent, I stumbled over the answers to his simple questions. We set a meeting place and time. I hung up the phone and did a happy dance in the middle of the kitchenette. Then a chilling thought stopped me mid-shimmy, I only had three days to settle the following crucial issues:

1. Should I attempt to look French and act a bit more suave and Euro-sophisticated? All French women, by definition, are sophisticated and have that *je ne sais quoi*. However, if I attempted any of this would I look like a *poseur*?

1. Should I attempt to speak French? This was easily answered. *Non.* I had been told that I have a cute accent but those French verbs are

tricky. *Merde.*

2. WHAT TO WEAR? Should I work the all-American angle? Perhaps Monsieur Josef was trying to distance himself from his homeland. He had an American ex-wife and had named his son Dallas. Jeans, a T-shirt, perhaps I could unearth the cowboy boots I'd begged Elaine to buy me in middle school. Given the American ex-wife, should I try to be less stereotypically American? Aargh!

3. Perfume. Must remember to wear perfume, the French love perfume. *Oui?* Would Paris by Yves St. Laurent be too obvious? Trying too hard? Frankly, the perfume collection sat collecting dust on my dresser, but for a Frenchman...

I'd always harbored a desire to be French. Or Russian. I had wanted to be a spy, a modern *Mata Hari* who could seduce nuclear secrets and emerging technology trade intel from burly Russian men. I never actually wanted to be me. Laura Ingalls (of the *Little House on the Prairie* books, not the TV series) could practically build a house and run a farm on her own before she was twelve. Harriet the Spy was my hero. Any one of the Little Women was much more interesting than me. School plays offered the chance to transform into someone else, but I was the only one who recognized my own talent and was unjustly relegated to playing the role of third tree from the left, and similar. My friends couldn't stand my fake accents, so I had to travel to distant shopping malls if I wanted some dialect practice.

On the evening of my first date with Josef, I'd experimented with dark red lipstick and a scarf tied around my neck. I looked like a stewardess, and a perfume mishap left me smelling like a whorehouse. So, I re-showered and re-dressed and tried to think of a reasonable excuse for my tardiness as I sped toward the restaurant, twenty minutes late.

Josef rose from his chair to kiss me on both cheeks. As I bent slightly for this maneuver I thought, *Note to self: No heels next time.* Happily, he stopped at two cheeks. Two were all I was prepared for, though I knew that in some parts of the world three or even four alternating kisses were customary. The pressure of knowing which side to go for first was hard enough. *There must be a handbook*, I thought and made a mental note: *Fodor's when I got home.*

First blind dates had taken on a pattern. I would meet the gentleman of the day at one of the five hundred or so chain restaurants on Route 355. Sections of that road have become interchangeable in my head. I couldn't remember which drab strip mall went where. Was TGI Friday's next to Bed Bath and Beyond or was that Appleby's? The first dates were always just a few steps up from fast food, nothing fancy, no great time or financial commitment on either side. We'd order drinks and an appetizer. If things weren't clicking, one could back out at that point. The convenient location of these restaurants meant that, should a date be a bust, one could always shop for household items on the way home. Over the past few months, Lainie had acquired new bath towels in a bright emerald green, and I had upgraded to five hundred thread-count sheets on a whim, but with a coupon.

Josef's small, neat hands fidgeted first with his napkin then his silverware. Not only was he petit, my Frenchman, but he looked rather like a little boy, his dark hair falling over one eye. He had a quick, shy grin and spoke softly. I liked him instantly, but this was wrong. The man was supposed to sweep me off my feet with his charm and sophistication, and, of course, his accent. Instead, I had to resist the urge to cut his hamburger into pieces for him. He was sad around the edges. His wife had left him.

"She wanted everything. My business is good. I make a good living, but still, it is not enough for her. She would not stay home with our son when he was born. I wanted her to, but she would not. She had to work because she wanted to buy this thing and that thing. Everything in the home had to be just like so. She wanted the perfect rugs and plates and dishes. All the best, and so my son had to go to the day care. Then I think she got tired of me. So she left," he said.

"How long have you been divorced?" I asked.

"Three years." He still looked bewildered, as if someone had just broken this news to him. He shook his head and stared into his drink, playing with his straw. I tried to lighten the mood.

"Tell me about your son," I said.

He brightened up. I watched and listened to him talk, trying to figure out how I felt about this date, this guy. I didn't have time to mess around. While he wasn't my fantasy French lover, he was a good-looking, sweet guy who was obviously devoted to his child. There was just no chemistry. None.

Zip. No pheromones, no twinge in the belly, no weakening of the knees. Just the same pleasant feeling one gets when spending time with a friendly yet distant cousin. But, perhaps, I rationalized, this could grow into something. It didn't have to be all passion and heavy breathing at the start. Right?

I had a policy of not exposing Lainie to the men that I was dating before knowing them for a decent amount of time. Even before receiving a lecture on that subject from my boss and self-appointed sage, Michael, I decided to keep Lainie out of the loop. I mentioned this to Josef. He nodded in agreement. So then, what did it say about the both of us that we each found the other so un-threatening, so un-mysterious, and probably therefor so un-sexy that we felt perfectly safe introducing our offspring to one another on our second date?

We met at the zoo on a sunny, blustery day. The wind buffeted the flags that lined the entrance to the park. It pushed the silky white clouds high above the trees and whipped the leaves so they shimmered as they flipped dark side to light and back again. The kids were shy and wary of each other for about thirty seconds then became instant friends. Josef and I studied the large zoo map, planning our route and discussing the pressing question of where to stop for lunch. We decided to go down the hill toward the sea lions before making our way back to the elephants and giraffes. We would hit the reptile house after lunch. I had brought Lainie's stroller and pushed it along empty as she and Dallas ran ahead, weaving back and forth in front of us, vigorously investigating things alongside the path.

"Kids," I yelled, "look up!" They did, and the sight sent them hurrying back to us. Lainie grabbed my jeans.

"Mommy, what's that?"

"That's an orangutan. It's like a big monkey. He can travel across the cables and go down into another cage, but he can only come down into places where he can't escape."

We watched as the orange ape swung arm-over-arm, high above our heads and across the path, graceful in motion. We stood and stared until he dropped out of sight, into another enclosure. Dallas and Lainie skipped all the way down to the marine mammal pool, swinging their arms overhead, pretending to hang from an invisible wire. Josef and I sat in the sun on the wide stone steps overlooking the sea lions. The kids stood transfixed as the trainer fed dead fish to the giant female sea lion.

"Well, I don't think we needed to worry about the kids getting along," I said.

"It's good for Dallas. His day care is pretty small but he loves other kids. He gets a little lonely on the weekends," he said.

"I know what you mean. If it weren't for Trixie, I don't know what Lainie would do."

"Who's Trixie?" Josef asked.

"Lainie's imaginary friend. She's usually getting into trouble. Lainie yells at her a lot because Trixie is not good at sharing."

Josef laughed. He closed his eyes and leaned back on his elbows on the concrete steps to absorb the sun, his hair falling back from his face. His polo shirt gapped at the neck and I could see the outline of his thin collarbone.

The trainer finished feeding the sea lions, and after a brief stop at the seal pool we strolled back toward the African safari animals. A squabble erupted.

"Mommy, Dallas doesn't believe I have African Granny."

"Well, you don't. You have a Granny who lives in Africa, which is a little different."

"Does Granny have giraffes in Africa?" asked Lainie.

"She doesn't have any of her own, but she sees some from time to time." I said.

Dallas looked skeptical. "She doesn't really see giraffes."

"Actually, she does and she's sent us pictures of them. She sees lots of monkeys too." I said.

"What about lions?" Dallas asked.

"I don't think she's seen any of those so far, and I am not sure if she wants to."

His face was a miniature of his father's, pointed and serious. He turned back to the animals. "Let's go see the elephants."

I read somewhere that elephants are pregnant for twenty-two months and give birth to two-hundred pound baby calves. I shared this helpful information with Josef. He laughed. "If my ex had to be pregnant for twenty-two months, Dallas wouldn't be here."

"I wouldn't blame her. Nine months were more than enough for me. And Lainie was eight days late. They would have had to commit me to an insane asylum if she hadn't come when she did."

My little girl, the love of my life, was busy flirting with my date's son, their dark heads were bent together, intently discussing something we couldn't hear, their words swept away by the wind. Thirty yards away, three elephants stood clustered together, looking like they'd rather be in Africa with African Granny.

When imagining this date in the days that preceded it, I had thoughts of the four of us sitting down to lunch like a real family. The children would sit at one end of the table, too engrossed in their juice boxes and French fries to notice as Josef and I held one another's eyes in a long, romantic gaze over zoo café fare. However, the wind turned what should have been a tranquil interlude into a comedy of flying napkins and soaring paper plates. I rescued Dallas' hotdog as it sailed across the table, the wind lifting the corners of its paper boat. Had it not been laden with extra Ketchup, all would have been lost. I dove across the length of the picnic table in an overly athletic attempt to save the boy's lunch.

"There you go. Just hold onto the bun and we'll throw the plate away. Can you hold it until you finish it?" I asked.

He nodded, his cheeks stuffed with food. Just as I sat down, Josef sprang up from the table to chase down the fluttering paper napkins.

"Ew Mommy, what do you have on your elbow?" Lainie pointed at a large glob of Ketchup which I had at that very moment wiped across my jeans. It took five napkins to clean up that mess, leaving an attractive reddish stain painted across my hip. Very sexy.

Lainie asked for popcorn, but I had a vision of popped kernels floating through the zoo like snow and suggested ice cream instead.

"Okay, next stop, the reptile house!" Josef announced.

The kids bounded after him. I trailed behind, pushing the stroller, trying to stack the jackets and extra water bottles so they wouldn't blow away. When I caught up with Josef and the kids, they were standing by the doorway, shoving the rest of the ice cream pops into their mouths. The large sign on the door said, "No food inside the exhibit. Thank you for your help."

"Slow down, the animals aren't going anywhere, we have plenty of time." I didn't realize how true that statement would turn out to be. They licked the ice cream off their fingers and argued over who had finished first.

"Here Mommy." Lainie shoved the ice cream stick, still dripping with chocolate, into my hand. "Throw this away please?" she said, dashing off to catch Dallas, who had managed to find a trash can under his own power. By the time I deposited the stick in the trash, a chocolate stain appeared on the hem of my white shirt, diagonally across from the Ketchup stain. I avoided catching my reflection in the glass door.

The pungent odor of the reptile house assaulted us as we entered, saturated with the smell of sodden woodchips and scaly things. True love for my daughter and the hope that things might turn out with my Frenchman were the only forces that could impel me into the reptile house.

My favorite reptile is the turtle. If you don't count snapping turtles, they are cute, slow and harmless. I do not enjoy things that slither. Dallas and Lainie, however, were enthralled. The glass cases were low enough for them to see into without assistance. They could get closer to the animals in here than they could anywhere else. A thin sheet of glass separated them from alligators and lizards, many of which liked to hang out at the front of their exhibits.

"Mommy, I can see his teeth. Come see! Come see!" Lainie and Dallas led us from one slimy creature to the next. They spent five minutes in front of one window trying to find the leaf snake which was perfectly camouflaged, curled like a gentle vine around a small tree branch. I spied it before they did, but waited, not wanting to spoil their fun.

"Oh! I see it!" Dallas jumped up and down and pointed.

"Where?" Lainie couldn't see it from her vantage point. I moved over and drew her to me, lifting her so she could see. Josef leaned in for a closer look. I could feel the heat of his cheek near mine.

"Oh, it's small," Lainie said and wiggled down. We were gathering our things and getting ready to move on to the Great Apes House when there was a loud bang from the entryway. We stood still. Then another bang echoed from the opposite end of the building and the large room became ominously quiet. There were three or four other families in the reptile house with us, and the adults cast concerned looks at each other over the heads of their children.

As Josef and I tried to get the kids to the exit, a large man in a green zoo uniform blocked our way. He stood, feet braced wide under his shoulders, a serious look on his face. Holding his hand up in front of him to fend us off, he announced, "I'm sorry folks, we're going to have to keep you inside the building for your own safety."

Oh my God, there has been some terrible incident. Who the hell would bomb the zoo? How are we going to get out of here? Is there a fall-out shelter in the Reptile House?

Before I could go into emergency over-drive, the zoo worker continued, "One of the orangutans has come off the wire and is loose in the park. They're generally harmless, but we can't take any chances. Also, human germs are very dangerous to orangutans, so we don't want them be exposed to us unnecessarily." General anxious chatter broke out. "There is really nothing to worry about," the man continued, "We have almost everyone indoors. It shouldn't take long to get our orang back to where she belongs." Our captor was about to abandon us to our malodorous fate locked in the House of Stink when he turned back and said with a smile, "Maybe I can get the guys to start feeding time a little early so y'all can watch!" A dozen little kids cheered and scampered among the displays see where the carnage would begin

It was the iguanas. Two of them began to scratch the dirt of their cage and move with uncharacteristic speed when they heard noises from behind their exhibit. I thought of it as "backstage". I wondered what the zoo-speak term is for things that go on beyond the public view. A panel slid back and a disembodied hand appeared. The scrum of children churned and held their collective breath. I stood back with the adults. The hand held the exact replica of the metal measuring cup in my kitchen drawer. They could have come from the same store. The cups were both worn and dented to a similar degree, but whereas my measuring cup was used to make lovely cookies and cakes, this one held a squirming mass of larva. A roiling cup of putrescence. My stomach lurched. My throat constricted. The contents of my lunch threatened to reappear.

I backed away from the horror movie unfolding before me and tried to block out the sound of the little Romans cheering in front of the glass colosseum. Larva to iguanas like Christians to lions. I needed air. My vision started to close in. I grabbed the nearest bench and lowered myself onto it, put my head between my knees and prayed to any god that might be listening to let me not throw up. *Please God, not now. Not on a date.* Bile burned the back of my throat, but I forced it down. *Think happy thoughts.* No happy thoughts came to mind. I stared at my shoes. They needed a polish. The floor of the Reptile House was reasonably clean. Maybe if I collapsed, no one would notice.

"Alex, are you okay?" Josef put his hand on my back. I had been waiting all day for him to make a move, hold my hand, anything. Now we were dangerously close to our first physical moment being his holding my hair back while I puked.

Breathe in and out. Slowly.

"I'll be fine, in just a minute." Through the curtain of my hair, I could see Josef leaning down.

"You look green."

"Great, I'll fit right in. Maybe they can put me on display."

In the end, it wasn't me who threw up, it was Lainie, suffering from a surfeit of sugar and lack of fresh air. The tell-tale flush came to her cheeks, and before she could finish the sentence "Mommy, don't feel good" I'd propelled her into the ladies' room. She held the side of the toiled and sobbed, "I hate this."

"I know baby, but you're almost done and you'll feel better in a few minutes." This was not the first time, nor would it be the last, where Lainie's fragile stomach would interfere with her mother's attempts at intimacy.

By the time I'd cleaned up my daughter (who seemed miraculously unscathed) and wiped green matter from my shoes, the orangutan crisis had passed, and weary patrons were filing out of the reptile house. Josef and Dallas were waiting for us just outside the door.

"I think we're going to call it a day," I said.

"I'm sorry you got sick," Josef said, crouching down to talk to Lainie directly. "We enjoyed meeting you."

At this, Lainie began the whimper that signaled the end of a good time and the beginning of a meltdown. We had to make a speedy exit if I were to maintain any shred of dignity. I could tell by the pitch and tenor of the prefit that this could lead to my having to carry Lainie from the zoo kicking and screaming if we didn't leave immediately.

"This was so nice. Thank you for coming." I tried to arrange my features into an expression that could convey the sentiment of I'm-sorry-my-kid-puked-and-we-had-to-spend-an-hour-in-the-reptile-house. Josef kissed me on both cheeks, and I knew, well, that was that. He wouldn't call again.

I believe, deep in my heart, that, had I been French, I would have weathered the zoo day without becoming a walking Jackson Pollack of food stains, that my hair would have remained perfect despite the gale-force winds, and that my perfume would have seduced my date. *C'est la vie.*

Chapter Seven
July, 1995

Before Ken and I called it quits, we went to a marriage counselor. His idea. The layman had been referred to Ken by a priest friend, and the sign on his door read "Timothy Conley, Catholic counselor." Did he counsel people about being Catholic? As ours was a mixed marriage, Presbyterian and Catholic, I thought Ken might be stacking the deck.

We had walked from the metro station in heat and humidity so thick it was like cutting a path through misdirected clouds. Ken plodded along, his feet in tattered sandals slapping the cement. Our shoulders brushed against each other as we were nudged together by the crowd. His hand brushed, but did not grab, mine. We pulled away.

In the waiting room, the air conditioner churned noisily and ineffectively on the windowsill. I did not want to be there. It couldn't possibly be me sitting in a moldy office being judged by a portly man ostentatiously brandishing his eight-millimeter wedding band. His tassel loafers had seen better days. I noticed this because I couldn't look him in the eye.

"Okay," Counselor Tim began, "why don't each of you write down why you came here today and what you think the main problem is in your relationship."

He handed me a yellow legal pad and another to Ken. The pressure behind my eyes made the lines on the page move, they wiggled and squirmed across the page until they took the form of a snake. The lines above and below wove together to make a diamond pattern on his back before he slithered off the pad. Stress hallucinations. That was a first for me. I gripped the blue ballpoint pen Tim offered. Ken refused to write with anything other than his black ultra-fine-tip pens. I hoped he might be crippled in his efforts to make me out as the perpetuator of all evil without the proper writing implement, but he'd come prepared and pulled his pen out of his pocket. As I sat pondering the biblical implications of my legal pad hallucinations, Ken was madly scribbling away and had filled half a page with his cramped writing. I was going to fail yet another marriage test. Ken paused, gave me an indeterminate look, and bent back over his pad.

I wrote, "I don't want to be here. I don't want to be married to Ken anymore."

Had Leon asked me to enumerate our marital troubles while I was standing on the treadmill, I would have held forth for hours, until my legs gave out and Leon would have to get one of the maintenance guys to help him move the towering machine after I let the treads suck me under. But there was nothing I wanted to say to Ken's face, and certainly not in front of this stranger who had already struck me as smug and self-righteous. I had gone from being in love with a really bright, eccentric guy to realizing that he couldn't be the partner I needed. I'd gotten myself into a mess and didn't handle it well. And this Tim guy was the last person I wanted to help us sort things out. I didn't want it sorted. I just wanted out.

Tim collected our papers and studied them. Pulling Ken's closer to his face, squinted and nodded. "Hmm, yes, I see." He turned to mine. "Is that all, Alexandria?" Silence seemed prudent. I waited. He continued. "The two of you have a child to raise together, and Ken wants to try to make this work, and all you have to say is that you don't want to be married anymore?"

Actually, I wrote that I didn't want to be married to Ken, specifically. I could easily see myself enjoying marriage. Preferably with Stuart. I sat.

"Ken says you had an affair."

"Yes."

"I think that is something we should explore here."

"I'd rather not, thank you."

"Alex, we're not going to get anywhere if you refuse to participate."

Tim was judgmental and Ken was annoyed. I really wasn't trying to be rude, the snake got my tongue. I'd said all I wanted to say on the topic, only I had said it to Leon and Cyn and Michael. I was talked out and cried out, I just hadn't included Ken in the process. I had tried, a few times, to ask Ken to do things, or to change something. Nothing changed. Nothing happened. So, I had made the journey from In Love to Out of Love and hadn't bothered to inform Ken of my itinerary.

I had had an affair. I was so clearly in the wrong, but so caught up in a whirl of passion that it didn't matter, the deceit, the immorality, none of it.

Most summers, I traveled, visiting relatives and friends, spending weeks at a time away from home. A year ago, Stuart and I had arranged to meet in Richmond. He had a credit card his wife didn't know about and made the reservation. I knew Ken would never find out, and that, as long as I called him every three days or so with a Lainie update, he would barely miss us. I rationalized that he would pass the days at work and the nights drinking and playing D&D with his buddies.

In the steamy Richmond evenings, Stuart and I meandered through the park near our hotel, Lainie riding on Stuart's shoulders. The saturated green of the park, the grass and trees, the white and blues and purples of the flowers still permeate my memories. We ate at a Greek restaurant. Lainie, full of energy, wanted out of the high chair. We let her down and she held onto the side of the booth, quietly bouncing up and down. The proprietor came by and swooped her up, like she was one of his grandchildren, and tickled her under the chin. He handed her back to Stuart saying, "You have a beautiful family."

All weekend long, people casually treated us as a married couple. We were somewhere we shouldn't have been, pretending to be something we weren't. We were in a bubble, with no thought of the past or the future, no thought of anyone beyond the three of us, no care for the consequences of our behavior. And no regrets.

The worn, fake, oriental carpet in Counselor Tim's office had four large blotchy stains. One was near Ken's feet. Ken spent the rest of the fifty-five minute session talking to Tim and at me. There were twenty-six yellow and white stripes on the upholstered arm of my chair. I don't remember anything that he said.

***

April 1996, Continued

In the perpetual quest for cultural betterment and a cultured man, Lainie and I ventured off to the National Gallery. The skylights in the main hall usually lent a warmth to the marble floor, but on this overcast day, everything was a bit dull. The security guards were having an easy time as the museum was practically empty. This didn't bode well for my man hunt, but Lainie was thrilled that she had the place to herself. She could comment and question freely, unconcerned about using her "Inside Voice."

Elaine used to haul me into The City to the Met once or twice a year. My enjoyment of those days was hampered by pinched toes inside of dress shoes and the icky feeling when the crotch of your tights falls somewhere halfway down your thighs. Therefore, I have a strict no tights in the museum rule. Unless Lainie really wants to dress up, and it's her choice, so if she has drooping crotch issues, there's no blaming me.

I was seven the first time we went into The City. I was getting ready for school one morning when Elaine came into the bathroom and said, "Forget school, let's go into The City." I vividly remember standing by the claw-foot tub in shock. Nothing, nothing ever called off school other than snow storms or strep throat.

We took the train, watching the colorful billboards and houses rushing past the windows. I sat as still as an excited child could, bouncing slightly in my seat, craning my neck this way and that. A conductor passed. I was eye level with his belt and stared at all the items hanging off it, like ornaments on a navy-blue tree. His hands with fingers thick as cigars took cash from Mom and made change from an ingenious contraption that dispensed quarters and nickels and dimes. While the train lurched violently he swayed gently with the rhythm. The conductor took the hole punch that was hanging from a chain on his belt and punched three holes in each of our tickets, the paper circles drifting like snow to the floor. I understood that this man's job was to ride the train back and forth to The City every day. I was enthralled. It seemed so glamorous.

Elaine led me by the hand through Grand Central Station, my neck straining to see the star speckled ceiling. Mom waited patiently for me to take it all in, then continued up the wide marble stairs, past the Oyster Bar through to the street. I halted, rooted to the sidewalk. Nothing in my bucolic upbringing had prepared me for this stark geometry, the unnatural canyon created by skyscrapers. Nothing had ever made me feel so small.

Lainie and I started with the Impressionist galleries. Lainie stood transfixed in front of Degas' dancers. She stared at the ballerinas, raising her hands into an arch high above her head and turned out her toes to plié. We giggled. It was becoming clear that Mr. Right & Cultured wasn't visiting the museum that day, so I tried to stop looking over my shoulder for him and concentrated instead on *being in the moment*, which is harder than it sounds.

In the Renaissance gallery, Lainie asked why Mary and Jesus didn't have halos.

"They do, they're just painted very lightly."

"I don't see them," she said.

"Look closer."

"I still don't see them."

"Okay." I hoisted her onto my hip and pointed to the faint outline of the halo. "There, do you see it now?"

"Oh, yeah." She wiggled out of my arms and stepped dangerously close to the canvas. The guard cleared his throat with unnecessary vigor. I pulled Lainie away and we headed to Nineteenth Century Portraiture.

"Oooooh Mommy, she's so pretty!" Lainie stopped in front of a painting of a young lady in a light blue gown, her creamy complexion glowing even on that dull day.

"Look Mommy, she has earrings and a bracelet and a necklace and a crown!"

"That's a tiara." I corrected.

"What's a tee-ah-ra?" she asked.

"It's like a little crown."

"Why?"

"Well, I think *tiara* is a pretty word. Besides, many young ladies back then wore tiaras, but you had to be a king or a queen to wear a real crown." *I think.*

"I am going to be a princess and have a hundred pink dresses and have cupcakes for breakfast, and lots of sparkly jewelry and you can come play princess with me on Saturday."

"Only on Saturdays?"

"Okay, Sundays too, and maybe Thursday."

"Thanks, Sweetie."

Is it genetic that all girls have a princess phase? I think the psychologists are missing this. Forget Piaget. The Smythe theory of female childhood development goes as follows:

    Princess stage
    Stuffed animals and puppies stage
    Barbie stage
    Pony stage
    Optional tomboy stage
    Social Causes stage
    Obsession with love

I'll let you know when I figure the rest out. All I know is that the princess and pony stages were a lot easier than the post-divorce-desperate-for-a-husband stage.

"Look, Mama!" Lainie dashed across the hall and performed an interpretive dance in front of Monet's *Woman with a Parasol*. This time it was a more understanding guard who smiled at my twirling tot. I find museum trips far more successful if I let Lainie lead the way. She traipsed across the big hall again and ended up in front of a large portrait of a lady with a King Charles spaniel.

"Ruskin!" She squealed upon seeing the dog in the painting.

An elderly woman in a wheelchair was also looking at the painting. She burst out laughing, caught my eye and said, "Everyone's a critic." It took me a moment and then I realized that she was referring to John Ruskin, the nineteenth century English artist and art critic. Thanks to a babysitting gig I once had, I knew what she was laughing about and we could share a moment of pre-Raphaelite humor. I didn't have the heart to tell her that it was just the name of Lainie's godmother's dog.

Walking back to the car we passed the merry-go-round. "Mommy, can I ride the carousel, please, please?"

I was somewhat unprepared for this as I was dressed in what I hoped to be a sexy yet refined museum-going outfit, a slim-fitting dress and walkable-but-dressy pumps. We climbed onto the carousel and Lainie immediately ran to a white horse with gold mane and tail wearing a pink bridle. There were only two other families on the ride, but I kept an eye out for single dads in the sparse crowd. I held Lainie by the waist, enjoying her happy giggles as we went around and around. I thought about the poor guys who ran the thing, all day, around and around. Stop for a moment and change the riders, then carry on. Never moving forward, never making any progress, and worse, listening to tinny music all day.

***

When I was thirteen, my summer camp went on a field trip to a museum in Sandwich, Massachusetts known for its barn full of antique cars, an art gallery and old-fashioned carousel. Most of our group didn't really care about the 'old stuff'. The ten girls were busy flirting with the three boys who were far more interested in the cars.

In the art gallery a folk-art painting of a family hung on the wall, their faces round and flat. The children were dressed in white dresses, even the little boys. The boys had bowl haircuts; wooden toys scattered behind them on the floor. I stared at this painting while other campers flowed past, wanting to fade into the canvas, into their lives. They probably had ponies in the stable out back, maybe a governess and a cook. I was suspended in the moment, not in their world, not in my own.

Thirteen is a miserable age. I was part intellectual snob (no one else on the field trip was appreciating the art like *I* was, thank you), part popular girl wannabe, part irredeemable geek. We rode the carousel that day, everyone trying to look casually disinterested, half hanging off the painted ponies. I saw myself in the mirrored panels of the carousel, bottle-thick glasses, freckled cheeks, Laura Ingalls braids. No sense of style whatsoever. Even the children in the painting looked better than me in their funny white dresses and high lace-up shoes. In the wavy mirrors of this carousel, sixteen years later, I still wasn't happy with the reflection.

Chapter Eight
September 1994 - May 1996

Ken and I had already drifted apart without any specific event signaling the beginning of the end. At the beach, playing in the waves, you think you're standing in the same spot, but the current pulls you farther and farther away from the place you left your towel and cooler. When you get out of the water, you end up shivering and wet, weaving through the maze of other people's beach blankets trying to find your own. I think that's what happened to us. I guess I was trying to find my way back to where we had fallen in love, but I'd drifted too far, and was led further astray by another man.

While I am not known for my clairvoyance, there have been three distinct times in my life when I knew, beyond all doubt, that a certain thing would happen. It happened once when my grandmother was very sick and I was studying across the ocean. My mother didn't tell me something was wrong, but I knew. Grandma had open-heart surgery, and Elaine thought it would be better if no one told me until I returned from my semester in France. But somehow, I knew something was wrong and sat, almost paralyzed, in a church on the shore of the Mediterranean, weeping unexpectedly with no explanation. The second time at a college party, I glanced across the room and knew instantly that my friend would marry the woman I saw in the corner of that restaurant. In that moment, they were strangers to each other. Six months later, they were engaged. So, at the risk of sounding overly dramatic, I knew the day I met Stuart how things would unfold.

It was the first day of school for teachers, the day each year we face the reality that we will be working for the next ten months of the year. I spent most of the staff meeting checking the school calendar against my Filofax, looking up only when the new teachers were introduced. There was perky Senorita Wendt in the World Language department, Stuart Driscoll in science, a new assistant in the Media Center and a terrified looking intern in Special Ed. After the meeting, I headed toward the main office to get the necessary paperwork and pull things from my mailbox. The name plates on the mailboxes had been moved to make room for the new staff, and I stood there trying to find mine, like a simpleton who had forgotten the alphabet. Clearly, I was suffering from summer brain. Then it happened.

"Hi, I'm Stuart."

He shook my hand, and in an instant, I saw it all. We would have an affair. It would be intense, wonderful and horrible. It would end badly. Even now, I hate to admit it, but I should have backed away politely and never spoken to him again. The school was big enough to avoid him if I needed to. My everyday memory may be faulty, but each of the three times I have glanced into the future, I remember every detail about the place where it happened. I can still see the white painted cinderblock wall next to the large bank of wooden mailboxes, the analog clock on the wall, the stacks of pastel paper handouts waiting on the counter for us to retrieve them, the elderly secretaries behind their desks.

For several weeks, nothing happened. Then, he took my face in his hands and kissed me. Imagine the trashiest romance novel you have ever read, secret meetings, passionate trysts, jealous spouse and ex-spouse, spying, stalking, lying. All of it. I would like to say it was love, passion, romance, but really, it was a psychotic, all-consuming infatuation. I was ashamed, but it didn't stop me.

There was something about the way his watch rested on his wrist. While not traditionally handsome, his masculinity was palpable. Maybe that's what drew me in and kept me there. When it was over, I realized that I had been living in a house of mirrors, and I wasn't the only one engaged in lies and deception.

The day it ended we went on a walk to settle the terms and conditions. I felt a little like Harry S. Truman meeting with Winston Churchill to discuss Stalin. The sun was shining as we walked through the neutral territory of a park. There were trees and flowers and kids playing, but my vision narrowed to the path of black asphalt winding along the man-made lake. Stuart reached for my hand. I pulled it away.

My insides were fragile porcelain and I would crumble into myself if it shattered. I could feel the cracks starting to spread and was amazed that I hadn't already disintegrated into a pile of sharp white fragments right there by the paddle boat launch. Stuart's wife had gotten pregnant, and he chose to stay with her. I chose not to ask obvious questions about how that came about. We decided that it would be too painful to talk to each other any-more. Like alcoholics, we determined to go clean, cold-turkey: no visits, no discussions, no phone calls, no email. He was moving back in with his wife.

We agreed to avoid one another at faculty meetings and the mailboxes. I would have lunch in the staff lounge; he'd eat with the science department. I'd do my Xeroxing in the morning before classes began. He'd do his during third hour. He'd do Prom, I'd take Senior Picnic. There would be enough staff to act as a buffer between us at graduation. Both miserable, we trudged along for weeks. Sometimes I'd see him walking out of the front office as I was walking down the hall. He would duck his head and turn away. My eyes would well up. His name would come up in the students' chatter as they set-tled into their desks for class, and my stomach would tie itself in knots.

After we had decided to part ways and Stuart had moved back into his house, his wife went into his classroom looking for evidence of me. Finding none, she left in her wake a half-dozen framed photos of her life with Stuart to celebrate their reunion.

One day, long after everyone had gone home, when the light was dim in the hallways and I heard the floor waxing machine whirring toward the op-posite wing, I crept into Stuart's room. Pulling my sleeves down over my fin-gertips, I picked up the biggest frame, a glittery eight-by-ten of him and the wife dressed to the nines, balloons in the background. Stuart in a tux. My breath caught on my throat. I turned the frame face down, holding it above the tiled floor, and then let it fall. The glass crunched as it landed. I closed the door gently as I left.

Chapter Nine
May 1996

One of our mutual students was beginning a steep slide from student-athlete to senior-slacker. Stuart was the track coach, so I was forced to break our détente. In the name of professionalism, for the sake of the kid, his scholarship and his future, I emailed:

> S: I know we have a moratorium, but this is about Gabe. He came to me after class and said he's thinking of quitting track. His grades have been slipping in my class, and I did a little checking, he's dropping the ball everywhere. I've given him the chance to make up some work. Trying to get to the bottom of it. Maybe his other teachers can give him a little extra-credit. He said something about his dad being sick again. I've let his counselor know, but you should know too. Maybe he'll talk to you. I'd hate to see him lose his eligibility.

> A

So there. Nice and professional.

> A: Thanks for the heads up. I'll get on it this afternoon.

> I bought a Diet Coke for you from the vending machine this morning. Then I realized I couldn't give it to you. I threw it away. I hate this. I miss you. I think of you constantly.

> S

Why the hell did he have to do that? I lost the little cool I had left and typed:

> S: I think about you every hour. In every place there is something that reminds me of you, good and bad. So, I started seeking out other places to be where the memories don't assault me. I tried eating lunch in the teachers' lounge in B hall, but the art teachers are so flaky I had to quit. You were everything to me. You showed me what a real

partnership could be. You were my soulmate and now I am wandering around like a person who has been lobotomized, unable to think straight or form a coherent sentence. I know what we're doing is the right thing, but it's killing me. Lainie misses you too. She keeps asking where you are. I have no answer for her.

A

I sat back in my chair, waiting for the tears to start. I had a tissue ready. But the tears didn't come. I got pissed. *Screw him.* I could have highlighted and deleted the message in one blow. Instead, I hit delete. Delete. Delete. **Delete**. And watched the words un-write themselves.

New Message:

S:

Don't go there.

A.

***

"You have twelve games this season," the athletic director said, "you will probably win these four." Ms. Jessup pointed to four teams on her list. "These six have established programs and they have more kids, so those will be your losses. The last two are anyone's guess."

I was sitting in her office among various sets of protective gear and piles of net-bags full of basketballs, soccer balls and volleyballs. It was my first time coaching girls' lacrosse for this team. Ms. Jessup didn't know anything about me, or my skills, or my strategy. What she did know was that none of that really mattered. It was a numbers game that she played well.

To my amazement, she predicted our season with one-hundred percent accuracy. We were halfway through and had lost and won games just as she had foretold. This athletic prophetess, with her short gray hair and tanned, muscled arms was the queen and goddess of her realm.

One day when I had to consult her wisdom about an upcoming contest, I sent the captains outside to lead the team warm-up. Ten minutes later I emerged into a beautiful spring afternoon, but something wasn't right. The men's team, in the field immediately next to ours, was neat and orderly, boys lined up in uniform rows of ten across and four deep, evenly spaced in a perfect grid. They went through their calisthenics with military precision, counting out one through ten for each set of exercises, shouting until they were red in the face.

And then there were the girls. As I walked past the boys toward my group, I had no idea what the hell they were doing. Several were crawling on the grass on all fours. A few seemed to be squatting and flapping their elbows like wings. Still others were hopping like frogs. One of the captains was standing off to the side, watching.

"Marissa, Angela, what the heck are you guys doing?"

"Oh, hi, Ms. Smythe! It's a team building exercise, we're all farm animals and you have to find your farm animal buddy without using words."

Then I heard it, the baaing and mooing and neighing. There was oinking and ribbitting too, accompanied by much giggling and occasionally toppling over. Soon, the cows and chickens had found each other, along with the sheep, pigs, horses and frogs.

"How is a frog a farm animal?" I asked.

"We ran out of traditional options."

"Ah."

And then, as if by magic, the girls had circled up and were going through their warm ups, quickly, quietly and efficiently. I looked from the circle of young women to the rows of young men and thought I'd take my barnyard any day, but I might have to leave them to save myself. I was coming to the realization that working in the same building as Stuart was unsustainable for my well-being.

***

"You should try going toward the city. Those close suburbs have good schools. Definitely better-quality singles than out here in minivan land." Leon gave me his opinion as he spotted me on the bench press.

"Einstein, Walter Johnson, Whitman, those are all good. You could get a cute apartment down by NIH, snag a doctor or a lawyer and scout for one for me too. You go jog around that campus, lots of military types." Leon sang in a high falsetto, "I love a man in a uniform!"

I was laughing too hard to push the bar up and he had to help me finish the last rep.

"There, at least I made you laugh," he said.

"You know, lonely minds think alike. I need a change of scenery."

"And a new pool of men."

"Yeah, that too. Your turn."

We switched places. I added more plates to the bar. Skinny Leon was stronger than he looked. I counted out twelve reps and thought that maybe my future did lie a few miles south.

There were three schools closer to DC that I was hoping would consider me for employment. I got a call to interview in early May. The interview rehearsals in front of the bathroom mirror and in the privacy of the Acura began immediately. I had five days to prepare and resolved that:

- I would speak in complete sentences.

- There would be no stains on my suit.

- I would incorporate the terms cooperative learning, authentic assessment, collaboration and technology in the classroom wherever possible.

- I would NOT mention that I needed this move to free my soul.

- I would NOT break into "I Really Need this Job" from *A Chorus Line*.

As I entered the room, the interview panel rose in unison to greet me. It was as though Sleeping Beauty's fairy godmothers had been sent to appraise me for the position of Social Studies teacher. All three women were in their fifties. All three had blonde hair in neat, chin-length bobs and each wore a welcoming smile on her face. One was tall and painfully thin, the next, shorter and plump, and the last so tiny and perfectly proportioned that my mischievous brain instantly named her "Thumbelina." This meant I would have to work twice as hard now at remembering her real name and using it appropriately throughout the interview. Of course, Thumbelina was the school principal.

They asked predictable questions and I gave them my rehearsed answers while trying to project likability and resourcefulness. Tall and Thin wanted to know how I felt about the internet and plagiarism. Short and Plump asked about curriculum development. Thumbelina wanted to know if there were any extracurricular activities I'd be willing to sponsor. I said I could run a Model UN, and tentatively mentioned coaching lacrosse.

Toward the end of the interview I was feeling pretty confident. I was wearing my stain-free lucky suit. Tall and Thin turned to Short and Plump, and then to Thumbelina. They nodded to one another, and then something happened that I had never experienced before. They offered me the job right there; no second interview, no anxious waiting for the phone call.

"We'd like you to join our staff," the principal said.

"I'd be honored."

Done. Maybe karma was turning my way. I would start at my new school in the fall. I only had to survive going to work in the same building as Stuart for six more weeks. Summer couldn't come fast enough.

***

For a divorced couple, Ken and I had a slightly unusual arrangement. Lainie's day care did not open until 7:00 a.m., but I had to leave my apartment by 6:20 at the latest to make it to school on time. So, to give Lainie and Ken a little more time together, and to reduce our day-care costs, Ken came over to our apartment between 6:00 and 6:15 in the morning, and then took Lainie to day care around 10:00. After a few strained weeks, we had gotten into the routine, and I had convinced myself that this made the divorce transition easier on my kid.

One morning, after Ken and I talked for a few minutes about Lainie's rapidly expanding vocabulary, I headed out for work at about 6:10. The dawn was pale, but light enough for me to see four police cars slide swiftly but quietly into the parking lot. No lights flashing, no sirens. Their speed and silence were chilling. I froze and watched as they stopped at the entrance to the apartment building adjacent to ours and four men leapt from each car.

Their black ball-caps were emblazoned with white block letters: DEA. They wore thick vests Velcroed over their uniforms and carried alarmingly large guns. The men fanned out, running on their toes, holding their weapons at their shoulders, ready to fire. Some toward the entrance, others towards the windows. Heart racing, I turned to run back into my building to tell Ken to hit the floor and take Lainie with him, but I was blocked by one of the men who shouted to me in a whisper:

"MA'AM. MA'AM. You CANNOT go back into the building. GO ON YOUR WAY."

"But my baby is in there!"

"Is the baby alone?" he asked.

I shook my head 'no'.

"Everyone will be alright; I just need you to vacate the parking lot NOW."

There was no arguing with this man or his gun, so I jumped into the Acura and sped out onto the main road. *Think, Alex, think.* I was freaking out. I pulled into the closest strip mall and sprinted to a pay phone. One of my recurring nightmares is that I have an extreme emergency, and I can't make my fingers dial the right numbers. I have woken up so many times in a cold sweat from this dream where I dial and dial over and over again and I can't get the order of the digits right, or I get the first nine right and my hand slips on the tenth digit and time keeps running out. Thankfully, I was able to dial my own number on the first try.

"Hello?" Ken sounded tentative; who would be calling at this hour?

"Ken, it's me. They are having a drug bust RIGHT NOW AT THE APARTMENT."

"Okay, what do you want me to do?" He asked, irritating me, but I conceded that it was a legitimate question.

"Just stay away from the windows for about thirty minutes, and keep your ears open. Look out the window and make sure they are all gone before you take Lainie out of the building."

"Okay."

"Just, be careful. Please."

"Yeah, we'll be fine Alex. I'll be careful. Don't worry."

I did worry. It took the whole drive to school for the adrenaline shakes to stop. I hit up the vending machine for a Snickers and a Diet Coke and considered going back for a Baby Ruth. We were supposed to be talking about the similarities between the Korean War and the Vietnam conflict in class. First hour was a mess, I could not focus, so between classes I found Judy in the Media Center to see if she had any good movies on the subject. She handed me something narrated by Peter Jennings which would have to do. I needed some time to think about this. I could NOT be raising my child around drug dealers.

At lunch I sat in my car, listening to the local news, scanning both AM and FM channels. There was nothing about a drug bust in my town, but still, I couldn't shake the feeling that we might not be safe. I did some mental math on what it would take to move to another place. I'd need first month's rent and security deposit, and possibly last month's rent as well, and I had to calculate that a safer location would mean higher rent. I'd also have to hire the U-Haul again. There might also be a penalty for breaking the current lease. Adding that all up, and subtract what little savings I had, I was short roughly twelve hundred dollars, a small fortune.

With Mom in Africa, there was only one place to turn. It probably wouldn't work, but I had to try, so after school, when there was no one in the staff lounge, I dialed the eight-hundred number.

"Hey Dad, It's Alex."

"Hey Honey, what's wrong?" he asked.

"What do you mean, what's wrong?"

"You're calling before the market closes and before you get home from school, so it must be important. What is it?" I should have waited another half-hour. Calling before Close of Business was *verboten*.

"Okay, I'll call you back later."

"Nah, you've already interrupted me."

Typically, when I ask my dad for something, anything really, I work up to it gently, preferably over the course of days or weeks. I build a case, and, if I play it just right, he ends up thinking that helping me was his own brilliant idea. In this case there just wasn't time for that game.

"Dad, I need twelve hundred dollars."

"That's a lot of money. Why?" His voice immediately took on a nervous tone. I didn't need to be there to see him start pulling at his left eyebrow with the hand that wasn't holding the phone.

"There was a drug raid at my apartment complex this morning and I really don't think it's a good idea for Lainie and me to live there anymore. I am very concerned for our safety." Had this been Elaine, had she not been in Malawi, there would be a moving truck at my door with a team of packers in less than twelve hours. But I wasn't talking to Elaine. I continued, "I need some help pulling together first and last months' rent and a security deposit so we can move." There was a long pause.

"Ah, geez, honey, I can't do that."

"Oh."

"I just don't have that kind of cash on hand." he said.

I let my breath out in one long, slow, disappointed breath." *No, of course you don't. All your cash is probably tied up in some high-risk stock or some half-cocked scheme to short something that is not going to work. Why do I even bother to ask?*

"Really? I was hoping you could help me out."

"You'll be fine. You don't need to move. If the cops are on it, those assholes won't bother you, they're probably on their way to jail right now. I gotta get back to work."

"Okay, well, thanks anyway." I mumbled.

"Sure. Love you Honey. Bye."

He would not call back to check on us.

***

Winter, 1975

I was six or seven years old. The girlfriend du jour thought skating might be a fun activity, and my dad agreed, so our visit that month took place in a run-down ice rink in New Jersey where everything, even fresh snow, was gray in the winter. The cooling system wheezed and coughed. The skate man handed me child sized double-bladed skates in exchange for my maroon corrective shoes.

I ventured onto the ice with a death-grip on the rink wall. I inched my way around, not afraid to fall, just determined not to. After a while, staying vertical ceased to occupy my entire mind, and I found myself making up little rhymes in my head because I couldn't understand the lyrics of the music being pumped over the scratchy sound system.

There was a tall dark-haired guy, too young to be a grown-up, too big to be a boy, practicing fancy jumps. Each time he landed, he chipped huge chunks out of the ice with his toe picks and sent them skittering across the rink. One landed at my feet and I stared at it. Could he break all of the ice? It wasn't fair, him hogging all of the ice and making enormous thumps as he landed. He scared me when he skated too close.

Making it around the rink became a game. There was a red line on the wall just where the door led you off the ice. Every time I made it around, I touched the stripe with my mitten-ed hand and said, "Got-cha!" Dad and the girlfriend were nuzzling at the snack bar, having given up on the skating ten minutes after they started. My dad had narrow feet that didn't fill up the skates. His ankles flopped like useless fish. The girlfriend's jeans were too tight for even the slightest athletic endeavor, so they sat snuggling while sipping coffee and occasionally remembering to look for me out on the ice.

When free skate ended, I'd lost count of how many times I'd made it around, but felt as though I'd pulled off an Alpine expedition. My knees were wobbly when I stepped off the ice and I was happy to sit down with them, the hot chocolate steaming up my glasses. I didn't even mind when my dad told me not to spill because the hot chocolate had cost him fifty cents.

May, 1996, Continued

Karma showed up again a few days later. Lainie and I went down to the duck pond, as we often did, for a little post-dinner, pre-bedtime stroll to visit our feathered friends. She had gotten out of her stroller and was venturing close to the water's edge. I hovered within arms-reach behind her, trying to let her have her freedom yet not fall into the water. The pond had a paved path around the circumference that was roughly one mile and a quarter around. Some industrious runners had marked the quarter mile intervals with spray paint on the pavement, and it was popular among the jogging locals. As Lainie communed with the ducks, a lanky figure caught my eye. He was rounding the bend at a respectable pace, his long arms and legs moving fluidly.

As he drew near, I thought I recognized him from the gym. He smiled a little as he passed us. I smiled back and returned my attention to making sure Lainie didn't go for an accidental swim. As dusk settled, I convinced Lainie to get back in the stroller so we could get home. As we headed up the hill, I heard the sound jogging feet come up behind us, slowing to a walk. The same runner was walking a few feet behind us, probably heading back to the gym, which was a few blocks down the street.

"Beautiful night for a run," I said.

"Yes, sure is."

"Do you go to Sol's gym?" I asked.

"Yeah, I thought I recognized you," he said.

Lainie was taking this all in, her neck cranked around to look at us. She piped up, "Hi! My name is Lainie, this is my mom, Alexandria."

"Alex," I quickly corrected. I was a little embarrassed that the two-year old seemed to have better manners than her mom.

"I'm Lester," the runner said. "I'd shake hands but I'm all sweaty."

"Do you live here?" Lainie asked.

"No, I live a few miles away, but I like to run down here from the gym," he said.

"Okay. Hold hands?" At this, Lainie stuck out her hand, reaching for her new friend. I was mortified. What kind of parent was I that my kid asked random strangers to hold her hand? How embarrassing was this? *What should I say?* Oh, the awkwardness.

"Okay," Lester said, and then he leaned down to take hold of her hand. He walked, bent comically sideways, for almost a block, and I tried to push the stroller at a pace that would make him holding hands with my tot possible.

I searched for something to say to make the situation seem more normal, but I needn't have worried. The two of them carried on without me, chatting about ducks and all the duck poop that was on the trail and how hard it is to avoid stepping in that poop. I estimated that Lester was over six feet tall; he had short, cropped brown hair. His running shorts were a bit out of style and he wore a faded sleeveless running top. Evidently, he spent plenty of time in the weight room. His running shoes were on the newer side, making me think that he took care of the important stuff, but wasn't too fussy in general.

I had no idea how to feel about this whole thing. My face flushed red and hot with embarrassment that my kid threw herself at this man with abandon. My heart was melting a little at the sight of this towering person contorting himself in a way that could not have been remotely comfortable just to humor a little girl, and my lips curled into an involuntary smile at the topic of their conversation. I admired how he matched her serious tone about duck excrement, and offered his opinion on the color of daddy Mallards versus mommy Mallards. The walk seemed shorter than usual.

"Well, this is where we turn," I interjected. Lester and Laine reluctantly dropped their hands.

"Maybe I'll see you at the gym," Lester said.

"Oh, I'm sure we'll run into each other. Have a good night," I said.

"Bye," Lainie said.

"Bye, you two. See you soon." And with a little wave, he jogged off.

Little did I know that my two-year-old introduced me to one of the best men on Earth.

***

Here is what I learned from two phone calls before the Longest First Date in History:

1. Lester was doing doctoral research at the National Institute for Standards and Technology, aka, NIST
   i. This meant he had no money
   ii. Being a PhD in Mechanical Engineering would, in the long run, provide a stable job
2. He had served in the Navy for six years before going to college.
3. He grew up in Vermont.
4. At thirty-five, he had never been married and had no kids.

Day of the Longest First Date in History
11:00 a.m.
Lester arrived to pick me up a half hour early. I could have sworn I'd said 11:30. At 11:00 I had just rushed home from the gym and was counting on having thirty minutes to, as my former mother-in-law used to say, "Perform my miracle." I'd peeled off my sweaty shirt and sports bra when I heard the knock on the door. Momentary panic. I grabbed my warm-up jacket and zipped it up to the chin. Through the peephole, I could see Lester standing in the hallway, holding a bouquet of flowers.

"Hi, you're early!" I said. He blushed.

"I thought you said 11:00," he said.

"I could have sworn I said 11:30." I smiled up at him, trying to make the situation a little less uncomfortable.

"Do you want me to come back?" he asked.

"No, no, don't be silly. Come in, make yourself at home. I'll just be a few minutes. I need to jump in the shower." He was still standing by the front door, clutching the flowers, looking around the apartment. "Are those for me? They are beautiful."

"Oh, here, I thought you might like them." He handed me the cellophane-wrapped bundle of bright red and yellow flowers. I should have turned and headed to the bathroom as quickly as possible, but I just stood there with him, holding the flowers. His shirt was pressed, his jeans faded, but very, very clean. His black loafers wore a shiny coat of fresh polish.

"Turn on some music if you like, I really need to shower if we're going to get out of here on time." I said this over my shoulder as I headed back toward the bathroom, stopping in the kitchen to put the flowers in a bowl of water in the sink to be arranged later. I took the fastest shower of my life and applied makeup like my shirt was on fire. The humidity dictated that my hair was just going to stay big and fluffy, so I accepted that fact and tried to move past it.

Planning for this date was tricky. A former student of mine, Ned, had made the lacrosse team at a local university, and he had invited me to come to one of his games. When he had called to ask me out, Lester thought that I might like to go to a screening of the newly restored Hitchcock classic, Vertigo. It could be a perfect day: lacrosse, lunch, early movie, and take it from there. However, this produced a wardrobe quandary. What to wear to go from a sporting event to lunch to a movie to whatever else, while looking attractive, slightly sexy and appropriate for each venue? After too much agonizing and some ice cream, I had settled on jeans, a white T-shirt, black blazer and black loafers with a stacked heel. Had I been daring I would have accessorized beyond the pearl earrings, but after the French scarf and perfume disaster, I had given up on taking fashion risks.

At the lacrosse game, fans cheered while pretty girlfriends winced and looked away when things got rough. People bounced up and down to stay warm when the breeze picked up. The ball flew from one stick to another with such speed I soon stopped trying to follow it directly and instead, concentrated on the field, the blue and white jerseys slamming into each other. The opponent was using an effective zone defense, frustrating our team. The man-to-man effort they were trying wasn't getting anywhere. Lester was surprisingly quiet.

"Are you okay?" I asked.

"This is the first lacrosse game I've been to. It seems a little like hockey."

"I think it has some football genes too. They say some Native American tribes played it to the death to resolve disputes without going to war."

"How would you kill someone out there?"

"They played with rocks instead of balls. One would target the goalie instead of the goal. But I also read that that was all a myth and it was just a peaceful game."

"Probably people like the bloody version of the story," he said.

"Like they say in the news, 'if it bleeds, it leads.'" I answered. He smiled at me. After we stayed for another half hour I said,

"Well, it looks like we've stayed long enough, I totally understand if you want to get going. It looks like our guys have no chance of pulling out from underneath this one."

"No, I'll stay as long as you want to, I'm fine." He smiled down at me again. A genuine smile, that told me he really was fine, and possibly enjoying himself, too.

"Let me go see if I can find Ned's parents, I'll be back in a minute.

2:15 p.m.

Lunch. We sat at a table by the window. The sun shone into Lester's eyes. They reminded me of the barrel-shaped, hard root-beer candies I had bought from the penny-candy bin as a kid, brown and clear, deeper than glass. His hands circled his coffee mug. They were hands that looked capable of almost any task. The afternoon stretched before us bringing with it an odd sensation, being relaxed and to not have a small person nearby to monitor. Lester was easy company. I dared venturing into personal questions.

"So, tell me about your parents."

"They both passed away. My step-mother is still living in Vermont."

There was a pause while the fact of the dead parents hung in the air. I had an evil thought, and then immediately sank deeper into my seat, hoping to be a smaller target for the lightning bolt I was sure was about to come crashing through the window and strike me dead because, God forgive me, the first thing that crossed into my head was *Thank you Jesus*. It was an awful idea, one I tried to banish as quickly as possible, but the prospect of marriage without a mother-in-law was, frankly, appealing. *Bad Alex! Bad.* Karma would get me for even *thinking* that way. She always does. I recovered my wits enough to say, "I am so sorry. You're very young to have lost both parents. How long has it been?"

"I lost my mom to cancer when I was twenty. Dad died about ten years later. Cancer, too," he said. Now I felt even worse.

"I'm afraid I never know what the right thing to say is."

"It's okay. It's been a long time." He signaled for more coffee. Black. "What about you?"

"My folks split when I was young. Dad is a stockbroker; Mom is currently living in Malawi."

"Really? That's surprising." He looked at me over the rim of his coffee cup.

"She's saving the planet, one village at a time."

"Admirable. How long has she been at it?"

"Hard to say, exactly. Mom has been going on mission trips with her church for a while. She liked going to Mexico and China, but something about Africa grabbed her. I think she's always had a secret fascination with wild places. She made a trip to Zimbabwe with her church, and then found another non-profit and has been spending lots of time in Malawi. She helps schools get supplies. I think she does home visits to families with young kids to encourage them to keep the kids in school. Especially the girls."

"Have you been there?"

"To Africa?"

He nodded.

"No."

"Why not?" he asked.

I had to think about it. "Now that I think about it, I don't think she's ever asked me to come." That was as much a revelation to me as it was for my date. I reflected on this insight for a moment. Lester remained quiet. "Maybe when Lainie is a little older and I feel up to an eighteen-hour plane ride, we'll go. Do you still miss your parents?" I asked.

"Sometimes. I was really glad that my dad was around to see me graduate from college."

The waiter, with a terrible sense of timing, interrupted us right then to ask if we would like some dessert, and rattled off the three items on the dessert menu. Lester asked if I'd like to share one. This won him major points. I hadn't shared a meal (beyond stealing Lainie's French fries) in forever. Elaine and I used to split both entrées and desserts. Ken and I rarely did, as our tastes were so different. Oh, how many signs I had missed.

"Which one would you like?" he asked.

"Is there more than one viable option for you?" I teased. If he picked anything other than chocolate, we might have to reconsider this thing, dead in-laws and all.

"No, not really." He held my gaze, as if dessert was the most important decision of the month.

"The chocolate thing?" I asked.

"Oh yes." He nodded for emphasis. "Crème brulé is for weenies."

"The brownie with ice cream, please," I stated with confidence. "And two spoons."

We shared a brownie topped with vanilla ice cream smothered with hot fudge sauce and whipped cream. He let me have the last bite.

4:40 p.m.

Movie Theater. The day was going well. Really well. We arrived at the theater in time to see the 5:15 show. In the age of the multiplex, *Vertigo* was playing at one of the last great old theatres in town with vintage movie posters flanking the walls and gilded moldings hung with heavy velvet curtains drawing us into the past. I should have been wearing a smart day suit and hose with seams down the back. Perhaps a hat and gloves. I could saunter down the hall like Grace Kelly, all cool and blonde with bright red nail polish.

As it was, however, the smell of popcorn threatened to undo my cool; I couldn't possibly be expected to sit through a movie without popcorn. But if I suggested popcorn after the lunch and massive dessert we'd just consumed, I'd look like a pig and feel like a bloated puffer fish. But that smell kept coming, kept distracting me from exuding Grace Kelly. I might drool. *Focus on Grace. Be classy. You don't need popcorn, you idiot.*

"Would you like some popcorn?"

Oh my God! Was this a test? Was he testing to see if I was a glutton? In Gone With the Wind, Mammy told Scarlet that she had to eat before the party so she would just nibble in lady-like fashion in front of her suitors. Why didn't I take Mammy's advice? Okay, stop, try to be normal. We like this guy.

"I'd share some with you," I said, so nonchalant.

"Soda?" he asked,

"Sure."

"Diet Coke okay?"

"Yes please."

"Raisinets?"

"Yes, thank you." *Yes! Yes! Yes!*

5:45 p.m.

Our fingers brushed against one another as we dug into the popcorn bucket, each incidental contact sending a little shiver through my abdomen.

Some guy in the movie was afraid of heights. That was all I was getting out of the plot. Also, Kim Novak's face was distractingly shiny; she needed powder. Whispering, we decided we'd had enough popcorn. I wanted Lester to hold my hand but now that the popcorn bucket was on the floor, I had no excuse to touch him. In the movie, someone was thrown off a building. I rested my hand on my thigh. Just let it lie there. Not a very natural or subtle position. I just left it there in a brazen attempt to be held.

5:55 p.m.

My lonely hand was still there. I felt self-conscious.

5:57 p.m.

Lester's hand slid over mine. I flipped my palm up to grab his. It was warm and dry.

6:01 p.m.

His hand was still holding mine. I stole a glance at him, and for an uninterrupted moment, gazed at his profile. His nose was straight, and he had a strong chin. He sat still, absorbed in the film. Then he felt my eyes on him and looked over. We smiled at each other in the dim light.

6:02 p.m.

I went back to watching *Vertigo*.

7:25 p.m.

Movie over. I didn't want the date to end.

"It's still early," Lester observed. "I can't believe it's not even 7:30 yet."

"Do you want to get something to eat?" I asked, realizing that this might seem a bit gluttonous.

"Food sounds good. That was hard work, watching that movie," he agreed.

"How about the Cheesecake Factory?"

"That would be nice, but I doubt we'll be able to get a table at this hour on a Saturday."

After we were told that there would be a two-hour wait at the Cheesecake Factory we ended up at Tasty Diner, one of my favorite dives of all time, greasy food and indifferent service. We settled into a cramped booth until late in the evening having one of those conversations that flow and bubble along, one topic melting into the next. We only paused when the waitress told us that we could have more coffee, but she'd have to brew another pot, and, from the looks of it, she didn't want to put in the effort.

Back at my apartment, I didn't want him to leave. We stood in the door-way making out like teenagers. I didn't want to have sex with him on the first date. Well, I did, but I didn't. On principle. Kim Novak wouldn't have invit-ed Jimmy Stewart to stay on their first date. What to do? I had found a per-fect (so far) man and didn't want to spend the night alone after the world's longest first date.

"I have a question for you," I said. He pulled back and looked down at me.

"If I ask you to stay, will you be a gentleman?"

"Within reason."

"Okay, please stay."

And he did.

***

Les made dinner for me at his place a few days later. He periodically consult-ed a tattered binder of his mother's recipes while he prepared country skillet chicken. As he cooked, I poked around. The dining table was set with forest green placemats and matching cloth napkins, a bouquet of daisies in a glass vase in the center. A group of framed eight-by-ten photos hung on the din-ing area wall, some he had taken in college. One featured Lester and his best friend in college, looking slightly drunk and very happy. Next to that was a photo of three men standing in front of a shack on a wooded lot. They wore flannel jackets of varying plaids and were gathered around a large pot. The three were holding forks, two had their eyes closed in sheer rapture, the third, a younger Lester, was waving his fork in the air and seemed to be in mid-sen-tence.

"Hey Les, what's this photo all about?" He came up behind me and slid his arm around my waist.

"Sugar on snow," he said.

"I think I read about that somewhere." *Little House on the Prairie*?

"My dad had a sugar house on the property. He made the best maple syrup. There's nothing like sugar on snow. You get the sap past the point that it becomes syrup, then pour it over the snow while it's still hot. It's almost like taffy." He paused. "That was the last sugar season we were all together."

"Looks like you guys were having fun."

"Yeah, the only time my brother is quiet is when he's eating."

Lester turned back to the kitchen and I stood in front of the photo a little longer. In the picture, cancer had cast its shadow over his father. Still as tall as his sons, his shoulders were smaller and shrunken, and shadows darkened his sallow cheeks. The men hung on to tradition with their forks, hoping that one sugar season would lead to the next, as it always had.

For dessert, Lester presented a chocolate torte with handmade chocolate leaves gracing the top. He had made the whole delicious thing from scratch.

We dated for two months. It was almost perfect. He met me at school with a bag lunch from my favorite bagel place. He fell in love with Lainie. He learned our schedule and fit himself in it wherever he felt he could be helpful.

In my head, I still have a snapshot of the exact moment I fell in love with Lester. I had a cumbersome stack of papers to grade, so he offered to fix dinner. There was a happy, contented interval while I graded, Lainie played in the bedroom, and Lester puttered around the kitchen. He leaned over the half-wall that separated the kitchen from the living room and asked, "What would Lainie like to drink with dinner?" Here was a man in my kitchen, looking pleased to be there. Not cooking a fancy, foreplay-dinner designed to lure me to bed, but a simple meal on a Tuesday.

"Milk, please. Thank you." I smiled back at him. I can still see him, big hands spread across the top of the half-wall, the breadth of his shoulders leaning forward, the tilt of his head. I didn't exactly fall in love. Love washed over me.

If I had been smart enough to carry that feeling with me, and hold on to it, I would have saved myself a world of trouble. Suffice it to say that within two weeks of that golden moment, Lester was out of my life. I was an idiot. It would be a long time before I could think about it without my cheeks burning and my stomach tying itself into knots.

Chapter Ten
July, 1996

Most younger teachers who were low on the pay scale did summer work, and one of my colleagues had referred me to a temp agency which kept me and Lainie in mac-n-cheese money through the lean months. The temp job helped me make enough money to keep Lainie's spot in day care over the summer, and I could choose when I wanted to work, allowing time for short vacations sprinkled throughout the summer months. Mostly, I subbed for low-level receptionists, and the slow pace of office work left plenty of time to go back to scrutinizing the personal ads. I was back in the newspaper business. The next contestant on Find Alex a Husband was Matt. Forty, outdoorsy, loved to travel, sounded mostly normal. After a little chitchat we decided to meet at a restaurant near my apartment. I hated the "How will I recognize you?" part of the process. I gave my spiel about being about five foot five and dirty blonde. He gave his spiel about being six foot two, fair-haired and "a little thin on top." I told him I'd probably be wearing black since that was about eighty-five percent of my wardrobe.

At the restaurant, I found myself, once again, with high hopes and jangly nerves on edge. I stood in the entrance between the two pairs of double doors, waiting for Mr. Wonderful to arrive and make me a happy woman. I tried, and failed, to push Lester's face out of my mind. Lainie missed Lester too, and she wasn't keeping that to herself.

A man who had to be Matt walked in. He took me by surprise as I was checking my reflection in the glass of the framed menu. He was the smallest six foot two possible, so thin and narrow that you wouldn't guess he was that tall unless you were standing right next to him and he wasn't slouching. "A little thin on top" was a bald faced lie. He did, however, have a smile that transformed his face from pallid and unremarkable to almost-good looking.

Drinks at the bar progressed to appetizers and dinner at a booth. He worked for *National Geographic* as a regional director, loved the outdoors, and liked to read, mostly biographies of explorers and World War II history. He had some family back in the Midwest. He had never been married.

Then came the make-or-break moment, the time when I hoped Dating Ref would appear and tell us what to do. I thought it had been a gratifying date, nothing off-putting on either end. Just before dessert, Matt reached into his pocket and pulled out a picture.

"I wanted to bring this along to show you. It is the photo I sent out in my Christmas cards last year." *This could be really cool, or really odd . . .* I know very few single males who willingly send out Christmas cards, and if they do, only to their close relatives under instruction from their mothers to do so, and that usually means a Christmas Eve dash to the card aisle at the grocery store. This man planned his cards and included a photo. Highly unusual.

The picture showed a darkly tanned Matt, which did help his general appearance, standing in front of a Mayan pyramid, wearing a fuzzy Santa hat. I sat up a bit in my chair. "Wow, where were you? Where was this picture taken?"

"I was in Mexico at Chichen Itza, about a year ago. It was a great trip. I did some regular beach stuff, then toured inland. It was a blast."

"Did you go with anyone else?"

"My brother and his wife met up with me for a few days. He took the picture."

"Do you actually carry that hat with you wherever you go?"

"I try to take one major trip a year, and yeah, I pack it along. It's become a thing with my friends. They like to see where Santa is going to show up next." That, I thought, was pretty cool.

***

"So, you're dating Waldo?" Cyn asked.

"I'm sorry?"

"You know, Waldo, from the *Where's Waldo* books. You find him by his hat."

"Are you freaking kidding me?" I asked.

"No. Obviously I need to buy that one for Lainie."

"No, obviously I need to stop telling you about the men that I am dating if you're going to degrade them," I said. I lay back on the couch, cradling the phone and reaching for my Diet Coke.

"What happened to Lester? I thought that was going pretty well."

"I don't want to talk about it. I was an ass," I said.

"Huh." She didn't press the issue. There was a pause and she continued, "So, now we're dating Waldo."

"Yes, and how is your love life coming along? How are the cowboys treating you?"

"Eh. I've been swamped with a few new accounts. I may have to hire someone. *No! No! Stop that,* she yelled, thankfully not directly into the phone.

"What has Buster gotten into now?"

"The ficus by the window," she said.

"Did he knock it over?" I asked.

"No," she said, "he keeps trying to dig in the soil. It's annoying."

"Okay, back to the new accounts. What are they?" I asked.

"The LBJ Library wants help developing a way to electronically catalog all their shit," she said.

"By 'shit' are you talking about his papers, or all the artifacts too."

"All that crap. It's pretty interesting. It presents a challenge. They're still not sure how they want to go about it so I actually have to get dressed in real clothes and go meet real people."

"So stressful." I jokingly commiserated.

"I know. And the University is asking me to do some stuff for them too."

"So, what you're telling me is that you could make your first million before thirty."

"Don't hold your breath. But it isn't helping my love life at all." We were quiet for a minute. Then she continued, "I am sorry to hear about Lester. He did sound like a good guy."

"It was my fuck up."

"You have to stop doing that to yourself. Isn't that what happened with Brian, the mountain bike guy?"

"Different kind of fuck up there. But I see your point."

"Yeah. I gotta go prep for this meeting. Kiss Lainie for me. Tell her Auntie Cyn needs a visit."

"Okay, give Buster a treat from me," I said.

"Maybe when he actually earns one."

I wished my friends lived in my state.

***

One day, about two weeks into dating, I talked Matt into watching Lainie in the playground so I could go for a run on the path that circled the park. Childcare usually confined my runs to the treadmill, so this was a rare treat.

I was thoroughly enjoying exercising in fresh air and sunshine when I glanced over toward the play structure and saw a dark stain spreading over Lainie's pants. Toilet training was still in progress and she had had an accident. Running on the far side of the little pond that was in the middle of the park, I watched as Matt picked her up and held her out at arm's length. He tried to hold her as far away from his body as possible, as though the urine-soaked pants contained a lethal venom. He set her down next to the car and went searching in the trunk for something for her to sit on. She trotted back toward the swing set. He repeated, dashing after her. Each time it got harder for him to carry her back to the car, holding her body away from his like a bag of stinky garbage. The look on his face was strained and buffoonish, so Lainie interpreted this as a delightful game of "run away!" I decided that this would be a good time to amend the check list for future daddy candidates. I should include the following:

LaQuaSH, Appendix A:

1. Acceptance of bodily functions as natural and not revolting
2. Ability to speak toddler after a ten-day immersion course
3. Ability to happily participate in appropriate playground behavior with the little tyke

Bonus points awarded for:

1. Presenting age-appropriate gifts
2. Reading stories without being asked, even the same book, over and over again
3. Automatically cutting the child's food into small pieces

Later that evening, the plan was for us to have dinner at Matt's house. I'd cut my run short to deal with the potty crisis and was keeping Lainie occupied in the living room while Matt finished preparing the spaghetti dinner. The pristine hardwood floor of the dining room glowed from a recent polish. Matt, sporting an apron and oven mitt, stood in the doorway between the kitchen and the dining room, surveying the neatly set table and make-shift high chair he'd assembled. He frowned, and I could see that a decision had been made. To preserve the floor, we would dine *al fresco* on the front porch instead.

Lainie and I balanced paper plates of spaghetti and red-sauce while sitting on rather uncomfortable plastic chairs. I was trying, unsuccessfully, to shovel the noodles into Lainie's mouth because they were too runny to stay on the fork.

Matt was oblivious to our food struggle, talking about his plans for renovating the house and improving the landscaping. I listened with half an ear, struggling to prevent tomato sauce drips on the slate patio. I had the creepy feeling that Matt would be out there under the light of the moon with a toothbrush scrubbing any food particles that fell.

I'd once overheard him on the phone trying to be calm as he explained to the lawn kid about edging the flower beds. "You need to do a thorough job with those edges, I want it to look really, really crisp. Please spend a little more time on that. I expect attention to detail. I am paying you because I don't have time to do it myself, but it's just no good if I have to come behind you and redo it if you've done a sloppy job." He listened for a moment, and nodded. "Yes, yes. Very good. Thank you. Goodbye." His jaw unclenched a bit as he hung up the phone.

In the basement of his house, Matt had an enormous pegboard about ten feet wide by six feet tall, where he hung the majority of his hiking, camping, exploring and diving equipment. Each item had a computer printed label with its name and the date and place of purchase beneath. He'd toyed with the idea of painting the outline of each object onto the pegboard so as to more easily and quickly identify where missing pieces should be properly placed, but rejected the idea knowing that each time he wanted to add or remove something from the collection he'd have to repaint or replace the whole board. I love a guy who is fully geared to hike or dive or ski at a moment's notice.

His tuxedo hung, neatly pressed and ready to go, in the back of his closet. I think he harbored a James Bond fantasy, imagining himself schussing down the slopes of Gstaad by day and dining in black tie by evening

While this may seem premature to a rational human being, Matt invited me to come with him to a conference out west. And, in my "trying to be cool, light-hearted and spontaneous" manner, I accepted. We would travel through Colorado and New Mexico and he had bought tickets to the Santa Fe opera. Therefore, I had to:

1. Figure out what to wear for activities ranging from hiking to attending the opera in an open-air theater.
2. Tackle how to make that all fit into a carry-on
3. Attempt to accomplish 1 and 2 without buying any new clothes or luggage
4. Lay out what I was going to pack for Lainie to spend a week at her dad's house
5. Alert day care that Ken was in charge for the week
6. Write down as many emergency numbers as possible for Ken because he lost the last list I gave him.

During the flight west, we passed over dry, open lands and I watched the shadow of our aircraft rippling across the ground beneath us. It was an odd sensation, the black outline of the plane representing the object that was carrying me thousands of feet about the earth. I was inside that black shape. I decided not to think about it. I hated flying and refrained from sharing my irrational fear of aviation with Matt as it might be a turn-off to someone who fancied himself a world traveler. Deep breathing. Crossword puzzles. A little wine. None of those kept away the image of the wavering, insubstantial silhouetted airplane skimming along below.

Matt's college roommate and his wife lived, conveniently, somewhere between Santa Fe and Breckenridge. As we drove through the desert, the swiftly changing colors of the sky at sunset held my attention, shades of violet and orange so vibrant and intense that I didn't realize we'd arrived until Matt stopped the car. The house blended into the surrounding landscape. I was surprised Matt had found it so easily; all the landmarks, boulders and cacti looked the same over the past three hours in the car. The path to the front of the house resembled a B movie set; overgrown, spiky, spindly plants crowded the walk to make it barely passable.

"Matt!" A tiny woman bolted out of the front door and flung her arms around his neck. "We're so glad you're here!" He bent to kiss her cheek, then picked her up and spun her around, letting out something between a grunt and a growl.

"Hey Francie! It's good to be here!" He set her down and stepped back to introduce me. Francie saw me standing behind Matt, and gave him a quizzical look.

"Francie, I'd like you to meet my girlfriend, Alexandria Smythe."

"Alex," I said, holding out my hand. Her hand felt like a small bird fluttering in mine.

With apparent effort, Francie transformed the look on her face from one of confusion to a welcoming smile and led us toward the house. Matt had briefed me in the car. Francie was a PhD botanist, and her husband, a PhD zoologist. Together they had made revolutionary observations about plant and animal life in the southwest desert. They were both tenured professors, and both were constantly publishing papers in highly prestigious academic journals. Matt imparted these facts in tones of admiration usually reserved for Nobel Laureates or baseball players.

I followed Francie through the front door and passed through a tastefully decorated but little-used living room. Everything was covered in a fine layer of dust illuminated by the low angle of the setting sun. At the back of the house, a large solarium ran the length of the building, lined with a dozen terrariums. A long desk was piled with papers and three computers, one of which was on and clearly in the middle of a project. We continued to the kitchen and into a prodigious mess. I couldn't see what color the counter tops were as they were covered in indiscriminate mounds of books, papers, newspapers, dirty dishes and plant life, which might have been the remains of a salad or an experiment, hard to tell which. A pot boiled on the stove, and something was smoldering in the sink.

"I got so wrapped up in what I was doing, I forgot about dinner! That's the casserole in the sink. It was so charred I'm surprised it didn't set itself on fire. I'm pretty sure the soup is ruined too."

She waved her elfin hands helplessly at the stove, staring at me from under thick, light-brown bangs cut straight across her forehead. Pale, and with delicate features, Francie could have been carved into an alabaster medallion and hung in a museum, but here she was, in her overalls, standing in the rubble of the failed dinner. There was a yelp, and a small body flung itself into Francie's backside. Her son had snuck in from the solarium where he'd been hiding. He had his mother's pale skin and big eyes.

"Jake, say 'Hi' to Uncle Matt."

The boy peeked around her hips.

"Hi Uncle Matt."

"Hey Squirt."

"Who's that?" Jacob pointed at me with the subtlety of a five-year-old.

"This is my friend, Alex."

"I'm sorry I'm so disorganized. Matt told me he had a surprise, but I had no idea what he meant. I'm a little embarrassed. Bart would have cooked, but he had a late lecture. He'll be back in a few minutes," Francie said.

"Well, let's just go out," said take-charge Matt.

"It's a weeknight sweetie," I said. "Maybe we could order in a pizza or Chinese."

"That would be great!" Looking happy to be relieved from culinary duties, Francie smiled. "They don't deliver out here, so we'll call ahead and send the boys out to get something as soon as Bart gets here. I can straighten up."

"Yep, Bart and I can be on food duty," Matt said. "You mind if I go check out the garden while there's still some daylight? Bart told me you guys did some new planting out back."

"Sure, go ahead. You know the way." Francie turned her attention to Jake. "Sweetie, Mommy has to clean the kitchen, please let go." Francie tried to wriggle out of Jake's grasp. He squeezed his arms tighter around her thigh. She started to turn toward the sink to start cleaning up the casserole mess. He swung around with her, and then squeezed himself between her and the sink. She tried turning back to the kitchen island, to make room for the take-out containers. Jake was in the way.

Francie looked at me, rolling her eyes in frustration.

"How can I help?" I asked.

"Maybe you can read Jake some stories?"

"Okay! I can manage that. Come on Jake, let's go read some books. Do you want to show me your room?" Jake eyed me through his bangs with suspicion, then turned and trotted in front of me down a small hallway to his bedroom.

He hopped up on his bed and began treating it like a trampoline. I feared more for the flimsy bed frame than for his head. The kid was a natural, bouncing from side to side with the regularity of a metronome.

"I've known Uncle Matt all my life," he said.

"So, how long is that? Sixteen years?"

"Noooooo." He giggled. "I'm five."

"Oh."

"Are you and Uncle Matt going to get married?" He asked. I opened my mouth to respond but he continued. "Uncle Jimmy has an Aunt Kay to go with him, and Uncle Walter has Aunt Corinne, but Uncle Matt doesn't have an Aunt to go with him."

"Well, I don't know if we're going to get married."

"Okay, let's play Legos." He jumped down, and, like so many men I'd met in the past year, kept the conversation going with no help from me. Superfluous though I may have been to any discussion, I was rather handy for propping up the tower while he constructed a buttress of blue and yellow blocks. We contented ourselves in this fashion for a pleasant interlude. Jake pulled out his Little Tykes. He handed me a dumpy little plastic person with lemon yellow pigtails declaring, "You can be the girl." I obliged.

By the time Francie called us to dinner, she had cleared the dining room table enough to accommodate copious little white boxes and several bottles of home brew. Ashamed of having never mastered chopsticks (Elaine didn't do Chinese food), or an appreciation of craft beer, I excused myself to the kitchen in search of a fork and a diet soda. The fridge was a mosaic of alphabet magnets sticking photos and Jake's colorings to the door. In the space above the ice dispenser, I saw it. Matt in the Hat. Matt smiled out from the pyramid picture wearing the Santa hat. I smiled back at it and went back to the dining room.

"So then Duff and Matt are out there in the middle of the lake in a row boat, and this huge snapping turtle grabs hold of the oar and won't let go. And Duff is like 'Get it! Get it! We can eat it!' and Matt's freaking out because Duff keeps swinging the oar toward the boat and the snapper is pissed and Matt's afraid the thing will come after him!" Bart continues on, but clearly, Francie has heard this story a few too many times. She smiles politely.

"Who's Duff?" I ask, sliding into my seat. Their faces shifted. Bart's from riotous to startled, like he had forgotten that I was there. Matt poked his chopsticks into a carton, pretending not to have heard the question. Silence.

"Karl Duffy, Matt's . . . friend." Francie finally answered. The pause between "Matt's" and "friend" was too long. A strained silence hung in the air until Francie thrust her wine glass skyward and cried, "To the Duffer!"

"To the Duffer!" the men echoed, raising their glasses. Then they changed the subject.

Was The Duffer a friend who had died? The toast had an air of finality, so I didn't ask.

Jake disappeared the minute he finished his chicken lo mein. He slipped off his chair, took his paper plate to the kitchen and piled it on top of the flotsam of a week's worth of meals. As he walked by his mother, Francie reached out an arm and circled him in for a kiss.

"I'll tuck you in in a minute."

"Okay."

When dinner was almost done, I excused myself to the bathroom and found it across from Jake's room. The light was still on in his room, Francie having forgotten her promise to be there "in a minute."

The little soldier lay where he had fallen on the floor after having waged a fierce battle between Power Rangers and dinosaurs. Jake was sound asleep, one hand clutching a T. Rex, the other tucked under his cheek. Clearing away toys and clothes, I pulled back the blankets and lifted him into bed where he turned on his side and curled up into a ball. Covering him up, I noticed something lumpy at the end of the bed. I scooped out a pile of lizards and farm animals, reptiles and mammals making strange bedfellows.

There were empty plastic bins on a shelf. Separating toys by genus and class, I filled one with pre-historic creatures, another with what I thought were more modern lizards, a third with Lego and a fourth with action figures.

Heartlessly, I threw the livestock in with the predators, then stacked up the books on the bottom shelf and gathered up the dirty laundry. *And I give Matt a hard time for being a neat freak.* Giving into my auto-pilot mom-bed-time-OCD ritual killed time and made me feel a little better about the "Duffer" incident. I stood in the quiet, listening to Jake breathe, missing Lainie. With the time difference, she should be starting her own bedtime routine soon and I wondered what book she would make Ken read four times in a row.

Laughter floated in from the other end of the house. I tried not to over-think the "Matt's . . . friend" comment. Why did that stick in my craw? It was odd. There was nowhere for me to put the laundry, so I set it in a pile in the corner, and slowly went to rejoin the party.

***

Matt patiently explained that a fourteener was one of several mountains in the Rockies that are at least fourteen thousand feet tall. He made an off-hand comment about my ability to keep up considering my lack of experience. "Don't feel like you have to keep up with me, honey. If you can't make it to the top, it's okay. It's your first time out there."

And that was the beginning of the end. *Okay, Sir Edmund Hillary, now I'm gonna kick your ass.* The little evil voice in my head started working her way into a frenzy. I should have squashed her, but I didn't. *Did ya forget that you have at least a decade on me old man? Elaine didn't raise a wimp. I'm gonna dog you all the way up this hill.* The voice was relentless.

My idea of a good hike is a shady trail with a gradual incline along a wide path where nice, tree-hugging people have thoughtfully cleared away the large brush and other obstacles. Ideally, there is also easy conversation, a backpack full of chocolate and cheese, and maybe a little trail mix, perhaps an adult beverage. But Sir Edmund had changed all of that with his little remark. This was the battle of the sexes. Billie Jean King vs. Bobbie Riggs. *Bring it on.*

About two thirds of the way up the mountain, the trees thinned until there were none and there wasn't much vegetation at all. There was no lovely wide path here, just some nasty stuff they call shale that slips out from under your Timberlands the minute you think you have a decent foothold. I imagine Bedouins trudging across the windblown dunes of the Sahara have similar problems, but they are smart enough to do it with camels.

Matt had no pithy conversation to offer once we got above the tree line. Much to my gloating self-satisfaction, I did pretty well on the shale. All those hours on the damn Stairmaster were finally paying dividends. I inched ahead of him. A dozen yards. Two dozen. I paused to let him catch up. Once I got the hang of it, it wasn't too bad. The trick was to take shorter steps with a fairly flat foot, almost like walking on an icy driveway. Too big a stride or too steep an angle and the ground would slip away. I found my inner mountain goat. The weather was hazy and gloomy, and there was a slight drizzle. What was supposed to have been a spectacular view only amounted to a grey shale ridge topped by a lighter grey sky with darker grey mountains in the distance. Alone, this would be drudgery. Together, it was competition. So, I let Matt catch up, and as he paused, gasping in thin air, I found some inane subject to rattle on about for a few minutes. Then we turned and continued upward.

"Don't worry if you can't keep up." HA! I realized that the tune I was whistling was the song from *Annie Get Your Gun*, "Anything You Can Do." I tried to stop it before the breeze caught it and carried it down to Matt, who I'm sure thought I was obnoxious enough already.

At the top, we stopped for a picnic, shivering the whole time. The unseasonable cold stiffened my fingers and started tightening the muscles in my legs. Matt went to retrieve the camera from his backpack and from its dark interior, something glowed fuzzy and white. He reached back in to get a different lens, and, as he did, I saw a flash of red. He'd brought the Santa hat! Was I going to be in the annual Christmas photo? What did it mean? Was this going further than I thought?

I began to get a little excited and nervous at the prospect of making it onto his Christmas card, but Matt shoved the fluffy object deeper into the pack and drew out only the lens and the mini tripod. Clearly, he didn't want me to see the hat. In the photo we took on the mountain that day, I have a strange expression on my face, like I had just misplaced something I thought I'd had. All the way back down the hill, slipping through the shale, I knew I had screwed up. I wasn't good enough for the Santa hat.

It ended badly. Think Scarlett O'Hara and Rhett Butler. Like Rhett, Matt was fed up with my antics and selfish behavior. Like Scarlett, I was shocked that anyone would have the temerity to break up with me, no matter how much I may have deserved it. There was a lesson in all of this. I knew it was my fault that things had turned out as they had. Scenes of my poor behavior (even worse than the mountain climbing, too embarrassing to share) replayed themselves in my mind for months after he dumped me, but I had to go on. Tomorrow was another day.

***

While my break up with Matt occurred after a few week's build-up, my break up with Lester happened in a flash of gross misunderstanding on my part. We had an argument. It was stupid and came about mostly because I misconstrued a comment he made about work. He used the phrase "just a paycheck." He was speaking philosophically, but I was listening literally. I interpreted his comment to mean that work didn't mean much to him, that he wouldn't put his heart and soul into his job. I projected this lackluster attitude through to what I thought was its natural conclusion: Lester working a mindless dead-end job because he lacked motivation, and me struggling to support us all. I wouldn't end up stuck in the same situation that I had found myself in with Ken. I needed someone who valued work and strived for upward mobility. I needed a partner, not another adult that I would have to take care of. My knee-jerk interpretation was that I was casting my lot with a slacker, and I didn't want to go down that road again. So, I broke up with him.

It must have hit him completely out of the blue. I can't recall the exact conversation (or just don't want to, I'm sure I was hateful). Lester sat on the stairs outside of my apartment and cried loud, heaving sobs. And I, shamefully, went back inside my apartment and closed the door. I watched him through the peephole, sitting hunched over, shoulders shaking, wiping his nose. I wanted to open the door and go to him, but resolved to be strong for Lainie. We needed a go-getter. We needed a man who could make a fortune; who *wanted* to go out and make a fortune for us. So, I tossed a good man aside to continue the hunt for our sugar daddy. It was the worst, most heartless thing I had ever done.

***

Lainie dove into her mac and cheese with abandon, shoveling yellow noodles into her mouth with her Winnie the Pooh fork. She paused only to take a drink. I watched her eat like a condemned man. Halfway through her meal, she came up for air.

"Mommy?"

"Yes?"

"You make better macaronis than Veronica does."

"Who's Veronica?"

"Daddy's new friend." *A friend?* Sure, a *friend* has control of my ex's kitchen? Having sated her initial carb craving, Lainie slowed enough to place one small noodle on the fork. She sucked it into her mouth. Her eyes half shut as she worked that noodle like a dog with a chew toy. She sucked off all the cheese sauce, wiggled her tongue until the noodle split lengthwise and then let it lay flat on her tongue for a second before she let it slide down her throat. She had painstakingly demonstrated these steps to me once. We had a discussion about how people don't like to watch other people dissect their food. We compromised: she could play her little game as long as she could do it with her lips closed.

"Daddy says that Veronica is going to live with him, and that we're gonna have lots of fun together."

"That's nice honey." Maybe having to keep my cool in front of Lainie was helping me process this new information. Maybe not. A weird feeling grew inside me which defied categorization. It wasn't jealousy. This Veronica person could have him. It wasn't anger, he had every right to date. I stared blankly at the placemat, the one I had inherited from Mom's last house purge. The blue and mauve flowers were just as they had always been. Maybe I was just angry at the situation.

"You have lots of friends, Mommy."

"Well, that's true."

"Are we going to have a friend to live with us?" She asked.

"No, I really don't think so. Not any time soon."

Dinner was cleaned up, a simple chore that included one pan, a salad bowl and a frozen dinner carton.

After her bath, I wrapped Lainie up in a big green towel. Rubbing her back through the damp terry cloth, I knelt and held her, feeling her damp hair against my cheek. Just the two of us, on the green rug, leaning into each other. In that moment, I wanted nothing more. We were whole. I breathed in the scent of wet hair and baby shampoo. Then she wiggled free, dropped the towel and ran naked into the bedroom squealing, "pink nightie, pink nightie!"

Pink nightie on, teeth brushed, stories read, she pushed the pillows into the right shape, and was half asleep before I turned out the light.

Out on the balcony, the air was calm. The trees in the parking lot were serene. Maybe I should just give up, eat whatever I want, get fat, give up stressing out about hair and make-up. Go totally bohemian. Seemed to work for my mom. Lainie and I could live happily ever after with a bunch of cats.

I'm allergic to cats.

Chapter Eleven
Late June - July 1996

That summer, I could sum up most of my stupid decisions as crimes of inertia rather than crimes of intention. Which is how I ended up with Quinn.

I had agreed to sail with him. He needed a crew, I needed adventure. By the time I realized something was off, I had committed to sailing in a regatta with him, arranged for Lainie to be at her dad's house for the weekend, and psyched myself up for a new thrill. The evening in his apartment should have made me run away, never looking back. But I'd promised I'd help him race, and it would be unsporting to back out. Sane, maybe, but not fair.

Quinn and I had met at a busy food court in DC. This was the nearest place to my current temping assignment to get a decent lunch. It was crowded with tourists in terrible T-shirts seeking nourishment and a respite from the heat and working folk pressed for time.

"Do you mind if we share?" I looked up from my book to see a slight man in a tan suit, indicating the empty chair with his elbow, his hands being occupied with a Styrofoam tray.

"Go ahead."

He fussed with his paper napkin and plastic utensils and then gripped his sandwich with bony hands, notable for a heavy gold class ring.

"Good book?" He wiped his mouth. I looked at him a little more carefully. Early forties, I guessed, geeky, but sincere. Too skinny. I could shut him down with a few choice words and my evil teacher stare, but I had learned at this point not to judge on looks alone, and the combination of his tan suit with a light blue shirt and subtly patterned tie indicated some class.

"It's pretty good. A friend of mine recommended it," I said.

"What's it about?" he asked.

"Eleanor of Aquitaine."

He gave me the expected blank stare.

"She was married to the king of France, then managed to divorce him and marry the king of England. Very powerful woman. Mother of Richard the Lion Hearted."

"When did this all happen?" (Points for recognizing this as history rather than fiction).

"Twelfth Century."

"You like history?"

"I should. I teach it." I had ordered a loaded baked potato, then regretted it. It sat half-eaten on a tray.

In a jerky movement, he extended his hand across the table. "I'm Quinn Haalstead."

"Alex Smythe." I don't remember how the conversation turned to sailing. I was bored and he seemed nice. His diction was excellent.

"Do you sail?" he asked.

"I did, about a hundred years ago, in summer camp."

"Would you like to help me sail my Hobie? It's a Twenty."

In my limited maritime repertoire, the Hobie 20, Sunfish, Swan and Laser were the only models of sailboat I could identify without help. The Hobie 20 was a favorite among my sailing friends. It was a sleek catamaran, fast and nimble. Did I want to sail one? Yes! Was I an idiot for not recognizing this as a pick-up line? Yes again!

For about three weeks, I learned how to handle the Hobie, meeting Quinn at the marina for weekend training sessions. It was hard work, but the adrenaline rush was worth it. In my mind, we were two teammates, just sailing, preparing for a big, end-of-the-season regatta. The third Saturday we sailed together, things really started to click on board. Quinn only had to remind me twice about the centerboards.

We cruised up and down a wide stretch of the Potomac in a medium wind. I soon learned to dread heading up wind where my job was to lay down in the bow and make myself as small as possible, sometimes holding onto the jib, but mostly responsible for adjusting the centerboards. Downwind was thrilling. We hooked into our harnesses, pressed our feet into the upper hull as it rose out of the water, leaning far back, flying high above the water as the bottom hull skimmed the surface. I was cool as an Olympian and graceful as a trapeze artist. The sun glinted off the water, the warm wind caressing my whole body. I was floating, weightless. In those moments, I could hardly believe I was me. If I looked out over the bow, I could even pretend I was there by myself, just me, the sun, the wind and the river, total peace.

Back on shore, we did the myriad tasks it takes to put the boat away: lowered the mast, stowed the sails and lines, cleaned metal things whose names I couldn't remember.

Quinn took a small leather folder out of his hip pocket, the kind that holds a replaceable notebook and pocket inside the cover for stray papers. He made notes about things he needed to pick up at the marine supply store, and noted the time, temperature and wind speed of the day's sail. I learned that this procedure went faster if I dispensed with small talk and simply followed directions.

When all was "buttoned up," we went to lunch at the marina and sat out on the deck, both of us too tired to say much. Food tastes so much better when you've worked hard, outside, for hours. I was thoroughly enjoying my salad, thinking that I needed to get out more. We talked about logistics for the race. Quinn only had one parking pass for the marina, so I rode back with him to the parking lot at his apartment to retrieve my car. "Do you want to come up for a minute?" he asked.

There was nothing in in his tone that warned me against this course of action, so I said, "Okay," curiosity getting the best of me. After all, he had bought lunch and it wouldn't do to be rude.

There was something a bit unsettling about Quinn's apartment. The *feng shui* was askew. He had a beautiful pair of tall, silver candlesticks, one standing sentry in the middle of a round dining table, while its partner held a lonely vigil on the coffee table, guarding a stack of books on Thomas Jefferson and the Founding Fathers. I fought the urge to reunite the two on the buffet. The apartment was spare. A leather sectional in the living area, dining set near the kitchen. All the wood pieces were carefully chosen (inherited?) antiques. There were no family photographs to be seen. Three architectural drawings of Monticello hung over the couch. There was a tarnished bronze of the second president on the buffet.

"Jefferson fan?" I ventured.

"Yes, what a genius. I wanted to go to William and Mary, but my parents wanted me to stay up north." Quinn was unloading sailing gear into a small closet by the front door.

"May I use your bathroom?" I asked.

"Down the hall, can't miss it." He gestured in the general direction.

Navy blue shower curtain. Navy blue rug. One toothbrush in the pewter holder on the sink. All very clean. I wondered how long I needed to stay at the apartment to be polite.

On the wall outside the bathroom hung three diplomas, an education haiku:

Philips Andover

Harvard University

Duke Medical School

Brains and money, but no family pictures. A mystery, but was it one I really wanted to delve into? There was something weird, I just didn't know what. I wandered back into the living room.

"Care for a glass of wine?" Quinn called out.

"Sure."

"Red or white?" I followed his voice into the galley kitchen. Immaculate. Nothing on the counters. He pulled a corkscrew from the drawer.

"White please." He turned and opened the fridge, which held a few vegetables in the crisper, three bottles of wine and some orange juice. Back in the living room, Quinn motioned for me to sit on the couch. I squeezed myself into the corner, he perched in the middle, close enough to touch me.

Okay, I thought, *I'll finish the wine, stay for about fifteen minutes, and get out of here.* The sterility of the place was giving me the creeps.

"Alex, how do you feel about having more children?" He leaned forward, resting his elbows on his knees and gently holding his wine glass in two hands.

I didn't see that one coming. I had been mentally preparing for a conversation about early American history, trying to remember what that whole Jefferson-Hamilton fuss had been about. Clearly, we were taking a more personal tack.

"Well, yes, I always thought I'd have more kids. I never wanted Lainie to be an only child." I answered. *Where was this going?*

"I want a family," Quinn said, looking intently into my face. "I bought that dining table with the vision of at least three or four children around it. It expands." We both looked at the table. I briefly wondered where he stored the leaves. He continued, "I want to debate the issues of the day with my children, have them read the newspaper before dinner and grill them with questions, you know, like the Kennedys did." (Actually, I didn't know.) "I want the kids to ski and sail and be on the debate team. I want them to play musical instruments and give little concerts in the drawing room. I've been saving for a long time to buy a big house, but I've been waiting for the right person to come along and buy it with me. What do you think?"

Oh no! Think fast! Change the subject! Diversionary tactic. I thought hard, looking around the room for inspiration. I had to pretend that I didn't get what he was hinting at.

"Quinn! You mean to say that you've been renting this for all these years? This isn't a condo? You're throwing money away every month! That's nuts. As soon as I can save a down payment, I'm buying a condo. I can't believe that someone with your brain power has been renting for what, ten years? Fifteen?"

I babbled on, ignoring the look in his eyes that said I was missing his point. I was intentionally missing it, I was skirting around it like a rabbit around a sleeping bear. I knew if I gave him one glimmer of hope, one inkling that I found his Rockwellian dream in the least bit attractive, he'd be all over me. The problem was that I did. I did want all of those things, just not with an intensely odd little man who would bring this up when we weren't even dating. I started looking at my watch.

"Would you like to go to dinner with me this evening?" he asked.

"Um, no thanks, I have plans with friends." *Must escape.* "Thanks for the sail, it was a lot of fun." I said all of this while making my way through the living room and depositing my glass on the kitchen counter.

"Oh, okay." He rose to let me out. There was an uneasy moment by the front door when I thought he was going to try to kiss me, but why a kiss after sailing? I ducked a little and made it out the door.

***

"I was at Daddy's last weekend, wasn't I?" Lainie asked from the back seat.

"Yes! Isn't this fun? You get to go see Daddy again, then you get two weekends in a row with me." I hated the child transfer thing. Traffic was already getting heavy.

"I want to go sailing with you!"

"Lainie, that sounded like whining. What do we say about whining?"

"Whiners aren't winners."

"That's my girl." She made a face, forgetting that I could see her in the rear-view mirror. "Tell you what, maybe if the weather's good next weekend I'll take you boating on the lake."

"Those are row boats, Mommy." *How the heck did she remember that? We were there a year ago.*

"Alright, I'll look into a place where I can take you sailing."

"How come I can't go on Mr. Quinn's boat?"

"Because it's a grown-up boat, and only grown-ups can sail on that kind of boat. I'll try to find us something kid friendly." *And after this weekend, Mommy's never sailing with Mr. Quinn again. Ever.*

Thankfully, Quinn had everything loaded and ready to go by the time I dropped Lainie off and met him in the parking lot. We cruised along the highway at first, the traffic and weather cooperating. Then, the truck's air conditioning began to falter, and gave out almost completely with two hours left to go.

After a long, sweaty drive, we stopped in an anonymous town in Delaware. Quinn filled the truck with gas, noted the mileage and number of gallons in his ever-present notebook, and suggested we have supper at the diner across the street.

I slid into a red vinyl booth that had seen better days. Quinn slid in across from me. The fluorescent lighting wasn't flattering to either of us. Quinn looked scrawny and wan. I probably didn't look much better. The waitress came to take our order, and I was fixated on the stains that danced across her apron, like an oversized Rorschach test. Further examination revealed slight gradations of color. Variations of stain drying time? Ketchup vs. spaghetti sauce? Hard to tell. Quinn and the waitress stopped talking. They were staring at me, waiting.

"Uh, cheeseburger, please. Medium."

"Lettuce, tomato, onion?"

"No onion, yes tomato and lettuce. Please." She waddled away. Quinn stared after her, then turned his bug-eyes on me. He looked like a kid who took a peek into his Christmas stocking and couldn't believe what he saw.

"Did you hear that?"

"No, what?"

"She called you 'The Missus.'" He grinned and gulped, his big Adam's apple bobbing in his pencil-thin neck. "She asked what 'The Missus" would like. She thought we were *married*!" He was delighted. It was disconcerting, but I was too hungry to think about it.

The morning of the regatta dawned clear and warm. I loved sailing Quinn's Hobie Cat, even if it did come with a crazy man and took over an hour to get ready to put in the water. It took another few hours to clean up and stow the boat every time too, but the hours between, especially when Quinn wasn't talking, were magical. I was in this for the boat, and because Quinn had convinced me that he really needed crew for this regatta. Here is a list of all the things I had ignored just to have a chance to sail:

1. What happened to the person Quinn used to sail with? A Hobie 20 can be managed by one person, but it's tricky.
2. He wanted to date me, but I didn't want to date him. At all.
3. He was a nutjob.

It was all about the boat. I secretly called her Sophie the Hobie in my head. Quinn hadn't named her. He informed me that twenties were referred to by their sail number alone. Evidently naming the boats was uncool, but Sophie and I knew different.

The first race of the day went well, considering it was my first race ever. I was still giddy over the beach launch. I hadn't given much thought about how we'd get the boat into the water until it happened. For our weekend sails, Quinn would back the Hobie on its trailer down the ramp into the still waters of the marina, and we would go from there. I was on the beach and noticed that there wasn't a handy dock or ramp, just sand and waves. We had to go in right over the surf. Open water makes me nervous in general. I prefer rivers, you can almost always see the shore. I looked out onto the breaking surf, the waves were relentless, crashing onto the shore, one after the other with hardly a break between them. Images of the Titanic came to mind. Truth be told, a ten year-old could have body surfed these waves, but I was working up to a full-scale panic. I checked that my life jacket was buckled tight. Other teams were on the beach, getting ready to launch, some of them smiling and waving at Quinn. Nobody looked concerned about the monster waves.

Quinn had hold of the rudder and the main sail as we waded into the water; I was at the bow. I realized that the only way we were going to get this small sailboat over incoming surf was by sailing right at it. The breakers continued their ceaseless, terrifying march, pounding against my body and the boat. Once I was up to my waist in the water, Quinn ordered me on board. I clung on to the edge of the tramp for dear life, convinced that we were going to die. I would drown a watery death, my body would be recovered later, bloated and blue. Quinn pushed us farther. When the water was up to his chest, he jumped on. It took about fifteen seconds to breach the surf, hardly long enough to practice deep breathing. I repeated my mantra *It's okay, it's okay, it's okay* and we were through.

Once past the breaking waves, the water stretched out smoothly before us. My nerves settled, and we sailed toward the start-finish line. Quinn yammered on about strategy and how we were going to approach the starting line. I knew from the past three weeks that he would repeat whatever directions I needed about six or eight times, so I tuned him out to take in the sights. I'd never been in a regatta, just watched them from afar.

The boats were so close to one another you could have chatted with the people on the next catamaran if it weren't for the wind. Some crews squinted at the competition with cold, steely eyes, taking their game very seriously. Others laughed and waved hello, but once the horn sounded, it was all business. I learned quickly that timing crossing the invisible starting line was key, and the boats struggled to get into position at just the right moment. If they crossed too soon, it would mean a false start and a penalty.

We had a good race. In a fit of testosterone, Quinn edged out another boat at one of the turns in a move that was legal but somewhat unchivalrous. We moved in closer, closer, until I could read the print on the crew's T-shirt. The other captain yelled, "Common Haalsey, give me a break." Quinn stared steadily ahead until we passed, and then smiled a little. On another man, that might have been sexy. On Quinn, it was snake-like. We finished sixth out of a field of about thirty. During our water break, Quinn started up with the endless stream of directions again.

"That was really good. Clean start. You're doing fine with the jib, but you have to move faster to get the center boards down. Try to keep a lower profile in the bow when we're sailing up wind. I think if we get a good start we can finish top three in the next one."

If I lay down any further in the bow, I'll be in the water. Mostly though, I was enjoying the breeze and the view before the next start. Too soon, the warning came from the Committee boat and we maneuvered to the start again. Quinn timed it perfectly and we crossed the line just as the horn blew. Our Hobie jumped ahead of almost the whole pack, we were just about even with a boat about fifty yards to the port side. Realizing that we might have a shot at winning this one, my competitive spirit kicked in. I tried to focus, what was my next move? Where could I put my body weight for maximum effect? How tight could I get the jib?

We rounded the mark and headed downwind. We hooked into our harnesses and hiked out over the starboard hull, throwing our full weight into the effort. Quinn had the main sail tight, and we were precariously high in the air. As we approached the turn, I felt my center of gravity shift too far.

"Let off, let off, we're too tight!" I yelled at Quinn.

"No! We are going to make it!" We were practically on top of the large buoy that marked the turn. We were going to go over, I felt it in my stomach and my knees. We rounded the mark.

"Quinn, let the main go!" I yelled again.

"No, I got it."

The wind swept his words away as we capsized. I felt the boat go over in slow motion. Still balanced on the hull, we rose high in the air. Sophie the Hobie tipped, casually, until the blue and yellow sail rested peacefully on the water, moving with the gentle ripples. I observed the sail from my perch, not noticing Quinn flapping around frantically in the water. His shouts broke through my reverie.

"Alex, unhook and get down now! Get your foot off the mast! Get in the water!" He was panicked. I felt an odd calm. It's a catamaran. They tip. Actually, it was kind of neat, I had wondered what it would be like to capsize. I wasn't dead, the water was warm and I had a trustworthy life jacket. This was okay.

"Come on," he continued to yell, "we have to get this thing up on our own before they help us." He thrashed about, realigning ropes and trying to position the boat so we could tip it up. "If they help us we get disqualified from this heat. (*Gasp!*) If we get up on our own, we get a DNF."

I followed directions and worked as hard as is possible while treading water. I was reassured that all these other nice people were out for a sail today. I'd hate to be doing this alone with no hope of rescue at all. Within minutes, we righted the boat and were getting ready to head back to the start-finish line. Two burly young men from the Committee boat approached on jet skis. They slowed to circle our boat.

"You guys okay?" a very attractive, well-built young man asked.

"We're fine." Quinn waved them off.

"You sure?" he pressed.

"Yes, perfectly," Quinn answered.

I wanted to interject, but too quickly the guy on the jet ski said, "Alright, good luck." They turned, spraying a donut of water in the air, and I watched their muscled backs bounce away across the waves, wishing I was riding on the back of one of the jet skis, my arms wrapped around a tanned waist.

Despite the setback, I was enjoying myself. I took a minute to look around at the brightly striped sails, the picturesque shoreline in the distance, the bright white clouds. The dip had been more refreshing than expected. Tipping over had broken the stress of the regatta. This was about the worst thing that could happen, and the best news was that it wasn't my fault. It was over and we could move onto the next race, I thought. I had no idea that Quinn was about to explode.

He was standing in the middle of the tramp, coiling the main sheet. Suddenly, he stopped and stood, his feet planted wide, looking like a demented Peter Pan in water booties and life jacket. I thought he was about to break into a rendition of *I've Gotta Crow*. Instead, he morphed into a skinny Stanley Kowalski. He looked at me, drew a deep breath and gave a plaintive cry, "Alex. Oh, Alex, I wanted this weekend to be perfect for you. I wanted everything to go right. I wanted to win for you. I wanted to show you how good I am. Oh Alex, I love you. I wanted more than this. I failed you. I love you Alex." He choked on the last phrase.

This was unexpected.

His eyes burned with irrational rage and sorrow. A little nervous, I glanced toward shore and decided it was too far to swim. The cute guys on the jet skis were nowhere in sight. I'd have to talk him down myself.

"Quinn, please sit down."

"No."

"Let's just get back into the race."

"But I . . . "

"It's okay. I'm not upset. Let's just get ready for the next race," I said.

"You don't want to quit?" he asked, his whole face stretched into a question.

"Of course not! Shit happens. Let's get on with it."

"But I failed you . . .

"The boat tipped." *And you are a typical man who doesn't listen to women when they're right.* "And I came here to sail the whole regatta, not just two races of it. Come on." He hesitated, looking at me with an unsure expression on his face. "I'm not mad. It was a little adventure. That's all." If I could just get his head back in the boat, maybe I wouldn't have to address the "I love you" part. *Stay calm, you're in a small boat with a crazy man.*

"Oh God, I'm sorry." He muttered to himself all the way back to the finish line. Somehow, we got through two more races and returned to shore to put the boat up for the night. Some of Quinn's buddies stopped by. Those who saw us capsize shook his hand and congratulated him on the quick recovery, others just stopped to chat. Some tourists asked if they could take our picture. I wanted to politely wave them off but Quinn wrapped an arm firmly around my shoulders and rotated us toward the photographer. Resigned, I thought, *I'll never see you people again, so go ahead, take a picture of me looking like a drowned rat. Whatever.* Quinn grinned broadly at the camera.

Quinn had booked us adjoining rooms at the local motel. I had an hour before we were to meet for dinner, and spent half of it in the shower. The salt water pickled my skin and there wasn't enough body lotion in the state to make it feel normal. My eyes burned from the sun and salt, so eye makeup was out of the question. With only a little lipstick and a passable outfit, I sat on the edge of the bed.

Another fine situation we're in, Ms. Alexandria Elaine. I've withstood worse for longer. Interminable visits to difficult relatives came to mind, when

I'd lay in bed at night and chant *Twenty-four more hours, twenty-four more hours. You can do it.*

I tried to call Lainie, but only got Ken's answering machine. "Hey Baby, it's Mommy," I said. "I miss you. The race is going fine. I'll be home late tomorrow night and come get you for school Monday. Okay? I'll try to call you again tomorrow. Love you Sweetie." I just wanted to go home, pick her up, and have a *Lion King/Little Mermaid* marathon.

There was a knock at the door.

"You ready?"

"Yep, coming." If I hadn't been starving, I would have passed on dinner entirely. I heaved myself off the bed.

There were only three restaurants in town, all equally crowded. We waited an hour for a table, giving two glasses of wine ample time to work on my empty stomach. Quinn was busy catching up with old friends. I leaned back against the bar and listened. There were a surprising number of women. A couple approached us.

"Quinn, how are you old man?" the husband asked. He had to be at least six feet, six inches tall. His wife also towered over me.

"Ed and Louise Kittridge, meet my friend, Alex Smythe." Quinn introduced us.

"Did you check the board?" Ed asked.

"Didn't get a chance to," Quinn lied. I knew he had gone back to the race pavilion while I was showering, and memorized the standings. He'd also written down race times in his notebook, but he was trying to play it cool.

"You two are about ninth, I think, after your mishap," Ed remarked.

"How about you two?" Quinn asked. He knew damn well they were in second place. I think Ed knew that Quinn knew. Evidently this was some polite male competitive ritual to which I was uninitiated.

"We're in second place and both of you damn well know it. Cut the crap." Louise interjected with authority. I decided I liked this no-nonsense Louise. Graceful, she wore her gleaming silver-blonde hair short. In addition to being taller and thinner than was fair, her nails were perfect, long and tastefully manicured. Once I'd started sailing, I had to cut mine all off. The water, ropes and general abuse to my hands did them in. I stared at her hands in buzzed amazement. Maybe they were fake nails.

Had it not been for two generous glasses of wine on an empty stomach, I never would have asked, "Louise, how do you keep your nails so nice? Mine are all broken and I'm really bummed about it." As the words were coming out of my mouth, I realized that Jackie Kennedy on no account ever would say something that vapid. Maybe if I continued on this way, Quinn would change his mind about me.

"Sailing gloves," she said.

"That's it?"

"Yep, and the longer you sail, the better you'll get at self-preservation." She pointed to the bruises on my arms. "After a while, you don't get quite so banged up."

"So, I guess it's pretty obvious that I'm a novice, huh?"

"No, actually I was asking Ed if he knew who Quinn had crewing for him. We saw how you guys handled your mishap, and we were right behind you at the start of the fourth race. It looked like you had a pretty good grip on things." She smiled.

"You're being very kind." I blushed a little, and knew I'd replay that compliment in my head for months. I was hoping that Quinn would invite the Kittridges to dine with us, but they were meeting other friends. Trapped at a table for two in a smoky corner, I hoped that, between ordering and eating, we wouldn't have time to actually talk to one another.

"Alex, I want to apologize for the way I acted today," he said.

"You were a little stressed. Let's forget about it."

"No, please, I want to explain." At that moment, we were interrupted by the waiter. I asked him to repeat the specials. Then I ordered the halibut but talked to him for a while about having the butter sauce served on the side and substituting steamed vegetables for the rice. Then I asked if I could have a beer with dinner. Then I changed my mind and asked, if he wouldn't mind, could he bring me a Diet Coke instead. Even after all those stalling tactics, Quinn still remembered what he wanted to talk about.

"Alex, I really think you're special, and I want you to consider the possibility of..." his voice trailed off. *What the hell is he going to say?*

"Of what?"

"Of giving us a chance, as a couple."

"Um, I um. You know that I just broke up with someone. Isn't that why we have separate hotel rooms? I don't understand."

"Just wait." He took the little notebook from his pocket and pulled a well-worn scrap of paper from the inside pocket carefully unfolding it on the table. I recognized it for what it was. He had a list. Just like my LAQuaSH list. He carried it in his little book. My jaw dropped. I took a large sip of wine to recover myself. He lay the paper down on the table to reach in another pocket for his pen. Quinn turned the list to face me, and, using the fountain pen as a pointer, carefully read each item aloud.

The Future Mrs. Quinn Haalstead

1. Well educated
2. Well read, at least one newspaper per day and all important books
3. Wants children
4. Conservative
5. No prior marriages or children
6. Willing to stay home with the children
7. Willing to support me and my work
8. Sails or is willing to learn
9. Country club compatible manners
10. Above reproach

Oh, Karma. This is rich.

"I thought I wouldn't consider a divorcee or single mother, but I can cross that one off." Which he did. Carefully. He looked up from the list. I said nothing, so he carried on. "The only thing we haven't discussed is number six. Would you be willing to stay home with the children? It's obvious that you would support me in my work if the way you've supported me here at the regatta is any indication." He waited for a response. I'd been leaning over the table, staring at the list. I sat back in my chair.

"Quinn."

"I know you don't think of me that way yet, but I think if you give me time, you can grow to love me. We would make a fabulous couple," he said.

"Maybe on paper."

"That's a good place to start." Maybe it was the wine, or fatigue, or hunger, but my brain was not functioning. Well, it was functioning enough to catch the Caesar reference. *Above reproach.* I certainly didn't meet that requirement. There were no witty comebacks or subject-changing options available. I had nothing to say that wouldn't be hurtful. He sat across from me, so guileless and prep-school in his blue blazer. What could I say that would get us through the rest of the weekend and a three-hour drive home tomorrow?

Saved again by the waiter who arrived with bread and my Diet Coke.

"Hang on a minute." I said to Quinn. I tore into the bread and drained the soda. He was smart enough to keep quiet while I refueled.

"You're a really nice guy," I said.

"I'm just asking you to consider the possibility, just the possibility that we could date for a while. Would you be open to that?"

My head nodded, "Okay." My brain screamed, *"No!"*

***

I started mentally composing the goodbye voicemail to Quinn on the ride home. I planned to call his machine on Monday, while he was at work, and leave a message that would state very clearly that we were not ever going to be a couple, or even make an effort at being a couple. I didn't want to write a letter and risk having it get lost in the mail. Back at home, I took a blank index card out of the box and started writing. This call would require a script.

> Hi Quinn, it's Alex. ~~I had a wonderful time sailing with you this past weekend.~~
>
> I just wanted to thank you for giving me the opportunity to learn how to sail. ~~It was so much fun!~~ It was quite the adventure. As you know, school is going to start back up again soon, and I need to focus on my work and on getting Lainie and me settled into a new routine, so I don't think sailing is going to fit into our schedule. ~~I never actually want to date you because you're certifiably insane.~~

You mentioned something about maybe dating, but I don't think that will work for me right now.

Okay, take care, Bye!

I called at 11:30 a.m. and recited the message, trying to strike a tone of congenial finality. Hopefully, that would be the end of Quinn.

Chapter Twelve

July, 1996

"I want a Cinderella cake and balloons and I want Katie, Violet, Graham and Asher to come. I want to have the party here and play with all my toys." Lainie was turning three and it was very serious business. "And I want Lori to come too." Our upstairs neighbor was Lainie's new favorite person. "And Daddy and Veronica too." *Oy.*

Having no money for a Chuck E Cheese party, and objecting to them generally, I invited the four children from Lainie's day care over to our place for kid-friendly food, games and cake. My plan had been to troop everyone down to the playground and exhaust them before having a late lunch and cake at the apartment. But of course, it rained. Lori came down to help, and Ken and Veronica arrived in time to be of no help whatsoever. Veronica had a wide face and thick, dark hair which she wore in a single braid that lay heavily down her back. While we were setting up the decorations, the couple tried to stand out of the way, which was a challenge in the cramped space. Ken slipped his arm around Veronica's waist (she was a few inches taller than him). He leaned in toward her neck and said, "How's my Rhiannon?"

Great, he's on the mythical goddess nickname phase. Ken had once tried to nickname me Athena, but I put an end to that. The party began. One by one, tiny tykes arrived nicely dressed, holding gift bags. The moms looked relieved to leave their offspring for a few hours. The girls alternated between giggling and shrieking. Then the boys joined in. As a hive, they ran into the bedroom to look at Lainie's toys, then, en masse, charged through the living room. They tumbled out to the balcony where Lori and I had hung the piñata. Then back to the bedroom.

Lori and I gathered them into the living room for party games. We played Tape the Tail on the Donkey. Then we attempted a short game of telephone. Short because the three-year-olds didn't really get it. Then there was the piñata. All I can say in my defense is, this was supposed to be outside, in the park, and yes, a smarter person would have realized that half the piñata loot would fly off the balcony to the lawn far below. I sent Ken down to pick up the errant candy and toys. Thankfully, there was a good mix of candy and toys left in the piñata carcass, so that kept the kids occupied for a few minutes, sorting and trading. The grown-ups took a minute to breathe. Then, the great birthday debacle struck.

Ken and Veronica were standing next to my modest dining table. Ken leaned into Veronica again (he seemed incapable of standing erect on his own power around her). He was going in for a big, juicy kiss, arching Veronica back, back, until she jostled the table. I watched, helpless from my position across the room, as a two-liter bottle of soda wobbled, then crashed down into the cake, flattening Cinderella and her pink castle, the *piéce de resistance* of the party, the creation of which had kept me up until 2:00 a.m.

Lainie, witnessing this, exploded into an ear-splitting yowl and skittered over to look at the cake. Her friends gathered around her and gently patted her back, their ministrations raising her sobs to a fever pitch. I rushed to assess the situation. Ken, unwinding himself from Veronica, lifted the offending bottle off the cake and, instead of trying to fix the damage, proceeded to clear the icing off the bottle with his forefinger and stick it into his mouth. I stared daggers at him. He looked back at me, finger in mouth, and raised his eyebrows to say "What?"

I grabbed a knife, and, instead of stabbing my ex as compelled, I gently pried Cinderella Barbie from her buttercream grave. For a moment I thought I might be able to salvage something, but the crater in the cake was too deep, and whatever icing I might have used for repairs was being licked up by Romeo over there.

Lainie broke from her friends and clung to my legs. I was afraid to speak and unleash the string of expletives in my head.

"Mommy, Mommy, my cake, my Cinderella, my cake!" The rest was lost into the edge of my shirt that she was using to wipe her nose.

"Sweetie it's going to be okay."

"NOOOOOO, it's not going to be okay! My cake is a mess! It's messy! Oh Mommy."

I pulled her the short distance into the bedroom and grabbed her favorite stuffed friend.

"Here's Lolly. Give Lolly a hug." Lainie took Lolly and promptly wiped her nose on his wooly head. "Now, I need you to be a big girl, and go play with your friends, they don't want you to be sad at your party. Go play with them and I'll send Daddy to get a new cake. Okay?" She nodded, her face still buried in the lamb's back. "Do you want to take Lolly with you?" She nodded again and I gave her a hug. She walked out in front of me.

I had almost calmed myself down but the sight of the ruined cake sitting among the plates of goldfish crackers, sliced apples and discarded pizza crust made me want to scream. Blessed Saint Lori, drawing from her experience as a Girl Scout leader had corralled the kids into a game that involved singing and clapping. Lainie looked like she would survive. I turned to my former husband and took a deep breath.

"Ken, I need you to go to the Giant and get a new cake." He and Veronica were standing helplessly in the kitchen.

"Um, okay. The Giant?"

"The one around the corner on Bent Tree road. The bakery is on the left toward the back of the store. I'll call ahead. Talk to the bakery person when you get there."

"Should I go with you, honey?" Veronica offered. I didn't trust the two of them alone together. They might end up necking in the parking lot and I'd never get the cake in time.

"No, I think I need you to stay and help with the kids." Ken and Veronica kissed like he was a soldier headed off to war. Barely resisting the urge to slap them, I found the phone book and headed to the bedroom.

"Giant Bakery, Joanne speaking."

"Hi Joanne, I need a big favor and I really hope you can help," I said.

"Okay, what can I do for you, hon." She pronounced it in the old Maryland way, it sounded like "hawn".

"My idiot ex-husband just sat on my daughter's birthday cake." (A little hyperbole never hurts when you're trying to win someone over to your cause.) "And I know it's a Saturday, but do you have any cakes left? He's on his way over now."

"What are you looking for?"

"Anything princess-y. Preferably Cinderella, maybe pink?"

"I can do ya a Snow White with yellow and blue."

"That would be great! My ex will be the confused-looking one. Whatever you do, don't let him walk out with a dinosaur cake or some GI Joe thing."

My new bakery friend laughed.

"Jesus, he sounds like my ex. What do you want me to write on it.?" I told her how to spell Lainie's name, and hung up.

Upon his return, Daddy was greeted with cheers and hailed as the hero who saved the day. When Lainie returned to preschool that Monday, she told anyone who would stand still long enough to listen that her daddy had gotten her the nicest, prettiest cake and she had the best birthday party EVER.

***

I was drowsily getting ready for bed on an uneventful Wednesday when someone started banging on my apartment door, the pounding so violent I thought the door would spring off its hinges. My heart hammered in response. I closed the bedroom door behind me and, as quietly as I could, padded to the door and looked through the peephole. I sprang back. On the other side was one of my former students. He had been in my World History class at my old school, a peculiar, quiet kid who hung around the lacrosse field. On occasion, he helped move goals and equipment. We had spoken a few times, but nothing too personal. I was pretty sure he used to have a crush on one of my offense players.

Ethan pounded on the door again. I snuck another peek. He had stepped away from the door and was pacing back and forth, the solid tread of his Doc Martens echoing in the empty landing, his hands jittery by his sides. The heavy chain that attached the wallet in his back pocket to the belt loop of his camouflage pants swung in and out, striking his thigh. He ran his hands through his crew cut. His face was taut, his eyes skimming the foyer.

I eased the deadbolt shut, praying it wouldn't make any noise, and stood there, away from the peephole, trying to calm my breath. Part of me wanted to open the door and help a kid in distress. The other part of me, the smallish, single woman protecting her child, was screaming in my head to keep the door locked. Ethan pummeled the door again, five quick jabs, every blow visibly rocking the door in its frame. Standing there I could feel the door pulse. I waited, still trying to breathe, blood thrumming in my ears, my whole body trembling.

Quietly, I went to check on Lainie. Finding her asleep, I went back to the door, counted to ten, and then looked again. Ethan was still there, still strangely quiet. It was unnerving; such ferocity should be accompanied with shouting, but it was not. Clearly something was wrong, but I couldn't tell what, I just felt his anger rolling off of him in palpable waves.

I waited for him to call out, announce what he wanted or needed. Instead, he walked to the top of the stairs, scanned the area, and came back to stand in front of my door, his face expressionless. I pulled away from the peephole and waited, trying to calm my breath. Finally, his footsteps receded and I could hear his boots stamp down the cement stairs.

After he left, I checked the locks on the bedroom window and the sliding glass door. Ethan would have to scale the wall to the second floor to get in there, but I wasn't taking any chances. It was too late to call a friend. If I called the police, what would I tell them? That a kid was knocking on my door? I went back to the bedroom, lifted Lainie out of her bed into mine, curled around her and tried to sleep, wishing all the while that we weren't alone in the apartment,

Hours passed. Every time I closed my eyes, I saw Ethan pacing back and forth in front of my door and wondered why he had come. I couldn't figure out how he found out where I lived, or even if I was the person he was looking for. If I hadn't been alone with Lainie that night, if I had a partner, maybe I could have opened my door and offered to help. Maybe with another person, a boyfriend or a husband, we could come to this kid's aid, together. Instead, I had acted in fear and ended up guilt-ridden that I couldn't reach out to a student. I never saw him again.

Chapter Thirteen
August, 1996

One afternoon, I dragged a reluctant Lainie out of the neighborhood pool and back to the apartment to find this message on my answering machine:

"Hey Alex, it's Becca, I know you didn't want to work the last few weeks of August, but I need a huge favor. Call me back please."

Becca was the manager at the agency. I called her back right away. I owed her.

"Hey Becca, it's Alex, what's up?"

"Oh my God, I need you."

"Wow Bec, didn't know you swung that way."

"Very funny. I have a client who needs a temp, and our usual person is out with a medical issue with her husband. I really need you, not just anyone. I know you wanted more time with Lainie, but I think you'll be interested in this one."

"Why?"

"It pays double, and it's just for two weeks," she said. I had knelt to strip off Lainie's bathing suit. I covered the mouthpiece and whispered to her to go get dressed, and then stood up, to better hear what Becca had to say.

"Why double?"

"It's a firm that does security for very wealthy people. You have to sign about forty pages of non-disclosure forms before they will let you in the door."

"I'm flattered. How did my name come up for this gig?"

"Well, Dwyer wrote an absolutely glowing review after you worked for him in June. It was so good that I showed it to my boss."

"Dwyer? The unholy terror of the insurance world? I thought he hated me. He was so obnoxious," I said.

"He's that way with everyone. He's the most difficult client we have. My boss thought if you could please Dwyer, you could do almost anything," Becca said.

My week working for David Dwyer was memorable in that the man's main mode of communicating with his office staff was shouting at them from his doorway or printing off blistering memos and slamming them on their desks. His son, who I took to be of college age, showed up one morning for his summer job wearing a button-down oxford that he clearly had just purchased and taken out of the wrapping. The sharply creased outline of the cardboard square to which the shirt had been pinned was blatantly visible across the young man's ample chest and belly.

Dwyer Senior stepped into Dwyer Junior's cubical and yelled at him for three solid minutes about the virtues of an iron and ironing board and the lack of moral fiber he, Dwyer Junior, was showing by arriving at work looking so disheveled. Dwyer Senior then went on to blame the ex-Mrs. Dwyer for his son's shortcomings before charging out of the cubicle like a bull from a rodeo gate, almost knocking over an assistant insurance agent in the process.

Becca told me later that the temp agency's unofficial policy was to leave their employees at that office for only one week to avoid burnout, or worse. Dwyer had wanted me back. On the phone he told Becca that I was the only one with the *cajones* to deal with him, but Becca had said no. I owed her for that, too.

"I need you to come in tomorrow morning and sign this ream of paperwork so I can get you cleared to start on Monday," Becca said.

"You're working on Saturdays now?" I asked.

"This account is really big, so yes, but the earlier you get here, the earlier I can go home. Bring Lainie, she can help me feed the fish."

"Okay, we'll be there at 8:30."

"Thanks, Alex," she said.

"No, thank you. For double pay, this is totally worth it." As I hung up the phone, I realized that, with this job, I might be able to pay off my credit card, and possibly stuff a few hundred bucks into savings. This called for a celebration.

"Lainie, Baby, put on a dress, we're going to Olive Garden!"

***

Upon arriving at M Street Security Services on Monday, I was immediately shown into a small back office by a skinny brunette who looked like she hadn't seen the sun in months and needed at least as much wardrobe help as I did. She wore a bargain-basement plum-colored suit with a short, tight skirt and boxy jacket that probably came from the same place I bought my bargain-basement suits. Her hair was pulled back in a severe low ponytail held by a clip with a black bow, and her glasses were big and round. Molly shut the door behind us and motioned for me to sit down. A few dozen Hello Kitty figurines lined the front of her desk.

"Look," she said, "Mr. Smith is not too happy that we couldn't get our usual temp, so try to keep your head down and don't draw any attention to yourself."

"Mr. Smith?"

"Our boss," she said.

"I thought his name was–" She interrupted me.

"No, we don't use his real name. You are not supposed to know it. He is Mr. Smith at the office. Okay?" I nodded. "Your job is to keep the security specialists happy, and to do so while gleaning as little information as possible about the actual operations that go on here." I stifled my thought that perhaps they had called the wrong kind of temp agency for that work. "Everything that comes out of the main printer and fax machine will have a cover page that will print last. You are not to look at the printer until it's done, and then you may ONLY look at the cover sheet. If it is a large print-out, you put it in a folder, then you deliver it to the specialist listed on the cover sheet."

"Okay, I think I can handle that. What else?"

"Often, our specialists will have their clients come here to discuss their security needs or updates. You are to do whatever is needed to make those meetings run smoothly, bring coffee or water, ask to order lunch or snacks if the meetings are running long. You know." Molly looked at me.

"What if they need me to make copies of something?"

"They should hand you whatever they need in a manila folder which you will take to Carmen, and Carmen will do the Xeroxing. Then you deliver it back to their office."

"That's a lot of running back and forth. Perhaps high heels may have been a bad idea?" I attempted humor.

"No," Molly said without humor. "High heels are always a good idea." The phone on her desk buzzed and she pushed the speaker button, clearly out of habit, not because she particularly wanted me to hear the conversation.

"Yeah, Drew?" she asked.

"Hey, I need the paperwork on the Qiao account."

"I gave it to you already."

"No, I revised it. I printed it off but I need four copies, we have more bodies at the meeting," he said.

"Where's Carmen?" Molly asked.

"Dunno, that's why I'm callin' you, darlin'." Then Molly said something to him in a language I thought sounded like Chinese. He shot something back at her. Even in a foreign language, it didn't sound polite.

"Fine, I'll have Alex do it. She's the new temp." Molly jabbed at the button to end the call.

"Were you speaking Chinese?" I asked.

"Yes, Cantonese," she said. And in response to my raised eyebrows she continued, "I've picked up a few phrases here and there."

"What was he saying to you?"

"He was mentioning an indecent act that he wished upon me and my mother, but that was in response to something I may have said about his manhood."

"Oh my."

"Let's get you started." Molly led me back down the hall and had me stow my things at a small desk tucked behind the reception area. "The guys will call you on that phone. Your extension is 317. You won't get any outside calls; Carmen handles all of those."

Moving remarkably quickly for a short-legged person in a tight skirt, Molly led me to the printer and showed me how to pick up the papers without peeking. Then we found Carmen for the Xeroxing. Molly introduced me.

Carmen took the print-out from Molly's hands and began methodically folding and tearing the narrow, perforated strips on the longs sides of the paper that fed it through the printer, then she gently separated the pages along the seams on the tops and bottoms. She handled it carefully, not wanting to tear the paper or chip her pristine ruby manicure.

"I could have done that part for you, Carmen," I said.

"And, risk having you see anything on the papers? Not yet, *mija*. I need to get to know you first." She turned to the copier and fed the pages in, narrating the steps of Xerox operations for my benefit. "If the boys decide you're trustworthy, you too, will be allowed the privilege of the Xerox machine." Finally, some levity.

"How will I know if I pass the trustworthy test?" I asked.

"Be unobtrusive, don't screw up their coffee order, and you'll be fine," she said.

"Okay. This is the same model copier as the one at my school, I think I can handle it."

"Good to know." She placed the copies in a manila folder and handed it to me with mock ceremony. "Your first assignment. You get to meet Drew. Follow me."

Through the sliver of a window on the door to Drew's office, I could see five people seated around an oval conference table. The desk at the other end of the room was rendered almost invisible by the four computer monitors on top and beige cables snaking like vines down the front and underneath. A tall, bearded man rose from the table. He smiled as he approached the door. As he opened it, I handed him the envelope.

"New temp?"

"Alex."

He took the folder from me, looked me up and down, and then nodded to Carmen and returned to the meeting.

***

Temping, up to this point, had only served to enforce my opinion that most people are not all that bright, but this job was different. My first day at MS3 demonstrated that each person there, at least among the support staff I had met, was very, very intelligent. Most had traveled widely, and none of them seemed to have personal lives. While Carmen served as the primary receptionist, she, Molly and a guy named Mo rotated duty on the front desk when the other two were in meetings serving as translators and liaisons to other organizations. Between them, they were fluent in twelve languages that covered much of the developed world.

I was uncertain on exactly what kind of security the firm was providing, but had been instructed, firmly, not to ask questions. A few clients came in with architects carrying blueprints in long tubes. Complex schematics on oversized paper stretched out on the conference tables, but I had the growing suspicion that building security was only part of the story.

MS3 Senior Consultant Drew was classically handsome and impeccably dressed. He reminded me of someone, and I couldn't figure out who, until I was standing in the shower, getting ready for work the next morning and realized: Barry Gibb, member of the pop-music sensation, Bee Gees. Barry Gibb had made an album with Barbara Streisand. The album cover was a picture of Barry and Babs, dressed all in white, gazing at the camera from the grip of a soulful embrace. It had been Elaine's favorite album for three years running. Take away the charcoal suit, put Drew in a white disco shirt, and voila: Barry Gibb with slightly shorter hair and blue eyes instead of brown. I imagined that Drew enjoyed watching his reflection in shop windows as he strode from the metro to the office.

To get to M Street Security Services, I dropped Lainie off at day care, drove to the Metro, and took the Red Line into DC. It gave me a precious thirty-five minutes to myself, but instead of taking advantage of that uninterrupted time for some serious self-reflection, or perhaps personal betterment through reading Great Books, I simply stared out the window. The suburbs drifted across the windows until we sank below ground as we neared the city. The air conditioning was ineffective against the muggy air when the temperature reached eighty-five degrees before 8:00 a. m., and the backs of my thighs stuck to the orange plastic seats.

On Tuesday, I was called upon once again to deliver a packet to Drew's office. He stepped out of his office and motioned for me to walk down the hall a little way.

"Stand here with me for a minute and let's pretend to be discussing something very important." He said this under his breath, turning away from his office door.

"Do you need a break?" I asked.

He nodded very seriously. "God, yes. I really need a cigarette and coffee," he said, "and I need these guys to just shut the fuck up and agree that I am right, because I usually am."

I nodded very seriously in response, staring down at the grey and black patterned carpet.

"What are you right about?"

"That they are leaving the client exposed with their current plan, and that, if they don't follow my suggestions, things could get very ugly for them."

"That does sound serious."

"They are just being cheap assholes," he said.

"Do you want me to come in and take a coffee order?" I asked.

"Give me another fifteen minutes and come back to do that. What's your name again?"

"Alex."

"Let's have lunch together, Alex."

"What?"

"You're cute, I'm frustrated, and I'll buy," he said.

"Okay, well, if you're buying, how can I resist?"

"Nod a little more. This is a very serious discussion we are having."

"So, other than the assholes, what, exactly, are we talking about?" I asked.

"The weather. It's very serious," he said. We were standing rather close for two people who had just met. I could smell the smell of his aftershave mixed with the scent of shampoo, and noticed that the blue in the paisley of his pocket square matched the blue of his socks. His tie was anchored with a gold clip. Over his shoulder, I saw one of his clients watching us through the door.

"I think they want you back now," I said, gesturing with my chin toward his office.

"I think this is going to take a while. Lunch when the torture is over, coffee in fifteen. Okay?"

"Okay," I said.

Drew went back to the office. I made a U-turn to hunt down Molly. I needed a girlfriend to discuss the lunch situation with, stat. In the absence of a girlfriend, Molly would have to do. I found her in her office, headphones on, plugged into a CD Walkman, head almost imperceptibly bobbing the

beat of music as she wrote on a legal pad with a fluffy pink pen. I waited for
her to look up.

Looking up, she lifted one side of the headset off her left ear.

"Um, Drew just asked me to go to lunch with him. Is that okay?"

"You're a grown-up. It's fine," she said.

"I was just wondering if there was any company policy about things like
that that I should know."

"Nope. It's fine." She clamped the headphones firmly back on her ear and
went back to writing. I had hoped for a little more information, like, is he a
good guy? Is he a player? Am I making a mistake? Am I reading too much into the situation? I was left to answer on my own, so I picked: possibly, probably, maybe, and definitely.

The clock dragged on, far past lunch time. Just as I was about to abandon
the idea of a free lunch with a handsome man and head to the local McDonald's by myself, Drew and his clients emerged from the conference room. He
escorted them past my desk to the lobby where they shook hands all around
and seemed generally happier than before. Drew closed the mahogany door
behind them and motioned me to follow him.

"We'll go out the back way."

He strode through the corridor and down the fire stairs. Once out on the
street, the heat of the day sucked the breath out of my lungs as I struggled to
keep up with Drew's long strides.

"It's a little late in the day for an actual dining; I thought we could grab
some sandwiches and find some shade if that's alright with you."

"It's fine"

Two short blocks later, he ducked into an unremarkable doorway.

"Hey ya Howard, how's it going my brother?"

Drew reached over the counter to grab Howard's hand. Howard, a short,
grizzled, veteran deli-man wearing a white apron and hat, grinned at Drew.

"Hot enough for you, friend?"

"Almost, almost." Drew ordered as I squinted at the menu board hung
high above the meat cases. "Just tell him what you want, darlin', he hasn't
looked at that thing in years."

"Tuna on rye with lettuce and tomato, please," I said.

"So, Howard, how's Norv going to do this season?"

"I don't know. I don't know, man. I'm still not used to him. I kinda want Joe Gibbs back," Howard said over his shoulder as he sliced the ham for Drew's sandwich.

"That is a familiar refrain, my friend." Drew and Howard commiserated over the Redskins for a moment.

Howard assembled our sandwiches together as we pulled drinks from the cooler and looked for chips. We had missed the lunch crowd, so the deli was almost empty. Drew paid for our meal with a crisp twenty he pulled from a silver money clip, and impatiently waved away the change. Then he led me a little further down the street to a small park and stopped in front of a bench, which, indeed, had a patch of shade from a tree that seemed to be thriving in the heat of the day.

"I like this spot. I've got to get out of the office at least once a day. That air conditioning is going to kill me. If you go to lunch too early, you can't get the good benches here."

Drew popped a chip into his mouth. We held the paper-wrapped sandwiches on our knees and balanced the soda cans on the slats of the bench. I finished the first half of my tuna on rye in four bites while debating if it would be okay to remove my suit jacket. I was wearing a pink silk T-shirt underneath, so not too revealing, and the sweat was beginning to pool in the back of my skirt's waistband. Drew had removed his jacket and folded it across the back of the bench. Gently putting down the rest of my sandwich on a bed of waxed paper, I did the same. Drew nodded.

"Feels good, right?"

I nodded.

"How are you liking MS3?"

"It's fine for a temp job," I said.

"So is temping your full-time thing?"

"No, I'm a history teacher. High school." I said.

Drew wiped mayonnaise from his mustache.

"Do you love it?"

"Yes, actually, I do. I love the kids and I love the subject."

"I loved history," he said, biting a chunk out of his thick sandwich.

"Oh, that's so good to hear. I've found that people either love it or hate it, and when they hate it, it's usually because they had a hideous high school teacher. My mission in life is to make people really enjoy and appreciate history, which I know sounds really geeky, but that's me."

"So, you temp in the summer to make extra money," he said.

"Yes, I have a daughter so there are two mouths to feed."

"How old is she?" He asked.

"She's three, going on fifteen." Drew smiled. We were quiet while we finished our lunch, watching the passersby. Then I asked, "How long have you been at MS3?"

"A few years."

"I'm not allowed to ask questions, but, well, what kind of security do you guys do anyway? Drew's face broke into a wide smile and he threw his head back with a loud laugh. It was a deep, throaty, joyous sound that I immediately knew I wanted to hear again.

"No, you're not allowed to ask that," he answered.

"Can we play 'Twenty Questions'?"

"You can try."

He took my sandwich wrapper and chip bag from me to put in the trash, and we started walking back to the office, his pace much slower now.

"It seems as though you guys aren't just installing burglar alarms."

"Well, we do some of that."

"But..." I prompted.

"But..." he encouraged.

"But it's more than that; it's got a lot to do with computers, and I'm not sure why. I mean, I know you use camera monitors, but there's something else, too, right? I am guessing money, something to do with people's finances perhaps." I was walking sideways, angled towards him, trying to read Drew's face. I had onlyt been at the company for two days, but I had lots of questions.

"So," he said, "let's just have a conversation." I waited. We had less than five minutes before we got back to the office. "You use email, right?" I nodded. "So, what the general public is using right now is just the tip of the iceberg as to what computers can do. Someday, you may use a computer for things you can't imagine now, but one of those things is banking." He paused. I looked at him, and he continued. "Security companies like ours are working on how to protect their clients' assets as those assets get tied more and more to computers. We need to understand how to protect access to assets."

"And, by assets, you mean money."

"For the most part, yes. And that is where our conversation about MS3 ends. On another topic, have dinner with me," he said. It was not a question.

"As in, a date?"

"Yes."

"You did hear the part about my daughter?"

"Yes."

"Okay. Dinner would be nice, but I will have more questions," I said.

"We'll see what we can do to alleviate your curiosity. Let's say Thursday. I'll pick you up."

"Thursday is good, but I'll meet you somewhere." I said. And there it was, out of the blue again, that marvelous laugh.

"You are absolutely right to be cautious. Don't ever trust anyone after only one lunch, especially not me."

And with that, we were back at the office.

***

Thursday night dinner came and by this point, I had bought a navy sleeveless sheath dress for such an occasion. I had a light cashmere wrap from Elaine's collection that was patterned with blues and greys and a hint of pink in the flowers. I felt suitably grown up for a date with a man sixteen years my senior.

I met him at a slightly upscale Italian restaurant in Rockville, where the waiter placed the napkin in my lap, saving me the effort. Drew sat across from me, wearing a casual linen summer suit, his white shirt open at the collar. Barry Gibb and I had a private chuckle in my head.

The evening passed in a whirl of candlelight and charm. And that laugh. I let myself be talked into a glass of wine to go with my penne in lobster sauce, and left slightly dizzy with more questions rather than less.

After the date, I picked up a sleepy Lainie from Linda, and as soon as I got my sweet baby girl into bed, I called Cynthia.

"He speaks Cantonese?" she asked.

"Yep."

"And he lived in Hong Kong for four years?"

"Yes, but he didn't talk much about that."

"What did you talk about?"

"Different stuff we like to do in DC. A little bit about computers, which I didn't understand. Lots about the zoo. He has a thing for zoos and aquariums."

"Do you know where he lives?" she asked.

"He has an apartment in Pentagon City, I think he said, and a beach house in Delaware. Which sounds promising."

"School?"

"Notre Dame."

"Family?" asked Cyn.

"Parents still alive, still married. One sister. That's all I know. No apparent former wives. No kids."

"Hmmm." She thought for a moment. "Wait, let's go back to Hong Kong." Cynthia paused and I could hear the wheels cranking in her head. She continued. "Think about this for a minute. What would a Chinese-speaking, computer-expert white guy be doing in Hong Kong a few years before reversion?"

"He didn't really say."

"Think, Alex. Come on."

"Oh, God," I said.

"Yeah, I'm betting CIA."

"Maybe. Honestly, I would believe almost anything at this point. He's definitely colorful." I said, my mental wheels spinning too.

"Mmmm hmm. Surprised you didn't catch that Ms. Georgetown."

"That's a little far-fetched, even for you. You've been reading too many spy novels again," I said. We left it there.

I tiptoed into MS3 the next day, worried that word had gotten around about our date. I needn't have worried. Each of the security specialists had meetings with prominent clients, and I spent the day running from conference room to printer to copier and back. I took seven different coffee orders and went out to pick up lunch orders for two of the groups. At one point, I went into Drew's office to take their lunch order, and he handed me a note:

Hey Darlin'

A friend of mine gave me opera tickets for tomorrow night that he can't use.

Meet me at the Kennedy Center at 7:30.

We'll go out after.

Let me know.

I scribbled across the bottom of it: *I have to get a sitter. I'll let you know if I do. A,* and handed it back to him with the bill from lunch. Then I consulted my Filofax for possible babysitters and made furtive phone calls during my lunch hour. Carly was free. Thank goodness for high school girls without boyfriends. On the next file folder I handed Drew, I stuck a little yellow note on the cover that just said, "Success!"

I didn't know that by midnight Saturday, I would have suffered from a severe case of cultural whiplash accompanied by an unhealthy dose of adrenaline.

And, as usual, there was the wardrobe question. I would have chosen the blue dress but had already worn that to dinner. I was out of grown-up-sexy-date clothes.

Feeling somewhat like Meg in *Little Women* who is sent off to society balls without proper gowns, I knocked on Lori's door, holding out little hope that my farm-girl Mormon friend might have anything appropriate for me to wear that would also fit.

I stood in Lori's doorway, explaining my predicament. Before I could get the whole story out, she had dragged me to her bedroom and threw open the closet. She handed me a hanger and said, "I wore this when Fred and I were courting." It was a forest green knee-length sleeveless dress with a thin ribbon belt at the waist.

"I thought you guys didn't wear sleeveless things." She dove back into the closet and pulled out a matching jacket.

"This goes with it. I wore it, but you should probably skip it; it's a little too matchy-matchy. But wait a minute," she turned to a small dresser and started looking through the drawers. I couldn't help but notice how beautifully organized her closet was. All the hangers matched. Dresses hung with dresses. Slacks grouped together, then blouses, arranged by color. Even her overalls were neatly arranged. Add closet beautification to my to-do list. "Found it! You might want to wear this in case it gets chilly." Lori was holding a shimmering silk pashmina in peacock colors, greens, blues, brown and gold.

"I can't use this, it's too gorgeous. What if I spill something on it?" I asked.

"It's dry-cleanable. It's survived seven years and two continents with me. It will survive a night with you."

"Did you get this while you were on your mission?"

"Yes, that and *Totoro* are my two favorite things that came back with me from Japan. Also," she added as she walked me out, "make sure your sitter has my number if she needs anything."

"Thanks. I gave in and got a pager a few months ago, I think it's worth the ten bucks a month." I said, with an abundance of confidence.

"True. Have fun tonight!"

Green dress, black high-heeled sandals, Lori's wrap and gold jewelry from the Elaine collection made a complete outfit. I put on a little extra mascara during the Metro ride to complete the evening look. At 7:25 p.m., I strolled along the expanse of the Kennedy Center's Grand Foyer, the red carpet tickling my bare toes through the sandals.

The sun was beginning to set beyond the Potomac, casting a golden glow through the tall windows. I walked taller, the crown of my head reaching toward the chandeliers, my feet automatically turning out more with each step.

***

On another humid summer evening, in 1977, Elaine and I had walked around the side of Lincoln Center, looking for the stage door, hoping for a glimpse of Baryshnikov. During the ballet, Elaine had put her hand on my thigh and whispered, "Close your mouth, honey." It had been hanging open as I watched the virtuoso leap, hanging in midair, as though suspended by invisible cables. His white tights flashed and shimmered as he spun and charged across the stage. His dazzling athleticism caused the audience to collectively, audibly, draw in their breath more than once.

Back outside, my eyes were still adjusting to the twilight. The pebbled concrete pressed through the soles of my white Mary Jane's. I was mortified that my mom would stalk the artist, my idol (second only to Gelsey Kirkland), and was relieved when she couldn't find the back entrance. I was easily embarrassed at nine.

Not much had changed. Inside, I was nine. Outside, I was trying hard to pass for an adult. It was harder than it looked.

Drew stood at the foot of the stairs to the Opera Theater, wearing a dark suit for evening. His tie clip sparkled with three large diamonds. He brushed my cheek with his lips and put his hand in the small of my back to guide me in; both movements made my spine tingle.

"Hi darlin'. You look great. We have time for a quick drink before the curtain, do you want anything?"

"Sure, a glass of wine would be very nice, thank you." Without further inquiry as to what kind of wine I might like, Drew turned to the bartender and ordered a chardonnay for me and a gin and tonic for himself. We took our drinks to a high table near the wall. Drew's eyes casually skimmed across the room before coming back to me.

"Green is a good color on you."

"Thanks."

"Are you a fan of opera?"

"I'm more of a ballet girl, but I just love being in any theater. There is something about it."

"It's good for the soul. But I haven't seen this opera," he said.

"I thought most operas were Italian."

"Many are. This should be interesting. I probably wouldn't have picked *Boris Godunov*, but I don't like to pass on free Kennedy Center tickets."

"Agreed," I said.

The wine was chilled to the perfect temperature, but a tad sweet. Drew threw back his drink and suggested we find our seats. I set down the wine and followed.

We slipped into the center balcony seats just as the lights were dimming. The orchestra started to tune and Drew leaned over to whisper, "This is my favorite part." His voice rumbled in my ear. Something we shared.

Tuning sounds random and untidy until the instruments resolve into one, united, sustained chord. The reckless cacophony fills me with giddy anticipation, every time.

I wished I had read the synopsis, I was grateful for the surtitles scrolling across the top of the proscenium. Evidently it was a political opera, but, being Russian, the plot was overly gothic and complex, so I gave up on keeping track of the actual story and began studying the extras as they reacted to the action on stage. Shortly into the first act, Drew made a noise.

"Hmm," I glanced over at him. His eyebrows drew together in a frown. I raised my own eyebrows at him in a question. He shook his head.

More singing. A few minutes later, we repeated: He made a noise. I looked at him. He waved me off again.

And then, he sucked in his breath sharply. He was staring up at the surtitle screen. I leaned over.

"What's wrong?"

Eyes still focused on the words projected over the stage, he whispered, "I don't like the translation."

I sat back in my seat. So, the man speaks at least one dialect of Chinese, Russian, and God knows what else. He was fidgety. About forty-five minutes into the opera, things slowed to a crawl on stage. Drew whispered, "I think we've had enough culture. Let's leave at intermission. I have an idea."

I nodded in consent. Feeling the rush of cutting class, we walked down to the garage and got into his black Lincoln Town Car.

"Where are we going?"

"I thought we might go from the sublime to the ridiculous."

"Oh? "

"Have you ever been to Tracks?"

"The gay bar?"

"It's open to everyone, especially on the weekends. It's a riot. You'll have fun."

He navigated the way as though he had done this many times before. We headed into an industrial part of town outside of my usual radius, past vacant lots and a few burned out buildings before turning into a parking lot next to a warehouse lit up like a landing pad for the Mother Ship.

"You're going to want to leave your purse and wrap in the car," Drew advised.

I took my new beeper out of my clutch and clipped it onto the thin belt of the dress, then shoved the purse and the silk wrap behind the seat. Once out of the car, Drew reached for my hand. I wiped my sweaty palm on my dress before slipping my hand into his.

He walked in like he owned the place. I tried to keep my gaping to a minimum. Tracks was a massive space, packed with all sizes and variety of humanity. People were pierced in places I didn't know one could be pierced. Some were tattooed on every visible part of their skin, but an equal number could have walked off of any preppy campus quad and modeled for L.L. Bean.

Drew left me at the edge of one of the dance floors to get us drinks. While I was waiting, a male Hare Krishna, complete with one tiny braid growing out of the center of his shaved head, took me gently by the hand and led me onto the floor, where two dozen dancers were gyrating to George Michael. He smiled at me and started dancing. I expected him to pull out tiny finger cymbals from the pockets of his robe, but he didn't. I played along, and started swaying to the music, trying very hard to act like this was the most normal thing in the world, school-teacher-toddler-mom dancing in a gay bar with a yellow-robed Hare Krishna while her super-spy boyfriend goes to get cocktails. No big deal.

I looked around for Drew. *Just keep dancing, it's cool,* I chanted to myself as I danced. *No big deal.* Through a door toward the back, it looked like people were playing volleyball on an outdoor court. Too many minutes passed. *Maybe he got turned around and is looking at a different dance floor.* A girl joined me and the Hare Krishna, creating a dancing triangle. She was taller than me, wearing ripped, no, shredded jeans. Her black hair was cropped short in the back, with long bangs falling over half of her face. Black leather jacket, black high heels. Silver and black bracelets stacked up her arm. Nose pierced with a delicate silver hoop.

She made eye contact with me, and I found I was unable to look away. *It's cool. No big deal.* She swayed closer to me. Then closer. The one eye not obscured by her bangs had heavy black liner and purple eyeshadow. The Hare Krishna faded off to dance with someone else. I was drawn into the strange girl until I could smell the beer on her breath. *It's cool, just be cool.* She slid her hands around my waist and pulled me so close that our knees bumped, her eye still locked on mine. Her skin was pore-less perfection, her lips dewy with clear gloss. She slid her hands further across my lower back, then slowly down over my rear end. Mild Panic. *Just be cool.*

Then another pair of hands came at me from behind, a pair of man's hands, slipped in under the girl's hands and slid up under my breasts. I felt his body start to move in rhythm with ours. Drew's beard brushed the back of my neck, his deep voice spoke in my ear, "Looks like you're having fun, darlin.'"

My whole being tingled, tensed up and caught on fire all at the same time. I thought I was going to melt, or faint, or have an orgasm right then and there. The girl smiled at Drew and moved in even closer. Hips grinding, her breasts brushing my collar bone. Too many sensations. My brain was on total overload. I thought Drew and the girl were going to kiss each other over my shoulder when something bit me in the waist. It bit again hard, and we all jumped to disentangle our human knot.

I frantically felt around the belt for a snake or tarantula then remembered. "My beeper!" I yelled over the music. I held it up so they could see, the little rectangle screen lit up with my home phone number. A whole different order of panic set in. The girl gave us a little wave and wandered off. Drew's eyes swept the room looking for a payphone.

"Outside," he said.

I followed him out, weaving through the crowd of revelers. There was a phone on the outside wall, but someone was on it having a heated discussion with his dealer. Drew marched up to him and said, "Get off." The man hung up and walked away briskly without even a backward glance or a "fuck off," which I would have expected. I looked at Drew helplessly, my purse was in the car. He handed me a quarter from his pocket. I dialed. Misdialed. Hung up. Fished out the quarter. Dialed again. Busy. Tried again. Busy again. Started dialing again.

"You try again. I'll get the car," Drew jogged off. Busy again. He pulled up and I jumped in. He didn't wait for me to buckle my seatbelt before hitting the accelerator.

"270 North?"

"Yes." I forgot that I didn't want Drew to know where I lived.

He tore through the streets of DC, pausing at stop signs and treating traffic lights like mere suggestions. As we neared the entrance of the highway, he reached over, and with a tearing sound, pulled up a piece of black fabric that had been Velcroed to the dashboard to reveal a radar detector, which he flipped on. We rocketed down the highway, Drew drawing up so hard on people's bumpers that one tap of their brakes could kill us instantly, then slipping around the cars like they were standing still. I silently berated myself for not putting Lori's number in my purse. This always happens when I try to change purses: I forget something mission-critical.

I began to get chilly and pulled Lori's wrap closer around my shoulders, trying to suppress all the horrific images running through my head, all the ways my precious daughter could have been hurt or abducted. Maybe the line was busy because Carly couldn't get through to 9-1-1. Maybe the emergency operator was talking her through baby CPR. Maybe someone had broken into the apartment, abducted Lainie and cut the phone lines as they carried her off. Maybe Carly had called 9-1-1 and the attackers left her bleeding on the kitchen floor, phone off the hook, as they bundled Lainie away. Maybe. Maybe. Maybe.

"What exit?" Drew asked.

I focused on giving him directions, and on not vomiting between my fear for Lainie and of his driving. We skidded into the apartment complex and the car hadn't come to a full stop before I vaulted out and flew up the stairs. I pounded on the door, and as I was trying to get my key out of my little, stupid purse, Carly opened the it.

All was quiet

Nothing out of place.

Carly held a piece of pizza drooping in her hand, and said with her mouth full, "Hey, you're back early."

Fear dissolved into rage. I wanted to smack her.

"You paged me! What was wrong?" I was trying not to scream. Thankfully for Carly, Drew had followed and was standing behind me, placing a calming, and yes, restraining hand on my shoulder.

"Oh, I just wanted to know when you'd be home. I was getting bored."

I stepped forward, choking on my words, "But I tried to call you and the phone was busy. Do you have any idea how worried I was? I thought something terrible had happened." My tone was on the verge of screeching. Drew stepped closer and put his other hand on my other shoulder.

"Oh, I'm sorry, I was probably on the phone with the pizza guy. He got the address mixed up." Carly said.

I stormed past her to the bedroom. Lainie was sound asleep, Lolly tucked in her arms. I didn't care if I woke her, I needed to feel the whole weight of her in my arms. I scooped her up and slid to the floor, smelling her hair, feeling my heart rate return to normal. I heard voices in the living room, and knew I should go back out, but I didn't.

After a few minutes, Drew appeared in the doorway. He came in and sat on my bed, watching the two of us in the street light glowing through the pink curtains.

"You okay?"

"Yeah," I whispered. "Sorry for freaking out."

"Totally understandable."

"I need to go pay Carly."

"I took care of it," he said.

"I'll pay you back."

"Nah." He waved it off like he had waved off the change from Howard.

"Thank you. For everything." I eased Lainie back into her bed, and we went back to the living room. "I'd invite you to stay for a drink, but I only have apple juice and Diet Coke." And suddenly, I was very, very tired. I just wanted to sleep.

"Come here, Babe." Drew wound his long arms around me and I leaned into his chest. I could have stayed there for hours. But Rational Alex still had her guard up and pulled me away. "That was a little more eventful than we planned," he chuckled. "Do you need help getting your car in the morning?"

"No, it's at a metro stop near here. I'll get Lori to take me."

We pulled apart.

"You should go to bed, you look worn out," he said.

"I am."

"Okay, I'll see you soon." He gave me a quick, soft kiss on the lips, and was gone.

***

Come to the beach house. Bring Lainie and she'll have a blast playing in the ocean. He said. It sounded like a great idea at the time: a calm, normal, weekend away. I thought it would be an old, rambling place on stilts with a big kitchen and bedrooms filled with lots of friends, and friends of friends. He gave me the impression that he invited people to the beach house all the time and that I was just one of many guests he entertained every weekend. I thought this was just a casual summer getaway. I should just stop thinking.

We had arrived late Friday evening. Instead of a well-worn beach bungalow populated by close friends eating barbeque, we pulled into the driveway of a modest colonial on a cul de sac with nary a grain of sand in sight.

I set up a bed for Lainie in the guestroom. Drew opened a window so we could hear her from the patio if she cried. We sat outside, Drew enjoying a cocktail while I drank a diet Coke and tried to affect a 180 degree shift in my expectations for the weekend. After about an hour, I kissed him on the cheek and went back to the guestroom.

I was roused from a deep sleep by a low rumble. As I woke, I slowly recognized the noise as the introduction to a song, seconds before it erupted into a full-scale rock concert. The walls shuddered. I feared the framed Elvis posters would crash to the floor. I groped my way across the guest room to Lainie's portable cot, thinking I'd have to comfort my child, but she was out cold, oblivious to the drunken braying emanating from the living room. I stumbled down the stairs, shielding my eyes. Every light was blazing in the house. I heard Drew sing,

I love you, baby, baby.

You are the most beautiful lady.

I fought against the tide of the music, wading into the living room.

He was standing in the small square of brown carpet between the couch and two armchairs. Drew posed, his back to me, clutching the microphone of his home karaoke machine in one hand, a cigarette and rocks glass balanced in the other. There was a musical interlude. He waited, head nodding low between his shoulders, arms outstretched, feeling the love of his imaginary crowd. His beard brushed against his hairless, shirtless chest. He wore bright red eighties-era jogging shorts and nothing else. The music throbbed into a crescendo and his head jerked up. I could see his ribcage expand, pulling in oxygen, and it started again. No human being should be able to sing that loudly outside of an opera house. It was deafening. The microphone was superfluous. His skinny hips swiveled. He sang,

Oh, never, never leave me
I can't take it. I'll give you my key
Can't you see, I'll pay the fee...

The scotch swirled precariously in the glass. Drew's knees buckled. For an instant I thought he was having a heart-attack. Instead, he performed the Elvis move of swinging one knee in and out with the beat. The knee swung, the head bobbed, the ice in the scotch rattled. Just when I thought I'd need to find the fuse box and flip the breaker on the electricity, the noise stopped. The song ended. In the pause between tracks, I tried to speak.

"Drew," I said. He didn't hear me. His eyes were glazed, lost in Graceland or somewhere. "Drew," I tried again. Nothing. I shouted his name again.

"What?" He spun to look at me. He looked irritated and annoyed to be pulled back from his fantasy stage into the living room.

"Sweetie, could you tone it down a bit? Lainie and I are sleeping. *You idiot, your neighbors are either deaf or on the phone to the police right this moment.*

"But this is what I do on Saturday nights. I like it loud." Drew's eyes swam in clear juice. He looked at me. He was petulant and very, very drunk. Odd that one can feel grateful for having a recovering alcoholic for a father at moments such as this. Few things shocked me.

So, instead of saying, *Look you bizarre Elvis freak-show, put down the microphone and get to bed,* I said, "Honey, I'm not asking you to stop, just turn it down a little, please. Lainie's not used to this kind of noise." Hell, Lainie could sleep through The London Blitz. It would take a lot more than eighty decibel karaoke to jar her from slumber, this was only upsetting to me.

The next day began calm inside the house and rainy outside. We took the ferry to his parent's house, again, something I was not warned about, nor did it fit into my paradigm for "weekend at the beach."

Last night's Karaoke King had vanished with the light, like a vampire. The ninety-minute boat trip brought back why I liked this guy so much. Standing at the rail on the deck, I saw again how his eyes were exactly the blue grey of an overcast sky. His smile was quick and easy, and he doubled over with laughter whenever I said anything particularly funny. In Drew, I found someone who was a bigger repository for arcane knowledge than myself.

"See that seagull?" he said.

"Yes."

"See the red spot on its beak?"

"Yeah"

"When mothers bring food back to the nest for their young, the chicks have to peck at the dot to get the food. It teaches them cause and effect, and beak-eye coordination."

"Get out."

"No, really." He smiled like a kid. Why did it always have to be the crazy people who were so interesting?

Drew bought Lainie a treat from the snack bar and chased her around the deck, giggling as much as she did at their game of dragons and princesses. I wondered why he wanted us to meet his parents. But it was an overcast day, not good for the beach, so I didn't mind. At the dock, Drew's dad met us in a gleaming blue Cadillac, a few years old but meticulously maintained. No one seemed to worry that I hadn't thought to bring Lainie's car seat. The previous night's activities had left me a little addled. I buckled her in as well as I could, the seat swallowing her until I thought she might disappear into the fine Corinthian leather. I kept up a silent prayer for the whole ride.

While a person's bookshelves tell you about their personality, a visit to a person's parents' house shortcuts the getting-to-know-you process by miles. Glenda and Greg were not minimalists. End tables were covered in doilies (the same pattern as in Drew's house, which answered that question). Doilies were layered with magazines accessorized by figurines who battled for space with ornate lamps in fringed shades. The top of Glenda's sewing basket was festooned with seashells. The Bible sported a needlepoint jacket, and the sofa donned a chintz slipcover. Wall-to-wall carpeting was smothered in throw rugs. Apparently, nothing was good enough in its natural state.

Every flat surface was embellished like a neo-Victorian movie set. We were introduced to Bitsy, the hyper Shih Tzu who wore a sweater knitted with miniscule toy poodles dancing across her shoulders. The smells came in layers too: mildew from upholstery exposed to sea air, something cooking, Glenda's perfume, and Pine-Sol clashed in the air. The house was a toddler parent's nightmare. I held Lainie on my lap. The only saving grace to the clutter was that everywhere I turned some object, oddity or photograph presented itself as a conversation life buoy. *How old was Drew in this picture? Where did you find this wooden Indian headdress? Did you make these macramé plant hangers?* Five minutes into the visit, I knew it was going to be a very long afternoon.

"You have a lovely home, Mrs. Dorr." I smiled at her.

"Glenda, please. Would you like a tour?"

"Oh, yes, please." I turned to Drew and asked him to keep an eye on Lainie. Bitsy and Lainie had hit it off and were playing, very quietly, on the carpet. He nodded and I began to follow Glenda up the stairs. We didn't get far. The wall in the stairway was covered with photographs.

"This is Drew at his high school graduation. This is Andrea, his sister, at their cousin's wedding. This is a picture of the four of us when we traveled to Greece. Two years ago now." She went on. And on.

We entered a small room to the left. "This is my sewing room. I do lots of other crafts here as well, as you can probably tell." On one side of the room was a sewing table with two machines and a rack holding spools of thread. A table covered with containers of seashells and hot glue guns was on the other side. In the corner was a rocking chair flanked by a needlepoint stand. Next to the chair was a basket full of yarn, and on yet another small table, a collection of crocheted baby items in pinks and yellows and blues.

"These are darling, Glenda. Who did you crochet them for?" I asked.

"My grandchildren, who are very slow in coming. But I also donate lots of them to the church." Her hands on her hips, she cocked her head to one side, looking at the little sweaters.

"And next door is the guest room. We ran out of room for all the kids' medals and trophies, so we keep them in here. I put the case opposite the window so the mirrors would reflect light into the room. It's very nice in here in the winter when the days are gloomy." The entire rear wall was covered with mirrors and glass shelves on which were dozens, maybe more like a hundred, awards and trophies. There were eight-by-ten frames with certificates and ribbons. In one of the pictures, next to a very large gold cup, a young lady held that same cup over her head in the middle of a tennis court, her racket at her feet. Andrea was also pictured in a ballet costume, and elsewhere, on stage, singing. There were awards and statuettes with Drew's name engraved on them as well. The photos showed a younger, but unmistakable Drew, one in formal attire at a piano. Another of him in a speedo perched on a starting block. Everything sparkled in the dim light. I couldn't help but think of all the dusting.

"This way, you can see the backs of the trophies too," Glenda said. Her children, were both over forty. Was this odd or normal for parents of adult children? I didn't know.

"That must have been a lot of work for you, too." *I have a hard enough time getting Lainie to dance lessons and affording that.*

"It was. Greg did side jobs and I took in ironing and sewing to pay for extra coaching and lessons. You'll do the same for Lainie. She is a precocious child. Loads of potential." She sighed and led me back toward the living room.

In the middle of dinner (which was served at 3:30 p.m. so we could catch the last ferry back). Glenda turned to me and said, "Andrew tells me you're di-vorced." She pronounced each syllable. I was taken aback. I didn't realize that Drew had spoken about me with his parents. It wasn't like we were dating. Did he think we were dating?

As for Glenda's query, I did know this from past experience: when people ask you that question, they really don't want to know what was wrong with your spouse, or the marriage; what they are really looking for is what is wrong with you. They want to know why you couldn't make things work out. Were you lazy, or immoral, or foolhardy? *Well, yes, but it's complicated.*

"Well, we were pretty young and it turned out not to be a great match." It also occurred to me that this was not an appropriate subject of conversation in front of Laine, but thankfully, she was very busy with her mashed potatoes.

Glenda grilled me further through dinner. She wanted to know about my *people*. Where had I gone to school? Where were my parents from? What kind of work did my father do? She expressed surprise that my mother had been a successful businesswoman. It appeared that I got low marks for not playing tennis or a musical instrument but gained a few for horseback riding and a brief collegiate stage career. I didn't think I measured up to her expectations. Drew and his dad kept a side conversation going to themselves. Drew got up from the table more than once to refill his martini.

On the ferry back to Drew's house, I let Lainie go nuts. She had hours' worth of pent-up energy and it all came out as she ran in circles on the deck, arms spread out like airplane wings, around and around. Back at the house, after I had read three stories and finally got Lainie to settle down, I stood in the bathroom, plotting my escape. If I'd left Lainie with her dad, I could have pretended to check my voicemail and created an emergency situation that would force me to drive home right then.

I was coming up empty. There was no reasonable excuse to drag a kid out of bed and drive home three hours this late in the evening. He would demand an explanation and he wouldn't like the truth. I am a wimp about the truth. As fun and sexy as Drew was, between the drinking, the cryptic things he couldn't, or wouldn't, talk about from work, the cloudy past, the multiple foreign languages and tactical driving skills, things weren't adding up to equal a quiet home life with a dog and two or three more kids. Especially the drinking. That, I couldn't get past.

I rinsed my toothbrush and was tapping it on the side of the sink when Drew snuck in behind me and grabbed my left hand. He squeezed, and when I looked down, to my shock and horror, there was a two-carat diamond ring on my fourth finger. It winked at me in the fluorescent light of the bathroom. I suppressed a shriek. What the hell was this? A proposal? In the bathroom? Was he joking?

Before I had time to really think, he pranced away shouting, "It fits! It Fits! I thought it would!" He waltzed back into the bathroom and grabbed my hand again as I was leaning over to spit the toothpaste out before I choked. He admired the ring on my hand for half a second, and unceremoni-ously yanked it off my finger.

"It's a sign, Alex! It's a sign!" he sang out as he went back to the bedroom to hide the ring away again.

I stared into the mirror, not seeing my sleepy faced self, but watching as my imagination unfolded a sick, fully formed scenario. Drew was not just the secretive security specialist I was not-quite dating, but possibly a sociopathic serial killer luring unsuspecting victims to his beach house where he would garrote them with piano wire and bury their bodies in the foundation under the cover of darkness.

Nothing. Nothing had prepared me for this. I was baffled. *One of us in this house needs Prozac, and I'm not sure it's me.*

Drew was already back in the living room. Once I had composed myself, I carefully approached the couch and sat down. He leaned forward and set his drink on the coffee table and then trained his deep blue eyes on me.

"I don't let just anyone try that ring on, you know," he said.

"Well, I would hope not." Try to keep things light. Deflect.

"Alex, I think you are very special." He leaned in and kissed me. His lips were gentle and his beard was soft. He pulled away. "What do you think?"

I think I am very special too, Mr. Rogers, is what my brain said. I said, "I think you're a very interesting person, and I enjoy spending time with you." *Mostly.*

"Do you think we could do more than just *hang out*? Eventually?"

This is where Dating Referee would come in handy, again. I had no idea what he was really asking me. Ten minutes ago, he had shoved an engagement ring on my finger. He had taken me to meet his parents, and, if my memory was correct, we had been out on a total of two dates and one lunch. This was not following any kind of recognizable pattern.

I weighed my options. If I left the house now, I'd have to wake up Lainie and piss off Drew. I was fairly certain that he didn't have any piano wire around and tried to reason with myself that I would live through the night. I leaned over and kissed him, and said, in my best movie star voice, "Eventually." I smiled at him and decided to stay until the morning, but I could not bear another Karaoke fiasco, so I sweetly suggested that we watch a movie.

I was solicitous and made sure his drink was never empty. By eleven o'clock he was out cold, and we all got a decent night's sleep, Drew on the couch and me curled around Lainie on the bed in the guest room. Between his drinking and the weird dynamic with his parents, this had to end quickly. But mostly because of the drinking. It was not good.

***

The last day at the temp job was the Thursday after what I thought of as the weirdest weekend of my life. The metro rides had given me ample time to contemplate the situation. Yes, I could be edgy. I could let strange, exotic women feel me up in the middle of a dance floor. I could appreciate opera and keep spy secrets. But really, I wanted to be a mom. A soccer mom or a stage mom. I wanted to dance in the living room with my kids and sing to the *Little Mermaid*. I couldn't see the intersection of that particular Venn diagram: Glamorous Alex and Mom Alex. I could stare out the train window for months and not make it work.

Drew had been busy with clients all day, so I waited until after his last client to talk to him.

"Hey," I said, walking into the training room as he was shutting down the computers.

"Hey!" He turned toward me with a broad smile and came toward me like he was going in for a kiss.

"Um, I just wanted to say that maybe we got our signals crossed."

"Oh, how so?" He glanced toward the door to make sure we were alone, then turned his full attention on me.

"I, um, well, I don't think anything could really work out between us. I just thought that we were having some fun, and you seemed, well, to take it a little more seriously."

"You mean the ring?"

"Well, that, and meeting your parents . . . it's all going very fast, and I just want to get back to my routine with school and Lainie, and all of that."

"Oh." He continued to hold my gaze but didn't say anything. So, I pressed on.

"There's also the age difference."

"It's only fifteen years."

"Sixteen."

"So?" he asked.

I was grasping for straws. I couldn't tell him that his drinking scared the shit out of me. Once again, I was trying to extract myself from a tricky situation. Houdini and his straight jacket. One more time for good measure.

"Look, Alex, I know last weekend was weird, and I know that you think things are going too fast. I get that. I'll back off. But I do love talking to you. Can I call you from time to time?"

I couldn't resist that Barry Gibb face, so I said, "Okay."

To ensure that this didn't go any further, and because I am not good at confrontation in any form, I wrote Drew a letter and mailed it to him at MS3.

Dear Drew,

It has been very interesting getting to know you. You are so intelligent, witty and fun. But, because above all else, I respect you, I am going to be frank. I don't see how things could work out between us. There are two things that are getting in the way. First, and I hate to admit this, I think our age difference is too big. You have seen and experienced so much, and I feel like I am just starting my journey. Second, your drinking is too much for me to handle. There is a great deal you don't know about my background, and, suffice it to say, I have been hurt too many times by people who drink too much for me to be comfortable having a long-term relationship with you. I am certainly not asking you to change because, of course, that would have to be your choice and your decision. Also, even if you quit drinking, that wouldn't guarantee that my overall feelings about you would change. Maybe if our timing had been better, things would have been different. As it is, I'd like to thank you for some interesting adventures and wish you all the best.

Alex

***

That Saturday, as Lainie and I returned from an evening hike at the local nature preserve, I saw the light on in my apartment, and Drew's car in a spot by the entrance. He must have talked Ed in the management office into letting him in. Ed and I were going to have a serious talk. *Drew must not have gotten the letter.* That was the only reasonable explanation for him to be in my apartment. The other reason being that he wanted to discuss the letter in person, something I just didn't want to deal with. *Why wasn't he at the beach house?* It was dark. I circled the parking lot and backed the car between two larger ones in a space where I could see the light in my apartment, but he probably wouldn't see us.

"Mommy, why are we parking here?"

"Hang on a minute, Lainie." *Mommy needs to think of something.* I waited and watched the apartment. "I am trying to remember if we have anything in the house for dinner," I said.

"Oh." Still no movement from the apartment. We waited five, then ten minutes. The light stayed on. I restarted the car. "Now where are we going?" she asked.

"Up to you!" Cheery Voice! "McDonald's or Taco Bell, where would you like to go?"

"Taco Bell! Taco Bell!" Lainie bounced in her seat. We killed time there, sharing a taco meal and doing our best to eat with a spork. When we pulled back into the apartment complex, our window was dark and Drew's car was gone. There was a note on the dining table.

Sweetie:

Thought I'd come by and take you girls out to dinner. Sorry I missed you. Call to let me know you got in okay.

Miss you,
Drew.

I didn't call. A week later, a letter arrived in the mail.

Darlin'

You've given me so much to think about. I appreciate your letter and understand why you couldn't say those things to me in person. That would be a very tough conversation to have, but I wish you had tried. I think you were correct in your assessment that the timing wasn't right for us. Perhaps if we had met at a different point in both of our lives, things would have worked better. You need to know that you are a very intelligent, wonderful person, and any man would be lucky to have you in his life. You are also correct in that I need to get a grip on some of my vices. Just remember, though, you have room for growth too. I know that you're trying to figure out what the future will be for you and Lainie, but take some time to really figure out who you are. You're not quite there yet.

You will always have a place in my heart, and a helping hand should you need it. You know how to reach me.

Love, truly,
Drew

P.S. You don't need to worry about the druggies in your apartment complex any more.

D.

That postscript kept me awake at night for week.

Chapter Fourteen
September, 1996

It was the first day of school.

I was awake an hour before the alarm was set to go off at 5:00 a.m. We were both going to new schools. Lainie was going to a preschool/day care that was so exclusive and expensive that my new boss put in two decades worth of favors owed her by the director to get Lainie in, and that I was going to have to sell a pound of flesh to afford. But its proximity to my new job and reputation for excellent made it worth every penny. I was headed to a new school where no ghosts of affairs-past lurked in the hallways. I couldn't wait.

I put on my serious but fashionable olive silk suit and an amber necklace from India that had been a birthday present from Elaine. I lay the suit jacket carefully on the couch. my briefcase, a canvas tote for larger books and papers, and both of our lunch bags were piled next to the front door. Lainie's Pocahontas backpack was loaded with an emergency change of clothes and her stuffed friend in case the going got tough. At 6:00 a.m., I woke her.

"Hey Pumpkin, time to get up." She burrowed further into the covers. "Come on sweetie, first day of school! Let's go!" I rubbed her back. She made a noise between a squeak and a groan. "Okay, now." I lifted her out of bed.

After a breakfast of frozen waffles and cereal, we had a debate over her attire. I had to convince her that the Cinderella crown and marabou slides didn't go with her hand-smocked blue First Day of School Dress we had picked out the week before.

"Besides, Lainie, I think there is a rule about the kind of shoes you can wear on the playground."

"Oh, yeah," she said, "wood chips."

"So, how about your Keds?"

"Okay."

The sky was beginning to lighten as we loaded everything into the car. The drive wasn't bad at that hour. Commuting with my child meant that I could use the carpool lanes, and as we flew past people in slower-moving vehicles, I worried that I might get pulled over, as Lainie's head was barely visible through the window of the Acura.

We listened to NPR as we cruised down the highway. As we turned onto the school's side street, the mown lawns and trimmed hedges looked crisp with anticipation. The first day of school: the feeling that everything is fresh and new, that pencils are sharp and notebooks are clean. The feeling that keeps me coming back every year.

Lainie's teacher was waiting at the gate. I hoisted my daughter out of the back seat and handed her the backpack. I knew some moms cried the first time their kids went to school, so, I stood for a moment, waiting for the welling-up to happen. It didn't; we were both too excited.

"Have a great day Honey! I love you!"

"Love you too, Mommy." She gave me a quick hug, then turned to her new teacher and unleashed a torrent of words, and I knew that she'd be fine.

First day at my new school was progressing nicely. I had three classes before lunch. The kids were on good behavior, and only one or two found themselves in the wrong classroom. At lunch, the phone on the wall rang.

"Hi Alex, it's Edie in the main office." She sounded giddy.

"Yes, is everything okay?"

"There is a delivery for you down here." There was a smile in her voice. My stomach did a flip-flop. It must be flowers, but from whom? I hustled down the stairs, and as I rounded the corner, I could see through the glass wall of the office that there was indeed a large flower arrangement sitting on the counter that separated the secretaries from the masses. Edie winked at me.

"Who are they from?"

"I have an idea." I pulled the little card from its envelope and my happiness evaporated. It wasn't Lester's spidery handwriting in black Flair Ultra Fine. It was the bold, all caps Mont Blanc blue-black handwriting that made my shoulders droop.

Good Luck on your First Day, Teach.

Quinn

"Teach." He was trying to be hip. I must have mentioned my new job during one of our sailing sessions. I was annoyed, but the flowers were beautiful.

"Here, Edie, these look very pretty on your desk. Happy First Day of School."

"You don't want them?" Her eyes opened wide.

"Nope." I strode out of the office before she had a chance to ask why, and walked back up the stairs, deflated.

***

According to Lainie, she has an African Granny who hasn't seen her since she was a little bitty baby, but she lives in Africa helping people, and it was alright that she didn't see African Granny all that often because Granny sent Lainie animals instead. They were lined up on a shelf over her bed. Not sweet Noah's ark animals, but fierce, exotic miniatures carved from bone or wood.

But now, African Granny was sitting at the small table that served as our dining room, talking to Lainie as if she stopped by for cookies and milk every afternoon after school. It didn't matter to either of them that this was their first visit in two and a half years. This time, Granny hand delivered the tiny Greater Kudu rather than sending it in the mail. I hardly recognized my mother. Since the christening, she seemed to be aging backwards like Merlin. Her limbs were strong and sinewy, and she wielded them with new grace. The remnants of *Beautiful You* hair color #48 had finally grown out, leaving her hair almost completely white, but I'd have sworn that there were fewer wrinkles on her face than before.

I was standing in the galley kitchen, making lunch, when my mom rose from the table and asked, "May I borrow a sweater? I have a chill." My hands were covered in mayonnaise.

"Help yourself, my closet is the one on the left." She walked the three steps into the bedroom.

"Oh my God, Alex, you still have all of these?" I wiped off my hands and followed her to my bedroom to find her staring into the closet at the three canvas shoe holders hung side by side, like an old-fashioned post office, with a total of twenty-eight cubbies. Each slot in the first two columns held what had once been my mother's prize collection of Ferragamo ballet flats, one in each color, plus neutrals. She and I wore the same shoe size and I had inherited the lot after Elaine's second mission trip to Africa. Once, when Lester had looked upon this vast collection of rainbow-colored footwear, he jokingly questioned if we could ever be happy together.

"Do you actually wear these?" she asked in amazement. I hesitated. It had been one of her great joys: endless excursions to Nordstrom's for shoes. I had been dragged across Manhattan to Bottega Veneta to Gucci to Bruno Magli. Salespeoplefawned over Elaine. She had curated an impressive collection. The shame of it was I hated wearing flats. I was too short to begin with, and the little bows just didn't work for me. They sat, neglected, in their little bins.

"Well, sometimes I wear the black ones. I do prefer heels." I cringed, waiting for the these-are-classy-and-expensive-shoes-you-should-wear-them lecture.

"Oh, for goodness sake, get rid of them." Before I could move, she had retrieved empty shopping bags from the hall closet and began piling shoes in. "You need more closet space anyway," she added. I watched, embarrassed that my mother was cleaning out my closet.

"Mom, I can do that, really."

"It will just take a minute. Hand me another shopping bag." I did. She methodically loaded it with thousands of dollars' worth of footwear. I stood feeling guilty, as though I'd rejected her largesse of hand-me-downs, or worse, rejected our shared history of shopping trips and fancy New York luncheons. As one pastel shoe followed another into the bags, I remembered the uniform my mom had created for herself when I was young. She greeted each day with a smile and a tailored suit, a pressed blouse and matching shoes. I couldn't tell what she was thinking.

"I can run them over to the Salvation Army in the morning," I offered.

"No, those cretins wouldn't know what these are. They cost a fortune. Good God, what was I thinking?" She paused, pulling a pair of chartreuse shoes out of a fabric case and waving them about angrily. "One pair of these things could buy a *case* of school books for the children." (She meant those in Africa, of course.) Elaine grabbed another pair, lost in thought.

"I've got it!" She brightened. "We'll take them to that resale shop in Bethesda, sell them on consignment, and then I can use the proceeds for the mission. The kids get supplies, someone gets to wear great shoes and you get more closet space!" She tossed the last pair into a bag. "That's so much better."

Lainie walked in the bedroom looking for Lolly. She stared at her mother and grandmother sitting on the floor in front of the closet surrounded by bags of shoes. She didn't know what to make of us. Neither did I.

**

That night I had a dream. I was walking in Central Park, mid-summer haze blurring everything. I came to a stone tunnel, and thought the air inside might be cooler, so I approached. A griffon stepped out of the shadows, blocking the entrance, his lion body and eagle head in silhouette. It was a short tunnel made by the road crossing overhead. Piled high on the other end of the tunnel were clear plastic shoeboxes, neatly stacked, blocking the way through. It should have been dark in the tunnel, but the translucent boxes were lit from behind. I could read the labels and see the pumps, flats and sandals outlined in each of them. The griffon looked at me with one of his beady eyes, and, in the voice of Robert DeNiro said, "Fugget about the shoes. Fugget-about-em." I walked away.

**

After the great shoe purge, the rest of Mom's visit went far too quickly. She wanted to take Lainie to the zoo. I was trying to block the whole Josef incident from memory when Lainie decided to recount the whole story, including the vomiting part, to her grandmother. They laughed hysterically at the part about the orangutan.

That week, while Lainie and I were at school, Elaine scoured thrift shops and secondhand bookstores for things she could take back to the mission. In the evenings, we were content with simple dinners and walks around the duck pond.

Too soon we were back at the airport, Elaine's suitcase full to bursting with used children's clothes and her carry-on bulging with books and old *Highlights* magazines. Lainie and I went through security with Elaine and walked her to the gate. We stayed for an hour, Lainie and Granny playing I Spy with My Little Eye.

"Good evening," said a voice over the speakers, "we are continuing boarding for Flight 283 to Harare. Those holding boarding passes from rows forty-five to sixty, please proceed to the jetway." Mom would catch a flight to Lilongwe from there.

"That's me." Elaine hugged Lainie, and then turned to me. I held my mother tightly. A great balloon of emotion swelled unexpectedly in my chest, accompanied by an equally unwelcome lump in my throat. This is how we had always behaved, conducting our independent lives at long distance; pretending that the ties that held us together were light and loose, that we could function as liberated women, loving and supporting one another at a distance, not acknowledging that it wasn't exactly what either of us wanted.

After a week of discussing every other possible topic, she finally addressed what had become my obsession. "Forget about the men, honey; the right one will come along. You just need to be patient. Stop worrying about it." She whispered this into my shoulder. We parted and I nodded.

"I know. I'm going to miss you." I managed to whisper.

"I'm going to miss you too, but you're doing fine. I'll be back in a few months. Love you." She kissed my cheek and walked briskly to the plane, only pausing to show her passport and boarding pass to the attendant. Elaine thinks she's tough, but I knew she was weepy too.

***

The phone was ringing as I walked in the door from the gym. Call it instinct, but I knew it wasn't good. Tonight was Ken's night to pick up Laine from day care. It was 5:50 p.m., which could only mean one thing.

"Hello?

"Hi Alex, it's Joan from preschool, Ken still isn't here." She was trying to be polite but *pissed-off* oozed through the phone.

"Is Lanie okay?"

"Yes, she's fine, just tired."

"I'm so sorry! I am on my way. It will take me thirty minutes at best, but hopefully he'll be there soon."

"Thank you," she said, not hiding her irritation.

I ran out the door and in ten minutes was flying down the highway in a fugue state. Enraged about Ken's total lack of dependability. Worried about Lanie. Engulfed by flames of mortification at the day-care lady's scolding.

Shit-shit-shit-damn-damn-damn-this-is -unbelievable-I-can't-believe-he's-fucking-doing-this.

Irresponsible-head-up-his-ass-can't-find-his-butt-with-two-hands-and-a-road-map-dick-bag.

Responsible Alex broke into my tirade.

If you don't slow down you're going to die and you don't want to give him the satisfaction.

The speedometer read ninety-seven. I eased off the accelerator just in time to make the exit. On the side roads, I slammed through the Acura's gear box as though Ken's head was attached to the other end of the stick shift.

Then Responsible Alex remembered that the neighborhood shrews loved to look out their windows and call the police on day care parents for speeding. Those biddies had nothing better to do.

As I pulled up, I saw that the gates of the day care center were chained and locked. I parked and tried to get out of the car on shaking legs. The building was dark. Everyone was gone. I had wasted my time for Ken. Again.

Back in the car, I drove very carefully to the closest 7-Eleven. Still quivering with rage, I dug a quarter out of my purse and jammed it in the pay phone. Ken picked up.

"Let me talk to Lanie." I said. He was smart enough not to say anything as he handed the phone over.

"Hi Mama!"

"You okay baby?"

"Yeah"

"What are you doing?"

"I'm helping make sketties."

"Ok sweetie, I love you. Give the phone to Dad."

"Hi Alex, look, I'm sorry–"

"Skip it. Just don't do that to me or to Lanie ever again." I hung up before the conversation could devolve in front of Lanie. No, I didn't hang up. I slammed the receiver into the metal cradle, one time for each syllable. You. Son. Of. A. Bitch. I shoved open the door to the 7-Eleven with equal fury. The clerk took a step further back from the counter. *Freezer.* Ben and Jerry's. *Fridge.* Diet Coke.

A young man rang me up, eyeing me cautiously. But as he took the cash out of my trembling hand, he held up one long thin finger and said, "Wait, please." He ducked behind the counter and produced two plastic spoons. As he handed them to me he said, rich Punjabi vowels dripping from his lips, "Take two spoons. That is in case the first one breaks. You need them."

"Thank you." I squinted at his name tag. "Naveen."

"You are most welcome." Naveen, my unexpected prophet of ice cream and kindness. I made a note to add him to my prayer list.

And yes, one can drive a manual transmission and eat Phish Food at the same time.

Chapter Fifteen
October, 1996

I wandered into the cafeteria of my new school for the second faculty meeting of the year, preoccupied with how I was going to rearrange my classroom and continue to plan for a course I'd never taught before with no textbook and a thin curriculum guide. There was a table by the door with plates of donuts and a pile of agendas. I was late and since there were no seats left at the table full of social studies teachers, I glanced around trying to a. be inconspicuous, b. grab a donut and c. find a vacant seat. As Dr. Hall (Thumbelina) was talking, I settled into a chair in the back. There was only one other person at the table.

"And at our first meeting, we ran out of time to introduce new staff..." the principal was saying. I had a mouth full of powdered donut when I heard her say, "And we welcome Alexandria Smythe to the Social Studies Department." I half rose from my seat to give a feeble wave and hoped that I only imagined that there was powdered sugar smeared across my face.

When the crowd turned their attention to Ms. Emily Sproat of the Math department, I turned to my tablemate, evidently a science teacher, and asked, "Do I have powdered sugar on my face?" He shook his head and gave me an off-centered smile. This marked the beginning of something strange.

During the fifth week of school, just when I was getting my bearings, small gifts began to appear in my teacher mailbox. They were small by necessity, given the dimensions of the mailbox and the public nature of its location. The mailboxes were in the main office, in full view of the secretaries and administrators' offices. It started innocuously: first a nice pen tied with a blue bow, then a fresh apple. A few days later, a little notepad tied with the same blue ribbon sat in the cubby.

At first, I thought this might be a welcome-new-teacher thing from the PTA, but when the notepad arrived, I checked other mailboxes and found only mail or piles of Xeroxed papers. Edie was pounding out an order form on an old typewriter that lurked in the corner of her desk, next to the computer monitor.

"Why are you using that old thing?" I asked.

"Book orders. The requisition forms have to be in carbon triplicate until we use up all of these forms they had printed back in the 1980s. They're a pain if you make a mistake." She was peering through her reading glasses, pecking out one letter at a time. "That damn computer with its backspace key has really spoiled me. Now I have to do this at a snail's pace or I have to drag out the whiteout. The correction ribbon doesn't work on the carbon copies."

"Wow, that is a pain. Um, Edie?" She looked up. "I've been getting little presents in my box and it doesn't look like anyone else is. Do you know what's up?" Seeing the notepad in my hand, she pushed her reading glasses up to rest in her curly gray hair and sat back in her chair.

"Oh my," she said.

"Oh my what?"

"How long has this been going on?" She crossed her arms in front of her chest.

"This is the third thing. They've been coming about every other day."

"Well, looks like he's at it again."

"Who?"

"Russell." She said his name like a dog might growl.

"Excuse me?"

"Russell Flusche." She was speaking between clenched teeth.

"Is he that science teacher who always wears a lab coat?" Edie nodded and gestured for me to sit on the wooden chair next to her desk. She looked around the office, then leaned close to me to talk in hushed tones.

"Russell is somewhat, uh, unbalanced. I was wondering which of you new girls he'd choose this year. There are three of you, fresh meat. He picks one to hit on each year. Sometimes they bite and agree to go out with him. They always regret it." She sat up and scanned the office like a periscope and then bent back toward me. "Just do yourself a favor and stay as far away from him as possible."

"Thanks for the warning. What should I say to him if he, you know, actually talks to me?" I asked.

"Lie. Tell him you have a fiancé in the military, or Canada, and you're waiting for him to come back so you can have five more kids together. Russell is a big wimp. If he thinks there's competition, he'll back off."

"I'll keep that in mind."

"Alex, he's not bad looking, and he plays a good game, but he's nuts."

"Thank you. I got it."

"No, I mean really, truly crazy." She warned.

"Okay. Thanks again. Have a good afternoon." *He can't be all that bad, can he?* I wondered why Edie's warning was so emphatic; he seemed like an affable guy.

A few days later, after my third hour students had left, I noticed a lunch bag under Miranda's desk. At the beginning of the school year, Miranda had approached my desk after class.

"Ms. Smythe, can I ask you something, or tell you something?"

"You can do both." I smiled at her. She looked concerned.

"I need to eat during class, if that's alright with you." I looked up from the papers I was trying to organize.

"Okay, but why?"

"I have Crohn's disease."

"Oh, the stomach condition that makes it really hard to eat?"

"Yeah. It's really uncomfortable, but I have figured out that if I eat a little bit throughout the day, it's not so bad." Her face was serious.

"It's fine by me. Just don't leave Cheeto dust on the desk, okay?" I got a little grin out of her.

"It's usually just crackers and water."

"That's totally fine. See you tomorrow." *So that's what it was.*

I had wondered. Miranda was so skinny that her hand was practically transparent when she raised it to answer a question. The petty cheerleaders in my class accused her of being anorexic, which she ignored. Miranda cultivated her aesthetic with a penchant for black clothes and heavy eyeliner, but she was a peach of a kid.

On this day, she had hurried out of class, probably trying to beat the traffic in C Hall. Fourth hour was my planning time. I didn't want to start grading senior essays about the impact of economics on historical decision making, so I set off to deliver Miranda's lunch.

The students' schedules were kept in a binder in the main office. If I read hers correctly, Miranda was in chemistry now, down in H wing. I hadn't ventured to that part of the building yet. I passed the gym and went downstairs.

I knew I was getting close when I turned the corner and was stuck by a terrible burning smell, probably from a chemistry lab.

Further down, the bank of lockers ended and was replaced by a row of hooks, precisely spaced and numbered. Light jackets and hoodies hung from the hooks. Beneath them, backpacks and book bags sat in a neat row on a pristine white shelf set two feet off the floor. The procession of belongings ended outside of Russell Flusche's classroom. I peeked in and thought I'd landed on another planet, or perhaps on the set of a science fiction movie. The students were wrapped in aprons that covered them from ankle to neck. Their heads and faces were distorted by huge goggles. They stood with their rubber-gloved hands resting unnaturally on the lab tables. The table surfaces were bare, and no one moved.

I had foolishly thought I could sneak in and give the lunch bag to Miranda, who was only about fifteen feet from the door. I didn't want to bother anyone or draw notice to the fact that I was being a little mother-hen-ish to a tenth grader who wouldn't appreciate that kind of attention.

I slipped into the classroom and was half-way to Miranda's desk when Mr. Flusche shouted from the front of the room. "STOP! What do you think you're doing?"

I froze. Russell was pointing at me with a set of tongs gripping a long beaker full of blue liquid. Twenty-five pairs of goggled eyes rotated to stare at me. Plastic aprons crinkled and crunched. My face turned red. I felt something in the pit of my stomach that hadn't been there since middle school.

"I, um, I was just going to give this to one of our students." I held up the brown paper bag. "I'm sorry, I was trying not to interrupt . . . "

"MIZZ SMYTHE, I realize that you are new to this institution," he paused to take a deep breath, "but I assumed that you would have the common courtesy not to come into this, of all classrooms, carrying a foreign object and interrupting my demonstration!"

The man was turning purple. I expected the students to start giggling at this point, but instead there was sympathy in the alien faces, as if they were trying to communicate silently: *We know, we think he's crazy too.* I began to back out of the room.

"I'm very sorry Mr. Flusche. It won't happen again."

"Fine." He waited, holding his breath until I was safely in the hallway before continuing his lecture. *What the hell was that?* This was going to take a trip to the vending machine for some recovery M&M's. I stood outside the classroom for a second to calm down. I found Miranda's backpack with the Nirvana and Rage Against the Machine buttons hanging on one of the hooks, and slipped her lunch inside.

I walked into the main office eating my M&M's. "Edie, I just had a little run in with our friend Russell." I relayed what had transpired.

"He can't get over his NIH days." She continued typing as she talked. "He conned the principal into hanging up the hooks and making his lab fancy. Did you notice the kids' feet?" She asked. I had, but it hadn't registered in the heat of the moment. They all had fabric coverings over their shoes, some floral, some pinstriped, a few plaid. "His mother makes a new batch of booties every year. He wanted his lab to be kind of like a cleanroom."

"For high school?"

"He has grand delusions. And a hell of a temper."

"That's for sure."

"Don't say I didn't warn you," she said.

The next day, Miranda thanked me before class started. "So, Ms. Smythe, you got royally Flusched." She grinned.

"Yeah, sure looks that way."

"Nobody can stand him."

"Do you guys get fully geared up just to watch demonstrations?"

"He's big into protocol. If we don't follow it, we lose points."

"That seems a tad draconian," I remarked.

"Yeah."

I love my students.

***

I stood at the back of an idyllic, white country chapel, patiently waiting my turn to march down the aisle. The heavy wooden doors were wide open, framing the view of a broad valley ringed with trees. Patches of gold peeked through the green leaves and a breeze carried the delicate scent of fall as it ruffled my navy chiffon skirt. Scenes from the previous evening ran, unwelcome, through my head as we awaited the bride's arrival.

Last night, after the rehearsal dinner, the men and women parted ways to enjoy a night of debauchery. As much as I wanted to go back to the hotel, my ride was the same trolley-limo that had taken us to the restaurant, so I was trapped.

After a twenty-minute ride, during which many in the party managed to down two or three Jell-O shots (conveniently placed in a cooler by the driver who was angling for a big tip), we stopped in front of an elaborately painted mint-green and white Victorian house in the older section of downtown. Gracefully curved letters etched in the oval window of the front door read, "Lady Vanda, Seer of Truth, Healer, Medium."

Unbeknownst to me, the maid of honor had made arrangements for us at a small tea shop/fortune-telling establishment. Our large group: bridesmaids, aunts, mothers of the bride and groom, and female cousins, crossed the expansive porch into a large parlor. We sat around several small tables topped with damask tablecloths and milk-glass lanterns. Winsomely mismatched teacups and saucers sat at each place. Dark brocade curtains hung in an arched doorway toward the back of the room.

The curtains didn't close completely, and from my vantage point, I could see another small table, this one decorated in typical new age fashion, draped with colorful scraps of fabric and a twisting brass candelabra holding six burning black tapers. None of us, other than the girl who had made the reservation, knew what to expect and the room was full of hushed speculation and light giggling. Because the only person I knew at this wedding was the bride, and she was sitting with her sorority sisters, I ended up sitting with the groom's mother and his aunt. They cooed over the crown molding and the classic bentwood chairs. The gentleman who ushered us in called for our attention.

"Ladies," he began, "I have very important introductions to make this evening. First, on my right, the two hostesses who will be serving you this evening. We have a selection of dessert pastries for you, accompanied by an assortment of fine teas. If you would like something to augment your tea." At this he gave an exaggerated wink in the direction of the bride's table. "We can provide that too, but it has to be our little secret." He winked again.

So, no liquor license, I presumed.

Though our Master of Ceremonies was wearing a suit with no tie and the shirt collar open at the neck, I thought he'd look more the part if he were sporting a top hat and red tail coat. The addition of a handlebar mustache would have been fitting as well. He looked back over his shoulder at the curtained doorway and seeing the figure of a woman silhouetted in the candlelight, gave a slight nod. He turned back to us and said, "Now, I present to you the clairvoyant Lady Vanda!" The woman parted the curtains and emerged looking like a medieval oracle. Black braids were piled on top of her head, wrapped in a green and gold patterned scarf; gold hoop earrings the size of bracelets hung from her ears. Enough beads, chains, baubles and ornaments to fill a good-sized treasure chest adorned her wrists and neck. Her dark almond shaped eyes and light brown skin glowed in the dim light. The soothsayer inclined her head slightly to her audience and disappeared back into her alcove.

"As you enjoy your tea, I will invite you, one at a time, to visit Lady Vanda. Bon appétit!"

The hostesses scurried about, bringing platters of desserts and tins with a collection of teas to each table. Large ceramic teapots full of hot water followed. One of the servers circulated with a bottle of brandy for those who desired a hot toddy. While we waited for our turn with Lady Vanda, Kyle's mother turned to me.

"Alex, please help me remember how you know Meg?" she asked, politely folding me into the discussion.

"She and I were in grad school together," I said.

"Why don't I remember you from the bridal shower?"

"Well, I was something of a late addition to the wedding party."

"Oh!" Kyle's aunt's eyes brightened. "You must be the one who had to step in for Millie! Poor girl. And you will be walking in with my son, Ross!"

"Yes." I smiled. "That's me." I'd been invited to the wedding and was still debating on whether or not to bring a date when Meg had called in a panic. I continued. "After Millie's accident, Meg didn't want Ross to feel awkward and have to walk down the aisle alone, so she asked if I could step in."

"That was so kind of you. Did Millie's dress fit you?"

"Almost. It just took a few alterations," I said. The three of us looked at one another in a wooden silence. Mercifully, a hostess arrived with our platter of delicacies and teacups, and the two older women resumed their own conversation. I glanced through the curtains to Vanda's room. One of Meg's cousins, Macy, was sitting with her back to me, gesticulating energetically while Vanda took notes in a spiral notebook, nodding, her earrings swinging vigorously against her neck.

As I was thinking that this process was going to take a very long time, and calculating the number of pastries I could eat each hour without consuming more than 3000 calories for the night, I noticed that the gentleman in the suit was standing near the curtains, looking at his watch. After a moment, he pushed a button mounted discretely behind the draperies, and I noticed the light inside of the crystal ball on Vanda's table modulate from yellow to red. Vanda looked up from her notebook. She spoke to the bridesmaid for a minute, then waved her hand dismissively. Macy stood and left the chamber, one hand over her mouth, the other at her heart, her eyes wide.

As soon as she sat down, her table-mates bombarded her with questions. Macy took a long swig of her enhanced tea, and then leaned in to share what she had learned. The evening continued along these lines for about an hour and a half. I observed that the rest of the house seemed to be off-limits to the public and wondered if Vanda lived here with the gentleman. The cabbage-rose wallpaper was peeling along the baseboards. The radiator hissed and popped as the night grew colder. Finally, after an eternity, it was my turn.

The back room was slightly stuffy. As I settled in my seat, Lady Vanda asked as she had of the others, "So, what are you looking for my dear? What is on your mind?" She spoke in an intriguing blend of French and British tones that I had not heard before.

Priding myself in being well versed in accents, I asked, "Where are you from?"

"I am from Mauritius." She looked at me, her gaze open and direct. "Nobody knows where that is."

"Isn't it an island off the coast of Africa?" I said.

"Yes." Vanda said. Her gaze lingered on my face. Then she set her notebook gently on the table and leaned back in her chair, closing her eyes. All was quiet, except for the scraps of conversation drifting in from the dining room. I started to say something, to ask if there was a good man in my future, but she held her hand up, palm toward my face. I stopped talking. One minute passed. Another minute. I began to worry that the gentleman would press the button soon and I would never learn my fortune. Then, Vanda gave a sharp, decisive jerk of her head and sat straight up, her light brown eyes fixed on mine again.

"You must stop," she said. "You don't need it, and the pursuit of it is," she searched for the right word, "destructive, or maybe that's too harsh, but certainly distracting. You have more important things to do with your time, and you will find what you seek, but not by looking for it."

"But, what..." This made no sense to me. She cut me off again with a gesture, the rings on each of her fingers flashing like gold nuggets.

"You are fine as you are. You are stronger than you realize. Carry that knowledge with you." She held my gaze for a long time, then pointed her chin toward the doorway. "Now go," she said.

I wanted to protest. I wanted more specifics, such as names of my potential husband, and the date that I would meet him, but the straight set of her mouth told me that the interview had concluded, and the crystal ball hadn't even turned red. As I parted the curtains to leave, she said, "Oh, and there is something about your car..." her voice trailed off as she waved me out.

At the chapel, my musings were interrupted by the arrival of a gray Bentley Continental Silver Spur. Meg's father, dressed in a morning suit, helped his daughter out of the back seat.

She radiated happiness, waiting for the bridesmaids to fan out her train. As we processed down the aisle, I reviewed the line of groomsmen, checking them off one at a time with the information I had gleaned from the rehearsal dinner: married, married, engaged, feckless, weird looking, too young. No prospects here. I ignored the minister's speech about love, etc., and tried to block out the Kahlil Gibran reading by closely examining every petal in my bouquet to avoid crying while on full display at the front of the church. It was a beautiful wedding.

After the ceremony, we loaded once again onto the trolley-limo and drove through verdant rolling hills to an expansive country estate for the reception. Toasts and first dance accomplished, the food started coming out of the kitchen one course at a time, with an agonizing wait between them. After I ate my predictable entrée of chicken with baked new potatoes and string beans, I went in search of a pay phone and found one near the restrooms.

I pulled out my calling card to place a long-distance call and pressed the dozens of numbers it took to connect to the service, then to Ken's house. Lainie was already sleepy, so it was a short goodnight. I picked up the receiver again to call Cynthia and got her answering machine. On a hunch, I dialed again, taking several seconds to dial the service, then her number, but she picked up on the first ring.

"Hey Cyn."

"Ugh, I just missed you before. I had my headphones on and only heard the last ring. How are you?"

"This weekend was a huge mistake," I said.

"Aren't you having fun? Are there no cute single men?" she asked.

"There are no cute single men, I don't know anyone other than Meg. Kyle's mom ignored me all last night and I am bored out of my mind."

"How's the band? Why don't you get out there and dance?" Cyn asked.

"Eh. The band isn't great." I hesitated, wanting to tell her about Lady Vanda, but I still didn't know how I felt about that encounter.

"Well, you're being a really great friend to Meg, and Virginia is pretty."

"Yeah, I guess so. I don't know. It's just not the fun time I thought it might be. I don't know why I'm complaining." I hesitated. "Something really strange happened last night."

"What?"

"Well, we went to this fortune teller..."

Cyn interrupted me. "You know all those people are big fakes, right? I hope you didn't spend a lot on that folly."

"No, I didn't pay, it was part of our rehearsal party, I guess. But she, the fortune-teller, wasn't what I expected," I said.

"She didn't tell you that you were going to win the lottery or marry a rich guy?"

"No, actually, she didn't tell me my future, really."

"Well, what did she say?" Cyn asked.

"She told me to stop looking for whatever it is that I'm looking for," I said.

"That is weird. But doesn't it sound familiar? This is what I've been try-ing to tell you," she said. "Look, I hate to do this to you but I can't stay on the phone much longer, I'm under a deadline."

"Okay, it's probably time for cake anyway," I said.

"Well, you have that going for you. Let's talk about this later, I do really want to know what happened, but I gotta go. Love you." And she was gone.

There was, indeed, cake at my place when I returned to the table. It was a small piece cut from the center with not nearly enough icing for my taste. My neighbor, who was out on the dance floor, had been given a corner piece with a healthy allotment of buttercream icing. When Ross, the only other person left at the table, wasn't looking, I switched plates.

Near the end of dinner, some guests went outside to wander the estate, some were dancing, a few had returned to our table. Over the music, I thought I heard Ross say something. The groom's nephew, as out of place as I was at the moment, seemed like a nice kid. I leaned closer to hear him better. "I don't feel so good," he said to no one in particular, his eyes glassy and dis-tant. Then he repeated, "I don't feel so good." Without any further warning, Ross collapsed out of his chair, his body thrashing out of control on the floor. For a few seconds, we sat, staring, and then it registered that Ross was hav-ing a grand mal seizure. My teacher-self kicked in and, moving toward Ross, I started shouting orders.

"You three," I pointed at the groomsmen at my table, "move the furniture out of the way so he doesn't hit it. You, Mary—"

"Marie."

"Marie, go call 9-11, the phone is probably near the office." Then others came to their senses.

"I'll go find his parents."

"We'll clear a path for the stretcher." A waiter shoved a wadded-up table cloth into my hands. "Put this under his head, he said. I nodded.

"When he stops," I said. I knelt by Ross as the thrashing subsided, and slipped the cloth under his head.

For a scary minute, I couldn't tell if he was breathing. Then, with a grunt, Ross began to snore loudly, and my breath came out in one long sigh. I felt someone kneeling beside me.

"How long was he seizing?" his mom asked.

"Oh, I'm sorry, I didn't time it," I said, "a minute, ninety seconds at most." She lay a hand on his forehead. "He'll be so upset," she said.

"There's nothing for him to be embarrassed about," I said, not understanding why this should bother him.

"That's not it. This means he won't be able to drive for another two years." His mom stated this in a tender but matter-of-fact voice. "He will be so disappointed, he was just finishing drivers' ed."

The paramedics arrived and loaded a still-sleeping Ross onto a stretcher. The bride and groom followed Ross's parents out to the waiting ambulance, and I thought *"well, this certainly wasn't on the list of images the photographer planned to capture today."*

After Ross's seizure, the reception wound down and I said my good-byes. As I drove out of the Virginia countryside and entered the inevitable beltway traffic, a novel serenity settled into my soul. According to Lady Vanda, I was going to be okay. I was going to find my way, eventually. And, according to Ross's dad, I was 'quite a cool character' under pressure. Things seemed to be looking up; I was calming down.

***

It was a beautiful evening when the Acura died. Lainie and I had driven down to the pond to commune with the ducks in soft autumn twilight. The air was still warm and the grass underfoot was dry and soft. Green trees had faded to the lackluster stage that precedes their bright fall colors. Having pulled Lainie away from her feathered friends and buckled her in the back, I turned the key in the ignition.

Nothing.

No indicator lights. No beeping. Silence.

Shit, Shit Shit. "Shoooooooot." I held my breath. Counted to ten. Uttered a prayer and tried again.

Nothing. Totally dead.

"Sssssssssssss-ugar."

"What's wrong Mommy?"

"Rosie won't start." Great flipping time to be stuck with a dead car, a hungry kid, and no cell phone. I popped the hood and got out. I don't know what I expected to accomplish by popping the hood as I was completely ill-equipped to handle a car emergency, but it did attract the attention of a good Samaritan who asked if we needed help. She was a woman a little older than me, out walking her dog, and appeared to be fairly nice, so I took a chance.

"If you could give us a ride home, that would be great. We're pretty close." We could walk, but the faster we got to a phone, the faster we could solve this.

"Sure, I'm parked three cars behind you."

While her standard poodle claimed the front seat, I climbed into the back seat and pulled Lainie onto my lap. Between giving directions to my new friend, my mind ran through the list of doom. *If I can't get this fixed, I have to miss work tomorrow, and Lainie will miss a day of school, or more. And I don't have any updated emergency sub plans and this is going to cost me a fortune, I am sure. I wonder how much room I have left on my credit card. Maybe I can call and get them to raise my limit.*

"Turn right here, our apartment is at the end of the parking lot." I thanked the lady no less than seven times as I was trying to extract myself and my kid from the back of the coupe. Like a true Samaritan, she shrugged it off like it was all in a day's work and drove away, her rear fender gently scraping the pavement.

Back in the apartment, Lainie shimmied up into her booster seat. I piled some grapes and crackers onto a plate to keep her occupied while I tried to figure this one out. I needed a man and some jumper cables, but maybe not in that order. In desperation, I called Lester knowing that, despite everything, he was a good egg and would come to our rescue. It would be nice to talk to him again. I got his answering machine. *Shit.*

The only other local male I could call was mountain-bike Brian. He seemed mildly annoyed, and said he would try to help, but he was on his way out to dinner with friends. When he showed up dressed to impress (in his case, out of gym clothes and into a freshly pressed plaid shirt and khakis), I recognized that *friends* was code for *hot date*. He picked us up and drove back to the pond, my guess was that he probably intended to jump the Acura and get on his way to his new hottie in fifteen minutes or less.

For all my love of cars, I'd never really learned much about them, preferring to believe that I would be protected by good mojo if I got the oil changed regularly. Clearly, I needed to reevaluate my doctrine of divine automotive intervention. Something didn't look right about the way Jarvo had attached the jumper cables. I had witnessed this operation on several occasions when my dad's clunkers broke down, but I usually buried my nose in a book when that happened. I should have paid closer attention. Brian ordered me back into the car and said, "Try it now."

Nothing happened. He jiggled the cables. "Try again."

Nothing. Brian was frustrated. He didn't want to be late for his date. Lainie was on cranky countdown. It was past dinner and she didn't understand why Rosie wasn't working.

I got out of the car. Brian and I stood in front of the bumper, staring hard into the engine, willing it to work. He looked at his watch for the umpteenth time.

"I really have to go, I'm late already. I can give you and Lainie a ride home on my way. Maybe you should call a tow truck."

Oh my God. I can't afford a tow truck, I don't have roadside assistance. My stomach balled up into knots. Then, a car that looked like Lester's pulled up behind us. Lester stepped out of his coupe and walked toward us. My heart leapt in my chest.

Desperate as he was to get to his *dinner with friends*, Brian sensed an incursion on his man-turf. We had a full blown Nature Channel moment. The two alpha males thrust out meaty hands for a firm handshake. Their voices dropped an octave. They pulled themselves up to their full height and, turning their heads slightly, eyed the engine and then one another. I realized that they must know each other from the gym.

"Hi Jarvo,"

"Hey Les."

"What do we have here?"

"Dead battery."

"I see. Do you need help?"

"Actually, I wasn't having much luck and I have to run..."

"I'll take over," Lester said. Brian, clearly torn between relinquishing marked territory and exploring greener pastures, looked from me to Lester and then unhooked his jumper cables.

"Okay then, good luck. See you guys around." Brian took off.

Lester and I were left standing there on the sidewalk. Nervous, I felt like I was standing on the top of a mountain, and which side I tumbled down depended on what Lester would say next.

He turned to me and grinned, "Let's get this old girl running!"

"Did you get my message?" I asked.

"What message?"

"The one I left on your answering machine."

"Nope, I was just driving by, I was going to pick up something for dinner."

"I'm sorry to interrupt... " I stood there, not knowing what to do.

"Don't be silly," he said, turning back to his car.

While Les rummaged through his trunk to get his own jumper cables, I went back to check on Lainie. Strapped in her car seat in the Acura, her eyes were at half-mast. She was plugged into her Walkman, *The Little Mermaid* lulling her to sleep.

"Hey Baby, Lester is here. He's come to help us with Rosie." (Lainie's name for the Acura.)

She perked up. "Lester with the black car? Where is he?"

"Over at his car, he'll be here in a minute. I have to go help, okay?"

"Okay."

When Lester finished hooking our cars together, the cables looked better to my untrained eye. He instructed me to sit in the driver's seat of his car. "Keep the RPMs at about two-thousand or slightly above." He reached in and with a sharp tug, pulled the seat forward so my feet would reach the pedals. Les got into the driver's seat of the Acura and started her on the first try.

He got out of the car, and I thought he was going to come back to talk to me. Instead, he flipped the front seat of my car forward and folded himself into the back to sit next to Lainie. I watched from Les's car, wishing I could hear them through the windshields and over the hum of two engines. Thrilled to see her old friend, Lainie's eyes flew open and she started talking at warp speed, her little hands making shapes and butterflies in the air, her legs absently kicking the base of her car seat. They were lit by the dome light, their fair skin in sharp relief in the interior. She giggled and his head nodded in agreement at something she said. There was a pause, then both of them shook with riotous laughter. For ten minutes, my whole world was in the back seat of my car. Little girl and big man in a happy tête-à-tête. Too soon, he appeared at my window.

"Get in your car and follow me to Sears. Keep the engine running and I'll go in and get you a new battery. We'll change it at your place. Okay?"

"Great, thanks."

"While I'm fixing the battery, maybe you can fix dinner?" he asked.

"I was thinking the exact same thing."

***

And then it all changed. Everything.

One morning, about a month and a half after Lester and I got back together, I rolled over to shut off my 5:15 a.m. alarm, and I felt it. My breasts were swollen. I stared at myself in the mirror. They were at least a cup size bigger than normal. It hurt to move. It hurt to put on my bra. The full impact of it slowly spread through my body, starting with a knot of dread in my stomach, then spreading out like ice freezing over a pond.

I have no recollection of that day at school. I have no idea what I said, standing in front of my students. The blessing of teaching teenagers is, however, that most of them are too wrapped up in their own inner drama to notice that their teacher is temporarily totally out of it.

Somehow, I made it to the drugstore to buy a pregnancy test. I bought three. I watched my hands take the credit card out of my wallet. They were another person's hands, pale and uncertain. I waited until Lainie was in bed. The little stick pregnancy tests hadn't changed much since we had tried to conceive her. My periods had been so irregular, I must have gone through twelve boxes of pee-on-the-stick tests. I had considered saving them. Some performance artist could make a statement, treat them like Lincoln Logs and build a tower of failed pregnancy tests as a commentary on society and its false sense of control.

Birth Control. It's a funny phrase when you think of it. There is little one can control. When it's time to give birth, it happens. I remembered wanting to crawl away from the pain when I was in labor with Lainie. The doctor had convinced me to kneel up on the hospital bed to hang on to the raised rail and let my belly swing free in an effort to turn Lainie around. She was facing the wrong way. In my delirium, I imagined that I could leave my body and the baby behind, and I started to crawl off the bed. The nurse turned me back. Babies come when they come. Parents who want them sometimes can't have them. Parents who should wait until they have their act together find them coming too soon.

I knew in my bones that I was pregnant. I even had a feeling it was a girl. As I waited the three minutes between peeing on the stick and looking for the matching lines, a kaleidoscope of images played through my mind, but someone else was spinning the cylinder, making the pieces move and the colors change before I had a chance to focus my eyes. The shapes shifted, blue and green triangles into yellow circles and green squares, sliding in and out of my field of vision. But one thing was constant. In the middle was a baby, curled into a ball, bald and pink and perfect. She didn't move. She was waiting there, waiting to see what I did and how it would affect our lives. She was calm and trusted me. I was petrified.

"Hi." I called Lester.

"Hey."

"I need to talk to you right now, please. Can you come over?"

The tone of my voice must have left no room for debate, even though it was 10:00 p.m. Eight minutes later, I heard his car pull into the parking lot. I sat in the middle of my bed, hugging my pillow. I hadn't moved, and had barely breathed since I'd hung up the phone. There was a soft thud as Lester set something down on the dining table. He appeared at the bedroom door and sat down next to me without saying a word.

"I'm pregnant." My mouth blurted it out before I could compose a preamble.

Still silent, Lester left the room. I heard him moving about the kitchen but was afraid to follow. I needed to hold perfectly still, hold myself together. He returned with a full glass of scotch, and he planted the bottle on the dresser.

"How did you know?" I asked, nodding toward the bottle.

"It had to be something big. I figured I'd need a drink either way."

"What are we going to do?"

"The only thing we can do."

"What's that?" I thought I knew what his answer would be, but I couldn't leave anything unsaid. This situation called for absolute clarity.

"Get married."

I had worried, for a split second, that he was going to say, "get an abortion," or "give it up for adoption." But there it was. Get married. Simple. I should have smiled and fawned all over him. Should have been grateful and immediately melted into his arms.

Instead I asked, "Are you sure this is something you want to do?"

"I am sure it's something I have to do." He looked at me, his deep brown eyes steady and resolved. "But there are two things."

"Okay."

"This isn't a proposal. I am going to propose to you when I'm ready and when the time is right," he said.

"That's fair."

"I don't know if I can promise to stay married forever, but we will do this," he nodded at my stomach, "together."

"Okay."

He stayed the night, but I don't think either of us got much sleep.

Chapter Sixteen
November, 1996

And so, we moved ahead, slipping into a routine, fitting our lives back together, whispering late into the night. We made some decisions: that we would keep this to ourselves for a while, and that we wouldn't move in together until we were actually married. But Lester spent more and more of his nights at our place. Each day, in small ways, we felt more like a family.

We were relaxing on a Saturday morning, trying to decide what to do with the day when we heard an odd rustling from under the front door of my apartment. Someone on the other side of the door seemed to be trying to shove an envelope under it. I glanced at Les. He held up two fingers in a "V" and pointed them first at his eyes, then at the door. *I've got the back. You recon the door.*

We rose from the couch and tiptoed to the door. I approached the peephole from an angle. Les followed with his hand on my back. When I looked, I saw Quinn bent over, trying to squash an envelope flat so it would fit under the door. I sprang back. Les and I, still on tiptoe, retreated to the bedroom for a whispered tactical meeting.

"It's Quinn!" I hissed.

"Let me at him!" Lester joked.

"No, I'll talk to him."

"I don't think this guy is stable."

"I know," I said, "stay close."

"Roger."

We crouched and tiptoe-ran back into the living room, SWAT team style. The envelope had made it a third of the way under the door. Lester stood with his back plastered to the wall next to the door. All we needed were earpieces and radios. Not wearing our jammies would have been good, too.

Judging that surprise was the best plan, I violently turned the deadbolt and flung the door open. Quinn jumped up from his position on the floor and looked at me with big startled-toad eyes.

"What the hell are you doing?" I stood with my feet planted wide, one hand on my hip, the other on the door, doing my best to channel Clint Eastwood.

"I just, I just wanted to give this to you," he stammered. He clutched the envelope to his chest for a moment, then thrust it at me. "Please, just read it. Read what I have to say." My Clint Eastwood persona faded. Quinn was simply pathetic, standing there in pressed khakis and a button-down shirt at 8:00 a.m. on a Saturday.

"Hi, we haven't met, I'm Lester."

Les had swiveled from his spot behind the door and stood next to me. Drawn up to his full height, he looked down at Quinn by several inches. Quinn shoved the envelope into my hands and scurried away down the stairs. My champion took a few steps after him. He planted himself a few feet in front of the door and didn't move until Quinn's car pulled out of the parking lot.

This was the moment in the movie where my character would move forward, thread her arm through his, and lay her head on his shoulder. So I did.

Back in the apartment, I opened the envelope and discovered why Quinn had such a hard time getting it under the door. The engagement ring got stuck. It was a Tiffany XO ring, where the X's were gold and the O's were diamonds.

The note read:

Dearest Alexandria:

> *I have had this ring in my possession for several months, waiting for the right moment to propose to you. I urge you to consider me as an alternative to the other man (men?) you have been seeing. I realize that you are expecting again, and I would welcome this child, and Lainie, as my own. Please consider this and contact me as soon as you are able.*

Yours, Always,
Quinn

Lester read this over my shoulder. We were both astonished.

"How did he know you're pregnant?"

"I told him." I was just as stunned as Lester was. "He had been bugging me via email, asking me to *come back* to him, even though we were never really together. He's been relentless. So I thought that would drive him off."

"This guy is unbelievable. If he really is harassing you, you should call the police.

"I'll make him go away. I'll handle it on Monday," I said, but my confidence was misplaced.

***

What happened next was horrible. I was horrible. In addition to dating so many men that I could accurately be labeled *slutty*, now I was knocked up and being a jerk. No, I was being an ass. I blame the pregnancy hormones.

To: Quinn
From: Alexandria Smythe
Re: Ring

> Quinn: I told you that I was pregnant hoping that it would, finally, convince you that there is not now, nor has there ever been, a future for the two of us. Lester and I will be married in the next few weeks. I have your ring. Please let me know how you would like it returned to you. Or, if you like, I have an appointment in a building near Tiffany's this week. You could call them and I could return it directly.

AS
To: Alexandria Smythe
From: Quinn
Re: re: News

> Alex, please meet me after school today. I will come to your work. It is imperative that I speak with you before you make your final decision.

Always yours,
Quinn

To: Quinn

From: Alexandria Smythe

Re:re:re: News

Fine

I waited for him in the parking lot after school. It was cold, gray and drizzling, but I didn't want him coming into the school. He rolled down the window.

"Get in, let's go for a drive."

"No, let's stay here. I have to leave soon. Park over by my car." I gestured toward an empty space by the Acura. I followed on foot.

"Please get in so I can talk to you."

"All right but we're staying right here." The sane thing would have been to have just sent the ring back via certified mail, but I wanted to put an end to this. I had granted this audience to clear my own conscience. I was going to give him ten minutes.

Quinn handed me a folded piece of paper. I tried to hand him the ring.

"No. Wait. Hold on to that." I put the envelope back on my lap. "Before you look at that, I want you to consider something. Lester is making, what, twenty-five, thirty thousand dollars per annum on his research fellowship? Top salary he can hope to make, ever, is what? Probably less than six figures. You need to consider your future. Yours and Lainie's and the baby's."

"What are you saying?" I asked.

"I want to marry you." He was determined.

"Quinn, you are totally out of your mind. Are you telling me that you want to marry me and raise two step-children? And deal with two other men who would be part of our lives for the duration? These babies have FA-THERS."

"Joseph was a good stepfather."

"Joseph who?"

"As in Mary and..."

"Joseph, stepfather of Jesus?" I shouted.

Quinn nodded and smiled, and then stopped grinning. It was only partially a joke to him. He was serious, convinced that we could overcome any obstacle and become a happy family. I opened the car door and tried to hand his paper and the envelope with the ring back to him.

"Look, I really need to get going. I came because I thought you had something to say. This is ridiculous." I started to get out of the car.

"Wait, Alex. Please look at this." His voice and face took on a familiar aspect, one I had seen in the middle of the ocean. It was time for appeasement. I sat back down and unfolded the paper.

> *Income: Currently $175,000 per annum, projected to double over the next three years as practice becomes established. Additional profits could accumulate and average over one-half million annually in as little as seven years.*
>
> *Current stock portfolio value: $163,000*
> *Retirement account and various mutual funds: $327,000*

My budget, after rent, car payment, and paying whatever Ken couldn't manage for day care, left me and Lainie about $315 per month to cover food, gas, ballet lessons, utilities, doctor's visits and clothes. God forbid the car need any work or there were any other unforeseen emergency. If we were careful, we could afford to eat at McDonalds or Taco Bell once a month. Comparatively, this man had a fortune. And I now had the futures of three people to consider.

"You see, Alex, I can do more for you than Lester ever could." His eyes bored into mine. "I could give you so much." He leaned forward and lay a bony hand on my thigh. The pressure of his lean fingers jolted me back. I jumped out of the car and dropped the paper on the seat as if it had stung my hand. I threw the ring down after it.

"Do not ever contact me again!" I slammed the car door and ran back to the school. The door by the service entrance was open, and I blew through it, barely missing the massive form of Jim, the afternoon janitor.

"Hey, hey, you okay?"

"Yeah, Mr. Jim, I'm fine." I looked past him through the open door, expecting Mr. Psycho to be following me. He didn't, but his car sat still, not moving from the parking space.

"Can I help you with something, Ms. Smythe?" Jim asked.

"You can call me Alex, to begin with."

He smiled. It was our running joke. He'd call me Ms. Smythe, I'd call him Mr. Jim, mostly because I could never remember his last name and I think he forgot my first one. I was still nervous about Quinn and didn't want to stay to chat. I told Jim I'd forgotten something in my classroom. By the time I made it to the third floor, and down the long hall to the windows that overlooked the parking lot, Quinn's car had gone.

I had a lot to think about.

There are two types of people. Planners and non-planners. My best friend in high school was a planner. He was going to be a doctor. He didn't just *want* to be a doctor; he was *going to be* a doctor. It was as much a part of him as my chocolate addiction was a part of my eternal soul. He took every science class available and spent his summers working in research labs. He had a short list of top-rated undergraduate institutions with good pre-med programs and was accepted into each one. College, med school, residency and fellowships all fell into place along the path he had set for himself when he was eight years old.

I, on the other hand, let Fortune be my guide. Not always successfully. I picked my college because it was the most prestigious one I had gotten into. I changed majors three times. I gave up my car to pay for grad school, so I picked the grad school that was within walking distance from my apartment. Caprice had led me here, and *here* was poor, pregnant, unwed and confused.

I used to like Caprice. She was cool, breezy. Adventurous and fresh. But had she been my enemy all along? Could I afford to marry a man just because I was carrying his child? For a moment during this period of insanity (which, fortunately would only last for six or seven days), I decided that Caprice was a flighty bitch, and I would do better to ally myself with her avaricious cousin, Cunning. Cunning, in her wisdom, dictated that I should calculate the financial needs of my children first and let the emotional stuff work itself out. After all, hadn't it been thoroughly researched that the number one reason for divorce was financial distress? Cunning led women to financial security and beautiful lifestyles. Was that history or in novels?

Sitting at my desk, I reconstructed from memory the figures Quinn had written on that scrap of paper. It had been a business proposal, and my new partner, Cunning, and I, were going to weigh our options.

How Lainie and I ate, dressed, and appeared at our respective schools for the next few days was a mystery, as I was totally absorbed with the pressing question of love versus money. I imagined what life would be like as Quinn's wife. I thought about the private schools I could send the girls to. (I was convinced this baby would be a sister for Lainie.) They would wear little plaid jumpers and blazers with the school crest emblazoned on the breast pocket. There could be riding lessons and tennis, in addition to ballet. Summer camps and country clubs. I could live the luxurious life of a trophy wife. If it only weren't for the nagging fact that I couldn't stand Quinn, and yes, I loved Lester. Ms. Cunning couldn't shove that aside.

Lester and I hadn't seen each other since the morning after the ring incident in the apartment. He'd gone out of town. Before his return, I committed the tactical error of describing my encounter with Quinn in detail. Then our phone conversation took an ugly, unexpected turn. Lester asked, "Well, what did you think of the whole thing?"

The answer he was looking for was the indignant shock I had displayed in the parking lot. Instead I stupidly said, "I think he had a valid point. I do need to think about the future and what the children might need." There was dead silence on the other end of the line. The temperature dropped about twenty degrees.

In his most chilly voice, Lester said, "Don't you think I could provide whatever the kids might need?"

I recognized the danger, but, instead of back-pedaling, and with my smarter self yelling *No, stop, fix this. Don't go there,* I said, "I don't know. It's not something we've ever discussed. I don't really know what your earning potential is, or where your financial priorities lay." The fallout shelter siren blared in my head. I was questioning his manhood. *What the hell are you doing?* I did not change course. I let the last statement hang in the air. I didn't have to see his face to feel the muscles in his jaw tighten. The silence came through the phone with deafening weight.

"When you're done with your decision making, you let me know. I don't want to talk to you again until you've straightened out your own head."

"But wait, Lester, that's not what I meant–" he had already hung up the phone.

***

The only accurate adjective for the first trimester of pregnancy was *shitty*. Instead of morning sickness, I got twenty-four-hour sickness. Saltines, bananas and ginger ale were about all I could stomach, and an after-school nap became a necessity. I'd sit in bed with Lainie in the evening and try to read her stories. Instead, she would recite her favorite stories from memory and didn't mind that her audience kept drifting off during dramatic interpretations of *Brown Bear, Brown Bear, What do You See?* Sleeping through the night, however, eluded me.

The night after the disastrous phone call with Lester I had fallen asleep for a little while in Lainie's bed, then woke to finish tidying up from dinner and get ready for school the next day. While I tried all the tricks I knew to fall asleep, herbal tea, fuzzy socks, even some soft music, I lay wide awake watching the leafy shadow pattern on the ceiling shift as the wind blew among the trees. Giving up, I decided to tackle the huge stack of mid-term papers sitting neglected on the coffee table. My students had each chosen an historical figure from world history. I had given them an extensive list of people to choose from, trying to select figures that might appeal to individual students on a personal level. It was no wonder that Alfonso, who was, in all probability headed to Juilliard to study cello, chose Bach, and that Andrew, honorary president of the Future Lawyers of America studied Machiavelli for his paper. I read paper after paper, using my green pen to note the students' great ideas and sentences or suggest adjustments for grammar or clarity. As I read, an idea began to grow in the deep, primal space in my brain, slowly and quietly at first, then gaining noise and momentum as the evening wore on. I graded papers on Isaac Newton and Louis Pasteur, then papers about Joan of Arc, Elizabeth the First, and Mary Wollstonecraft Shelly. Papers by the boys about men. Papers by the girls almost uniformly about women. Charles Darwin followed by Florence Nightingale. One student informed me that

Queen Victoria managed to rule England and have nine children and carry on when she was widowed. The noise in my head expanded to a rumble. And then, Marie Curie. I remembered that one of my students had asked to study the physicist for her paper even though Madame Curie lived well into the twentieth century. While I was aware of Marie Curie's many scientific accomplishments, I didn't know that she had two daughters, and that, tragically, her husband was killed by a horse-drawn carriage while he was walking down the road, leaving Marie to raise the very young girls by herself. Marie Curie was a single mother who won two Nobel Prizes and radically changed life for all humankind. The noise in my head amplified into a deep bass drum. I set the papers aside, fanned out on the sofa next to me.

I didn't need Quinn, or his money. I didn't need any man. I could make my own damn money. Lady Vanda's words sang to me with the beat of that bass drum, "Stop looking. You don't need what you're looking for." I handled Ross's seizure while others stood around doing nothing. I found myself this good new job with a robust pay scale. I was a good teacher. By most measures, I seemed to be doing a fairly decent job of raising Lainie. I could make things, improvise, grow tomatoes on my balcony, get by on a budget. I could put together Ikea furniture by myself and had my own tool box if the little allen wrench that came with the *kallax* bookcase wasn't up to the job. If there was anything I couldn't do myself, like plumbing, or jumpstarting my car, I knew how to call people.

"I can do this myself." I said the words out loud. I needed to try this idea, to make sure it was real and that I could verbalize it with conviction to another person. I capped the green pen and reached for the phone. Cyn didn't object to late-night calls.

"Hey, it's me," I said.

"Hey, what's up, Me?" Cyn asked.

"I'm pregnant."

"Get out. How did that happen?" she asked.

"Mittelschmerz."

"Fred Mertz? What?"

"No, Mittelschmerz when you bleed when you ovulate. I thought I was having my period," I explained.

"Ovulation is a far fucking cry from a period my friend." She said.

"No kidding."

"How could you not know when you're having a period?"

"I've never been really regular." This line of questioning was making me feel stupid on top of miserable, anxious and depressed.

"I thought you were on the pill?"

"I was giving myself a break, from everything." I said.

"What does that mean?"

"Cleansing the system." I realized how stupid it sounded as I said it.

"Did you go all organic?" Cyn asked, "Tell me you gave up Diet Coke and ice cream too, genius."

"No, just the pill, and the antidepressants."

"Well, shit, you might want to reconsider that second thing."

"Yeah, I know. It seemed like a good idea at the time." There was a long pause between us.

"You have options." Cyn said, gently.

"There are no options here," I said. "This is a done deal. I am going to keep this baby."

"Are you sure?" Cyn asked.

"Yes. I've done a lot of thinking. Here's how I feel; Lainie, this baby and me, we're a triumvirate. We're in triplicate. We're a trio. We're going to be the Three Musketeers, or, if it's another girl, we're going to be the Three Graces." I said.

Cyn interrupted, "You can be Larry, Moe and Curly for all I care. I just wanted to say that by 'options' I meant that you can always come stay with me if you need to, if worse comes to worst, so calm down sister. But I totally agree with you, you can do this by yourself."

"Yeah. I don't need Quinn, or Lester, or anyone. I can raise this family by myself." I stated this again because I needed to hear myself say it, I needed to stamp it indelibly in my being. I knew it was true, but saying out loud made it so.

"Yes, you can!" Cyn agreed.

"The thing is, I don't need Lester, I want Lester. I want him in my life and I think he is going to be a great dad, but if it doesn't work, it's going to be alright."

"Yes, it is." Cyn said this in the strong, affirming tone I needed to hear. "You are totally capable of doing this. You have lots of people who love you and will help. If Lester does flake out on you, do you want me to come for the birth?" She asked.

"Definitely, if my mom is still in Malawi. That would be awesome." I said.

"If it's a girl, you have to name her Cynthia." I smiled at that.

"I will take it under advisement for a middle name." I replied. "Thank you. I needed to hear your voice to make sure I'm not crazy. I owe you, as usual."

"You're not crazy," she said. "You'll be fine. All three of you will be fine."

I went back to bed and, while I waited for sleep to come, started planning.

***

On Thursdays, Ken usually picked Lainie up from school for an overnight visit. That Thursday, after work, I went to the grocery store and loaded the cart with apology food: two pints of ice cream in decadent flavors, a bottle of chocolate sauce, crushed peanut topping, two large steaks and salad makings. I didn't call first; I just drove to Lester's place. The door was locked. I thought about using my key, but decided against it.

I sat on the stoop, big paper grocery bag at my feet, and waited. It was a quiet evening, and the sky was turning gentle shades of pink and orange, tinting the edges of feathery clouds. For the first time in days, I was alone and quiet, and I felt a new combination of calmness and confidence. I loved Lester. I loved the fact that he was willing to do the right thing, even though he had no guarantees that this would work out. I loved his big hands, his honesty, his laugh. Viewed objectively, I was being a psychotic, materialistic bitch. Any other man would have turned and run in the other direction, and I wouldn't have blamed him.

"Hey, are you okay?" Lester snuck up on me in his running shoes.

"Yeah," I said.

He lowered himself down on the stoop next to me.

"I came by to apologize." *Oh crap, I am going to cry.* As my composure weakened, I choked up. He waited. "I've been a total jackass," I continued, "and I am really sorry." He didn't say anything. The tears rolled down my cheeks. "I don't know what I was thinking. I was really hoping we could call it temporary pregnancy insanity and forget this whole thing ever happened."

He was quiet for a moment, then stood up. He went into the house and reemerged with a towel and bottle of water for him, and a box of tissues for me. I blew my nose and waited while he wiped down the sweat and drained half of the bottle. The sky was growing dark.

"I can't promise that I'll forget. You really pissed me off." He stated this in a matter-of-fact tone.

"I know." I had stopped crying at this point and said, with honest determination,

"I understand if you want to call the whole thing off, and I can be ok with that. I've been giving this a lot of thought and I know can do this on my own. If you want me to sign something to let you off the hook, or..."

"Don't be ridiculous," Lester said, sounding annoyed. "I love you and that's my kid. Period. We are doing this together." He folded me into his arms, and I could have stayed there all night, sweaty shirt and all. "Come on, I'm getting cold and I have to stretch. Let's go inside. What's in the bag?"

"Dinner."

"Excellent."

***

After our make-up dinner (and other things), we talked about logistics. Les still insisted that I would have a proper proposal. So, for days that turned into weeks, I waited for the big moment. I felt like a character in a Jane Austen novel. I didn't want to tell anyone that I was pregnant until I was married. I couldn't tell anyone I was getting married until Lester proposed. I had no great explanation for my boss when she found me napping in my classroom on my prep hour, head down on my desk. I think she knew. Finally, on a glorious fall Saturday, Les came to pick me up to go hiking.

Yes, going hiking. That had to be it! Proposal Day! What does one wear on a proposal hike? And I was at that in-between stage where pants were starting to get tight. I finally settled on hiking boots, black leggings and my favorite red sweater.

He picked me up and when we got to the trail head, he fiddled with something in the trunk. I tried not to look. But then I did look, and I saw nothing. No square bulge in his pocket. He put on the ball cap that he had grabbed from the car and started up the path. The trail was full of couples and families enjoying the foliage and crisp weather. We hiked up and up. My heart was thumping with excitement and exertion. Slightly more than halfway up the hill was a rocky outcrop with a beautiful view of the valley below. Les drew me aside, and I thought *Now! It's going to happen now! Oh my God!*

"Well, that's a nice view. Let's keep going," he said, and turned up the hill.

I stood, rooted to the spot for a moment. Shocked. Then trotted after him, deflated. *Oh no, maybe it won't be today. Maybe I was wrong! Must keep from crying. Enjoy the day. Beautiful Day. It's okay. It's okay.*

We continued up the hill. The trail narrowed, so he marched ahead, and there wasn't much conversation. When we neared the top, Lester stopped and looked around. There was a clearing and a convenient fallen tree. He sat and patted the log.

"Sit down." I sat next to him. Then, he dropped to his knee. My heart was pounding right out of my chest.

"Alex," he started. "Oh, wait." He flung off his baseball cap and started again. "Alex, would you do me the honor of becoming my wife?" He had pulled a little black velvet cube out of his pocket and was presenting it to me when I tackled him with a hug and we both fell into the dirt. Luckily, the ring stayed anchored in the box until he slid it onto my finger.

***

There are many things a woman fantasizes about when it comes to her wedding. Horse-drawn carriages, rose petals, harps or maybe even bagpipes. Putting my bouquet through a metal detector at the courthouse was not one of them.

Lainie was thrilled with the idea of Mommy marrying Lester. In true three-year-old form, she was so concerned about our future happiness that the first words out of her mouth were, "Can I be the flower girl?" Followed by, "Can I have a pretty new dress for the wedding? And can I invite Sara? And will there be cake?"

"Yes, yes, no and no."

"What?"

"Yes, you can be my flower girl, and yes, I think we might be able to get you a new dress. No, Sara can't come and there won't be a cake."

"NO CAKE?" (She certainly is my child.)

"No honey, we're going to elope. That means it will just be you and me and Les at the wedding."

"You can get married just by yourselves?"

"There will be a justice of the peace who will marry us."

"Piece of what?" Lainie asked.

"Pardon me?"

"Justice of what piece?"

"That's just the title of the person who has the job of marrying people." I explained.

"I think you should have a cake."

"I'll think about it."

Lester told me to pack for a long weekend (Lainie too) in a similar climate to ours, and that he would be picking us up on Wedding Day at 10:00 a.m. Our appointment at the court house was at 10:30 a.m., Friday morning.

My first wedding had contained all the elements of a modern nuptial celebration with myriad details and headaches. We had lists upon lists: wedding guest list, bridal shop list, catering list, flower list, out of town guests list, thank you note list, and on and on. Wedding number two had one list:

1. Call Mom
2. Look for a dress
3. Put in a request for a substitute and leave lesson plans
4. Pack for weekend

I stared at the paper. It can't be this easy. I must be forgetting something.

1. Get some flowers for me and Lainie.

That was it. Number one on the list was going to be the most problematic. How to tell my Christian missionary mother that I had gotten knocked up and was engaged, and oh, by the way, the wedding is in ten days? No, not in the church, but by a justice of the peace?

I tried for a half hour to find the right words but had to call before it got too late. I felt nauseous. Dialing was a challenge. I confused the thousand-digit number it took to reach her village twice, and had to start over, each time choking back bile. I perched on the wooden stool in the kitchen. If one kept the cordless handset close to the base, one had better luck with intercontinental telecommunication.

Finally, contact.

"Hi Mom! It's Alex!" *Who else would it be?*

"Hi Honey, everything okay? It's not like you to call this soon, we just talked last month."

"Everything is fine. I have some big news." There was a faint echo across the line. "Lester and I are getting married!" My stomach started to lurch. I thought it was the adrenaline from telling the most important person in my life the news. The cramps came on like a train.

"Alex that's great! I'll come home for the wedding!"

"Well, actually Mom, it's going to be next week, so I'm not sure that will work."

At that very moment, I threw up. Not wanting to break the connection, I had moved over to the sink and tried to muffle the mouthpiece. I couldn't hear what she said. I could tell that this was only my body's opening gambit, and that more vomiting was on its way. I had to finish this call, please God. "I'm sorry Mom, what did you say?"

"How far along are you?"

"What?"

"You must be pregnant if you're getting married next week. Are you feeling alright? How many weeks are you? Have you been to the doctor yet? Do you have your prenatal vitamins?"

Just hearing her voice made me wish she was here with me in this yellowish kitchen, patting my back.

"Hang on a sec."

Two more big heaves caught me off guard and I couldn't cover the phone. I was breathing heavily now, wondering if I would die while on this long-distance phone call. If I collapsed without hanging up, it would be a huge bill.

"I'm okay. I just wanted to make sure that you knew. I hope you're not too upset or disappointed in me." Now the tears started. Great.

"Is this the same Lester you wrote me about? The engineer you liked so much?"

"Yes."

"And you still like him?"

"I love him, Mom."

"Does he like Lainie?"

"I think he probably loves her more than he loves me." I smiled.

"Will he take good care of you?" she asked.

"Absolutely."

"Then I'm happy for you. Take a few pictures so I can see what my new son-in-law looks like."

The lump in my throat was so big I could barely speak. My powers of speech were also impaired by the taste of vomit in my mouth and shock at Elaine's equanimity. She was so calm. Her only daughter, divorced, now had gotten herself pregnant and was having a shotgun wedding. Old Elaine would have been furious. This Elaine was acting like I had announced that I was hosting a ladies' tea at the junior league next weekend.

"Are you going on a honeymoon?"

"Just a long weekend for right now. We'll probably go somewhere over spring break.

"Do you need me to come home?"

YES! PLEASE! "No, I think we'll be okay. Why don't you save the trip home for when the baby comes?" My stomach started again. "Mom, I've got to go, I don't feel well."

"Write soon sweetheart. I love you."

We said our goodbyes and I stumbled toward the bed, grabbing the bucket from the laundry closet on the way.

Chapter Seventeen
December, 1996

Not morning sickness, stomach flu. This was the diagnosis my doctor gave me over the phone when I described the acid green slime that appeared in the toilet after I thought there was nothing left to throw up. I didn't think such a color existed in nature.

I was confined to bed for three days and was instructed to take one-half cup of any form of liquid every hour. Ken took Lainie for a few days so she wouldn't catch it, and Les arrived with popsicles and chicken broth. My time passed either sleeping or worrying. There was the normal worrying about how this illness would affect the baby, and the stupid worrying about what I would wear to my wedding in six days, and the psychotic level of worrying about the state of my eternal soul now that I had rounded out getting a divorce with an out-of-wedlock pregnancy. This last worry floated in my brain at the height of feverish dehydration.

I needed an outfit. I wanted a natty little suit that I could wear more than once, maybe in a light blue. Something serviceable yet bridal. It was too bad there wasn't time to order coordinating mother-daughter dresses from my favorite catalogue. We could stop up at the children's department after we found my outfit. I fell back into a drowsy haze.

T-minus eighteen hours to the wedding. I had managed to get back to work for two days and sat slumped in my chair, sipping water, and supervising quiet cooperative learning. On the day before our wedding, I picked Lainie up from school and we went to the mall. The plan was to go to Macy's, get two outfits and have a celebratory bachelorette-toddler dinner at Chi Chi's. I was still woozy and worn out, and vowed never again to underestimate how debilitating flu and pregnancy could be. We barely made it to the dress department. Predictably, the perfect wedding ensemble did not present itself. I found a sales girl, half-heartedly straightening out hangers.

"I was wondering if you could help me?"

"Sure, what can I do for you?"

"I need a nice little suit or dress." She stared at me blankly. "I'm getting married tomorrow, and I need something to wear." The girl laughed out loud.

"You're kidding, right? No one shops for their dress the day before their wedding."

"I've been sick." Lainie was sitting in her stroller, preoccupied with her *Curious George* book. The sales girl took a closer look at my face and determined that I must be suffering from a critical illness or mania.

"Hang on." She trotted over to the cash register and grabbed an older lady. The two of them whispered. The older woman took charge.

"Hi, I'm Lorena. What can I help you find?" she asked. I described what I had in mind. Lorena made a concentrating face. "Wait here." She bustled off, happy to have something to do on a slow weeknight.

"How are you holding up?" I asked Lainie.

"Good."

"How's George?"

"He's a good little monkey, and always curious," she quoted. I smiled with my lips, but something wasn't right. I'd lost my bearings. The department store liquefied around me, shapes melting in Dali-esque fashion. Translucent spots floated into my field of vision, iridescent pink, greenish yellow, blue. I swayed and grabbed the arm of a clothes rack. *Don't fall down. Don't fall down.* The cluster of spots was growing thicker, I couldn't see. I felt my way to the handle of the stroller and lowered myself to the floor. *Head between knees. Breathe, breathe.* I felt Lainie's hand pat my head.

"You're okay, Mommy."

I heard some voices. I closed my eyes and squeezed my temple with my knees.

"Here, drink this." Someone, I guessed it was the sales lady, wrapped my hands around a paper cone cup.

I tried to remember her name through the spots. The water was cold and metallic. Lainie's hand was still on my head. I drank. The cup was taken and refilled. I drank again. After a few minutes, I looked up far enough to see a knot of stocking covered knees. Many concerned people. So kind. So embarrassing. I heard voices drifting above.

"Do you think we should call an ambulance?"

"What about the baby?"

"I'm not a baby, I'm three."

"She said she was sick."

"She told me she was getting married tomorrow. Doesn't that seem weird?"

"Maybe she has cancer?"

"I don't know, she still has all her hair."

"Yeah, but why get married on a Friday?"

"It's cheaper. My fiancé and I looked into it."

"Do you want more water?" Lorena was crouching next to me.

With some effort, I raised my head. "I think I can stand up now." I said. Two ladies bent to help me up.

"Are you okay?"

"I think I just got a little faint." I answered. Lainie sat serenely in her stroller. If she was so unruffled, of course I was going to be okay.

"Is there someone we should call?" I thought about that. Tomorrow I could say, *Yes, please call my husband.* Tonight, I was just going to handle it.

Lainie and I made it home in one piece. I fed her half a grilled cheese sandwich and a hotdog. We sat in the living room and watched *Jeopardy* for a treat. When I tucked her in I asked, "Lainie, did that frighten you when I got sick in the store?"

"Nope."

"Why not?"

"Because we're all getting married tomorrow and I know you're not going to be sick for that."

"I love you baby."

"Love you too, Mommy."

Exhausted, I fell asleep in Lainie's bed as she "read" us *The Very Hungry Caterpillar.* I made it to the point where the caterpillar ate five strawberries and have a faint memory of Lainie turning out the light and giving me a kiss on the cheek.

I awoke in the dark, Lainie's knee in my ribs. It took a moment to identify an odd sensation. Healthy. I finally felt healthy. Extracting my legs from the tangle of stuffed animals and blankies, I stood up and didn't have to immediately sit back down. I took a few steps and realized that I was hungry. No, famished.

The fridge contained grapes, some American cheese, a half-dozen hot-dogs and Pedialite. The cabinets weren't much better, but I found some tomato soup and crackers. When the soup was warm, I crumbled in enough crackers to turn the soup practically solid, and savored every spoonful. Thinking that my wedding wardrobe problem wasn't going to solve itself, I went to the bedroom to reinvestigate the closet. I could wear a work suit. No. I could wear a skirt and a pretty sweater. No. Why was this always so hard? I skimmed past a black graduation gown that I had saved to no apparent reason, and there it was, the perfect wedding-day dress. It was a navy-blue raw silk coat dress with dyed-to-match navy lace trim at the sleeves and collar to give it texture. How had I forgotten about this dress? It was classy and understated, a ladies' luncheon kind of dress. It would complement the plaid Christmas dress that Lainie was wearing for the occasion. Even better, it was a dress Elaine had bought for me years ago to wear at a professional women's networking tea, so, even if my mom was in farthest Africa, I would be able to wear the dress she had given me. I could get away with wearing black pumps, and, as luck would have it, I had a fresh pair of nylons too.

At midnight, I lay in my own bed, wide awake and excited. Just like a real bride.

***

Lester, Lainie and I sat next to each other on red plastic chairs that lined the waiting room inside the courthouse. Across from us, next to the door marked "Weddings," the other bridal party had staked out their territory. Les squeezed my hand and nodded in their direction, a smile dancing at the corner of his lips.

The men of the group were wearing black concert T-shirts with the names of heavy metal bands blazoned across the back. To their credit, their jeans were clean and intact. At some unseen signal, they pulled out white dress shirts and stood buttoning them while joking with the groom. The bride arrived and shrugged off her heavy coat to reveal her dress, which could only be described as a slip. I could hear Elaine's voice in my head, *We don't wear underwear as outerwear, dear.* The bride must have gotten it in the lingerie department. The garment had spaghetti straps and ended just past her rear, the hem skimming the bottom of her buttocks. I worried that she might bend over in front of Lainie and prayed that she was at least wearing a decent undergarment. Rapunzel-length hair, frizzy from too many bleach jobs, hung straight down her back. She took out a compact and applied blood red lipstick. The groom leaned in to kiss her. She shoved him aside.

"I count four tattoos." Les whispered.

"On him or her? I think I see five on the bride alone."

"Did you catch the one on her neck?"

"Very dainty, for a rattle snake!" We giggled.

The bride's maid of honor, resplendent in a shiny purple taffeta dress recycled from another wedding, or perhaps prom, indicated that they should get ready to go in. There was a commotion at the entrance to the waiting area.

"That goddamn idiot almost didn't let me in. Tami, Tami, here, here are your flowers!" A huge woman pushed her way past the groomsmen and thrust an enormous cellophane wrapped bouquet into Rapunzel's hands. The pink, white and lavender flowers dwarfed the bride, and her mother smiled with delight. "I thought I was going to miss it. Jesus, what do they think this place is, an airport? For Chrissake."

Lainie stood leaning on my crossed legs, gripping her own small bouquet, staring at them, mouth agape.

"At least you made it, Ma." Said Tami.

The door marked "Weddings" opened and we all turned toward it. I expected a man in black robes to call in the biker wedding party; instead, a skinny middle-aged couple emerged holding hands. They were wearing faded jeans and matching plaid flannel shirts. They both had equally long, stringy hair and looked as though they had just dropped their car off at Jiffy-lube down the street and that this was as good a time as any to stop in and get married.

"Looks like they dressed up for the occasion!" Lester whispered wickedly. I elbowed him in the ribs. Lainie continued to stare.

An unremarkable man stuck his head out and said, "Corbet-Samuels, you're next."

The groomsmen filed past, Def Leopard and Metallica logos visible through their white dress shirts. One thumped the groom on the back saying, "Here we go, big guy." Tami followed her friend in the purple dress, and her mother, still complaining, brought up the rear. When the door closed behind them, the waiting room fell quiet.

Lainie asked, "Are we next?"

"I think so." Lester said. And she climbed into his lap to wait.

Acknowledgements

Thank you to Mel Corrigan and Peggy Terhune, my very patient editors, and Julia Timko for the final read-through and cover concept. Thanks also to Hannah Kroesche for her beautiful cover design. I am grateful to Wendy Bomers for her help navigating indie publishing.

Many thanks to the women in my life who are always there to listen, support, and laugh: Jennifer Gottlieb, Peggy Best, Peggy Terhune, Lisa Tucker, Wendy Bellermann, Blake Wood, Renee Myers and all of the SB2 4EVA crew. Thanks also to the women of UPC, whom I can't wait to see again post-COVID.

This book would never have been possible (or finished) without the support of my amazing family: my daughters, Julia and Jessa, always available for honest feedback and therapeutic shopping, my son, Ian, whose determination inspires me every day, and my husband, James, who keeps us all fed, well-rested and happy.

About the Author

J.P. Gebbie was born and raised in New England but has been a happy transplant to the Midwest for many years. A full-time educator, she loves spending her free time with her family, traveling, hiking and kayaking; however, her love of the great outdoors does not include camping. Jennifer is passionate about reading, writing and the arts, and could not be more proud of the fact that two of her adult children work in museums. My Year of Dating Crazy is her first novel.

Connect with the author on line:
Email: jpgebbieauthor@gmail.com
Website: www.jpyegebbie.com

Made in the USA
Monee, IL
01 January 2023

24173797R00142